One agent is already missing,
and  most
confiden... lling into
a ... ds.

The t... are the

Agent Robert Davidson: He's never let anything distract him from a mission, but finding Lily Scott—the woman he loved and thought he had lost—still alive has shaken him to the core. He wants the truth—and her—and is determined to have both.

Lily Scott: She'd never thought she would see Robert again or feel that familiar surge of desire. But now he's here, asking questions about her life and her son that she isn't prepared to answer.

Samuel Hatch: Though pleased to be getting closer to finding his missing operative, the astute ARIES director is troubled by the ominous undertakings of the Rebelian government. If only he could reach Morrow and learn the meaning of the doctor's last message…

General Bruno DeBruzkya: The power-hungry dictator isn't only interested in possessing rare jewels. He wants Lily Scott and her son in his clutches—dead or alive.

Dear Reader,

"In like a lion, out like a lamb." That's what they say about March, right? Well, there are no meek and mild lambs among this month's Intimate Moments heroines, that's for sure! In *Saving Dr. Ryan*, Karen Templeton begins a new miniseries, THE MEN OF MAYES COUNTY, while telling the story of a roadside delivery—yes, the baby kind—that leads to an improbable romance. Maddie Kincaid starts out looking like the one who needs saving, but it's really Dr. Ryan Logan who's in need of rescue.

We continue our trio of FAMILY SECRETS prequels with *The Phoenix Encounter* by Linda Castillo. Follow the secret-agent hero deep under cover—and watch as he rediscovers a love he'd thought was dead. But where do they go from there? Nina Bruhns tells a story of repentance, forgiveness and passion in *Sins of the Father*, while Eileen Wilks offers up tangled family ties and a seemingly insoluble dilemma in *Midnight Choices*. For Wendy Rosnau's heroine, there's only *One Way Out* as she chooses between being her lover's mistress—or his wife. Finally, Jenna Mills' heroine becomes *The Perfect Target*. She meets the seemingly perfect man, then has to decide whether he represents safety—or danger.

The excitement never flags—and there will be more next month, too. So don't miss a single Silhouette Intimate Moments title, because this is the line where you'll find the best and most exciting romance reading around.

Enjoy!

Leslie J. Wainger
Executive Senior Editor

Please address questions and book requests to:
Silhouette Reader Service
U.S.: 3010 Walden Ave., P.O. Box 1325, Buffalo, NY 14269
Canadian: P.O. Box 609, Fort Erie, Ont. L2A 5X3

The Phoenix Encounter
LINDA CASTILLO

Silhouette

INTIMATE MOMENTS™

Published by Silhouette Books

America's Publisher of Contemporary Romance

Special thanks and acknowledgment are given to
Linda Castillo for her contribution to the
FAMILY SECRETS series.

This book is dedicated to my husband, Ernest, for his never-ending love and
support. To my agent, Jennifer Jackson—you're the best in the business.
To my editor, Kim Nadelson—for thinking of me and always having
the best ideas. To the team of talented editors at Silhouette who worked
so tirelessly on this immense project—you guys are a true class act.
And to my sisters in crime—Cathy, Jenna and Vickie—
thanks for always being there.

SILHOUETTE BOOKS

ISBN 0-373-27278-2

THE PHOENIX ENCOUNTER

Visit Silhouette at www.eHarlequin.com

Printed in U.S.A.

Books by Linda Castillo

Silhouette Intimate Moments

LINDA CASTILLO

grew up in a small farming community in western Ohio. She knew from a very early age that she wanted to be a writer—and penned her first novel at the age of thirteen during one of those long Ohio winters. Her dream of becoming a published author came true the day Silhouette called and told her they wanted to buy one of her books.

Romance is at the heart of all her stories. She loves the idea of two fallible people falling in love amid danger and against their better judgment—or so they think. She enjoys watching them struggle through their problems, realize their weaknesses and strengths along the way and, ultimately, fall head over heels in love.

She is the winner of numerous writing awards, including the prestigious Maggie Award for Excellence. In 1999, she was a triple Romance Writers of America Golden Heart finalist and took first place in the romantic suspense division. In 2001, she was an RWA RITA® Award finalist with her first Silhouette release, *Remember the Night*.

Linda spins her tales of love and intrigue from her home in Dallas, Texas, where she lives with her husband and three lovable dogs. Check out her Web site at www.lindacastillo.com. Or you can contact her at P.O. Box 670501, Dallas, Texas 75367-0501.

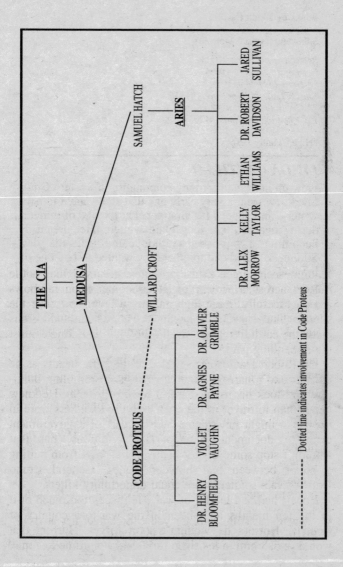

THE CIA

MEDUSA

SAMUEL HATCH

WILLARD CROFT

CODE PROTEUS

ARIES

DR. HENRY BLOOMFIELD

VIOLET VAUGHN

DR. AGNES PAYNE

DR. OLIVER GRIMBLE

DR. ALEX MORROW

KELLY TAYLOR

ETHAN WILLIAMS

DR. ROBERT DAVIDSON

JARED SULLIVAN

- - - - - Dotted line indicates involvement in Code Proteus

Prologue

Luminescent green cruise missiles streamed like bottle rockets across a violent night sky. Dual neon rainbows arced gracefully, their high-pitched whistles piercing the silence like a widow's keening. The distant explosions made the earth tremble, a frightened giant huddling against the impending pain.

Dr. Robert Davidson marveled at the eerie beauty as he ducked into a narrow alley between two crumbling buildings and took his usual shortcut toward the pub. He knew better than to travel in the open when the soldiers were in town. He might have come here as part of a government team to document humanitarian conditions, but that wouldn't stop some trigger-happy young fool from putting a bullet between his shoulder blades. General Bruno DeBruzkya's soldiers were equal opportunity killers.

Robert had had his fill of war. He'd seen too much of it in the ten months he'd been in the war-torn country of Rebelia. Horrors he wouldn't soon forget. Horrors that would revisit him in his sleep for a very long time to come.

He'd done what he could to ease the pain and suffering of the innocents caught in the crossfire, but time had run out. After months of unrest, civil war had finally erupted. Just that morning DeBruzkya had ordered all Americans out of the country—or suffer the consequences.

Robert didn't have to be told twice.

But it wasn't the war raging all around that claimed his thoughts as he passed by the deserted marketplace and jay-walked toward the old church across the street. His harried pace had absolutely nothing to do with the dangers of traveling at night in an area teeming with hostile soldiers, small-weapons fire, and the occasional blast of a mortar round. Robert had to reach Lily. Had to convince her to leave with him. To get on that last plane out.

Before it was too late.

He knew her well enough to expect an argument. American journalist Lily Scott was not the kind of woman to duck and run when the going got tough. She thrived on hardship; she was at her best when the chips were down and the odds were stacked against her. Give her a cause, and she would fight to the end.

But while Robert admired her courage and tenacity, he wasn't going to let her overdeveloped sense of responsibility put her life in jeopardy. Lily might be fighting the good fight here in this tiny country, but Robert wasn't going to let her get herself killed. He wasn't going to lose her to a war nobody seemed to care about.

She was the best thing that had ever happened to him. The only good thing that had come out of this ten-month stint in hell. Lily had kept him going on days when he'd wanted to quit. Days when he'd seen enough and wanted nothing more than to take the next plane out and forget about the hungry children and grieving widows and a political system run amok with corruption. Lily was an oasis of goodness in an ocean of despair. He'd only known her for two months, but even surrounded by a devastated country and indiscriminate violence, they'd been the best two months of his life.

Robert was going to get her on board that jet. He was going to take her home whether she wanted to go or not. Then he was going to spend the next fifty years showing her how much he loved her. The thought made him grin. And he felt like an idiot tromping over the ruins of what had once been a café. No one smiled in Rebelia.

At the end of the street he entered the church through the front door. The roof had collapsed and burned the pews. Tendrils of smoke rose from the destruction like ghostly fingers as he made his way along the wall toward the rear exit. He looked up to see another missile streak across the sky, its eerie whistle making the hairs at his nape prickle uneasily. It was a breathtaking sight, frightening and awesome at once and powerful enough to unnerve even the most seasoned soldier.

Breaking into a run, he left through the rear door and crossed the small cemetery where the headstones glowed ethereally in the darkness. At the next street, he checked for soldiers then headed toward the edge of town where he could see the spire of the boardinghouse and pub where she rented a room on the second floor. The light in her room shone like a beacon from the single window above her writing desk, and he smiled again. Anticipation stirred at the thought of seeing her. He wondered if she was sitting at her desk, staring at her laptop screen, her brows knit in concentration as she tapped on the keys and poured her heart and soul onto paper.

The need to see her, to touch her, sent him into a dead run. He could hear the rumble of tanks in the distance, closer than he'd thought but not dangerously so. But he knew the soldiers would be here soon. And he knew all hell would break loose once they arrived.

All he had to do was convince her to leave with him. Not an easy task considering she'd taken it upon herself to save the country single-handedly. Damn stubborn woman.

He could do it, Robert told himself as he climbed the stone steps and crossed to the pub's entrance. Damn it, he loved her. And she loved him. She may not have said those words, but he could see it in her eyes. When she smiled at him. When she touched him. When they made love. Just because she'd refused to leave with him that morning didn't mean she would again now that she'd had time to think about it. Now that the bombs had started falling. Lily Scott might be on a crusade to save the people of Rebelia, but she wasn't a fool.

He shoved open the heavy wooden door. A German polka played merrily from the ancient jukebox. The impact of a mortar striking the earth nearby rattled the windows and the glasses hanging above the bar. Hans Pavlar, the old bartender, looked up from his miniature television when Robert walked in and grinned. "Hey, American, I thought you would be on your way home by now."

Robert grinned back. "I've got one more thing to do, old man."

Hans looked toward the stairs leading to the rented rooms above. "She's a stubborn one, our Miss Lily."

"Yeah, well, so am I."

"She will not go with you, my American friend."

Aware that his heart was pounding hard against his ribs, Robert started for the stairs. "We'll see about that."

He took the stairs two at a time to the second level. Yellow light slanted from beneath her door. He crossed to it and rapped hard with his fist. "Lily, it's Robert."

He closed his eyes, refusing to acknowledge that he was shaken. That he was terrified because deep down inside he knew she was going to refuse.

The door swung open. The world shook a little beneath his feet at the sight of her. Iridescent hazel eyes. A complexion as fine as German porcelain. Wavy strawberry-blond hair pulled into an unruly ponytail.

She blinked once as if his presence surprised her, then a

slow smile pulled at her full mouth. "I thought you would already be on the plane."

He wanted to devour her in a single bite. "I can't leave without you." He closed the distance between them, backed her into the room and slammed the door behind him. "I want you to come with me."

He saw the answer in her eyes before she uttered a word and he heard the message as loud and clear as the bombs dropping outside.

No.

Feeling desperate and scared and a little out of control, he leaned close to her, slid his hands through her hair and kissed her. He wasn't sure why he did it. Maybe because he felt so goddamn helpless. Maybe because he was scared. Maybe because his entire world revolved around this woman, and he couldn't bear the thought of walking away without her.

She kissed him back. Heat mingled with desperation and fused into something volatile and unstable. Fear and desire and a hundred other emotions pounded through him with every beat of his heart. He poured all of those emotions into the kiss. Mewling, she opened to him. Dizzy for the taste of her, he used his tongue, wanting her with an urgency that was insane at a time like this. They'd made love just that morning, but he was already hard and pulsing and wanting her all over again. He knew it was crazy, but that's the way things had become between them, and he was helpless to stop. He could never stop when it came to Lily.

He slipped his hands beneath her blouse and cupped her breasts, brushing his thumbs over the erect peaks of her nipples. Gasping, she arched into him, her hands going to the waistband of his jeans where his erection strained uncomfortably against denim. He groaned when her fingers closed around his shaft.

Realizing belatedly that the moment was going to get out of hand if he didn't stop now, he grasped her wrists, then broke the kiss. "Don't tell me no," he growled. "Come with me."

She pulled back slightly. Her pupils were dilated. Her nostrils flaring. He glanced at her mouth. Her lips were kiss-bruised and wet, and it took every ounce of discipline he could muster not to kiss her again.

"I can't," she said. "I'm sorry."

"I'm not going to take no for an answer."

"You don't have a choice."

"Damn it, Lily." He glanced at the clock next to the bed. "The last plane is leaving for London in less than an hour. We've got to go. Now."

"The soldiers won't hurt me."

"The tanks are coming. They'll kill you without even seeing your face."

"No. I talked to DeBruzkya less than an hour ago."

Anger stormed through him. "I told you to stay away from that son of a bitch."

"He promised to spare the orphanage," she said quickly.

"Then you've done your work."

"My work is just beginning. I'm sorry if that hurts you, Robert. But I can't leave. If I hadn't been here to contact him, the soldiers would have... All of those beautiful children—"

"Lily, you can't save this country all by yourself," he said, surprised by the emotion in his voice. "You sure as hell won't be able to save it if you're dead."

"I may not be able to save Rebelia, but I'm not going to run away."

Suddenly furious, Robert turned and paced to the opposite side of the room. His heart raged against his ribs, a tormented beast prodded by a cruel owner. "I love you," he said and closed his eyes against a hot burst of emotion. He'd never said those words to anyone before, knew in his heart he'd never say them again if she didn't change her mind and come with him.

"You can come back when things settle down," she said

quickly. "In a couple of months." Moving toward him, she put her hand on his shoulder. "When things settle down here, I can fly to Paris. We can meet there."

"You're an American," he snapped. "DeBruzkya has sworn to kill all Americans."

"DeBruzkya and I...have an understanding—"

"He's a psychopath, damn it! He doesn't make deals."

"Robert, please, don't make this any more difficult than it already is."

He turned to look at her, felt the sight of her like punch to the stomach. God, he loved her so much. How could she expect him to walk away? How could she refuse to go with him if she loved him? For an insane instant, he considered forcing her out of the room and down the stairs to his hotel across town. He was a doctor; he could drug her if he needed to. He could carry her to the jeep where an armed escort waited to take them to the airport in Rajalla thirty miles to the south.

But Robert knew forcing her wasn't the answer. Lily wasn't the kind of woman to give up something she'd set her mind to doing. Evidently, she had her mind made up, and there wasn't a damn thing he could say or do to change it. The thought terrified him.

He stared hard at her, loving her with all of his heart, furious because he knew no matter what he said or did this stubborn, infuriating woman wasn't going to bend to his will. But dear God, he couldn't bear it if something happened to her.

Abruptly, he took her arm. Her eyes widened as he dragged her over to the door, yanked it open and shoved her into the hall. "I'm not going to let you get yourself killed," he snarled.

Shock shone bright and hot in her eyes. "I'm not leaving with you."

He muscled her down the stairs with her fighting him the entire way. Cursing and struggling, she fought to extricate herself from his grasp, but Robert was stronger. At the foot of the stairs he shoved her through the double doors and into the bar.

Hans Pavlar glanced up from his television, his rheumy eyes widening at the sight of them. "Dr. Davidson?" He looked from Robert to Lily.

Robert barely spared the old man a glance. "Now might be a good time to close up shop for the evening," he said between clenched teeth. "Soldiers are on the way."

The old man came around the bar and began closing the interior shutters.

As if that was going to help if someone decided to send a SCUD missile this way, Robert thought bitterly, and forced Lily toward the door.

"Damn you! Let go of me!" Halfway there, she jerked free of his grip. "You have no right!"

Robert released her. For several long seconds he stood in the center of the room, breathing hard, so shaken he didn't trust his voice. Guilt punched through him at the sight of the red marks he'd left on her arms. Christ, what was he *doing?* He'd never manhandled a woman in his life. Never put a mark on another living soul.

"Come with me," he said, realizing he was pleading, that his voice was shaking. "Please."

"I'm sorry." She backed away, raising her hand as if to fend him off. "Just…go."

Robert felt the words like a dull knife being shoved between his ribs. The pain was so sharp he couldn't take a breath. He felt it, flowing like blood from a wound that would never heal.

He stared at her for an interminable minute, loving her and hating her—and more terrified than he'd ever been in his life. She stared back, eyes wide, breasts rising and falling with each labored breath. "I'll be okay," she said. "I promise. I'll be fine."

He crossed to her, pulled her to him and kissed her hard on the mouth. It was a kiss born of desperation and the very real fear that he may never see her again. Closing his eyes against the barrage of emotions, he poured his heart into the kiss, trying to absorb her, all the while hoping desperately that she would change her mind and come with him.

Robert didn't know how he found the strength to pull away, but he did. Tears shimmered in her eyes, but there was nothing he could do to staunch her pain. She'd made her decision.

"I love you," he said, his voice little more than a whisper.

She offered a wan smile. "I'll see you in Paris."

"I'll be there."

"Go before you miss your plane."

Because he didn't want to break down in front of her, he turned away and started toward the door. Hans shouted a farewell, but Robert didn't respond. Mechanically, he walked through the door, down the steps and onto the street. Around him, snow fell gently, a sharp contrast to the violence snapping in the air. He put one foot in front of the other, barely aware of his feet touching the ground. He counted the steps. One. Four. Ten. A missile streaked across the sky, filling the air with the whistle of impending destruction. Robert barely noticed.

He turned to take one last look at the pub. Lily stood in the doorway with her arms crossed, watching him. She waved, and he wondered how it was that they had come to this point. How he could go on without her. Raising his hand, he waved and felt the rise of grief like a bayonet in his heart. Vaguely, he was aware of the high-pitched whine of a missile. The night sky glowing eerily.

An instant later, the world exploded. The concussion whacked him like a giant baseball bat. He cartwheeled through the air, aware of the heat burning him, of tiny debris tearing through his clothes, searing his body. He hit the ground hard. The violence of the impact stunned him, knocking the breath from his lungs. Pain flashed brutally through his left thigh. He heard bone shatter, would have cried out but there was no air in his lungs.

Disoriented, he lay in the snow and watched another missile glide overhead. Trembling and nauseous, he mentally tallied his injuries. There was a vague sensation of heat in his left thigh. But when he tried to move his foot, pain like he'd never known screamed through him. Groaning, he rolled onto his side and glanced down to assess the damage. He immediately spotted the large piece of shrapnel jutting from his thigh. He stared in disbelief at the growing circle of shiny black blood.

Robert had seen enough shrapnel wounds in the last ten months to know this one was bad. Life-threatening if he didn't get immediate medical attention. The piece of metal had hit him with such force that he'd sustained a compound fracture. The femoral artery had been spared, but he was still in danger of bleeding out if he didn't get medical attention soon.

Cursing and groaning as pain radiated up his injured leg, Robert struggled to a sitting position only to have the dizziness and nausea send him back down. He lay silent and still in the snow for a moment, aware of the growing circle of blood, the symphony of pain singing through his body and felt a moment of panic.

Damn it, he didn't want to die like this.

He rolled onto his stomach, worked off his jacket, then eased out of his shirt. Every movement sent ice-pick jabs of agony shooting down his leg. He spotted a narrow piece of wood nearby, looped his shirt around it and formed a tourniquet. Grinding his teeth against the pain, he twisted the makeshift tourniquet around his thigh, praying he didn't pass out before he could stanch the flow of blood.

Lily.

Raising his head, Robert looked quickly around to get his bearings. Thick smoke belched from the crater where the bomb had struck ten yards away. He squinted through the smoke and flaming debris, trying to locate the pub. Hor-

ror swept through him in a flash flood when he realized the
building was gone.

Robert blinked, disbelief and horror rising inside him like
vomit. *"Lily!"* He heard panic in his voice but he didn't
care. The terror ripping through him overrode the pain, giving him the strength he needed to struggle to one knee, his
injured leg dragging behind him. He got one leg under him,
but when he tried to move his left leg the pain sent him
spiraling into blackness.

"Lily…"

Holding his broken leg, he went down in the snow and
mud and floundered like a turtle on its back. Agony and
terror streamed through him like a cold, black tide. He rode
the waves, struggling to stay conscious, struggling even
harder to keep his head.

"Lily." He'd intended to shout, but her name came out
as little more than a puff of air between clenched teeth.

Dear God, she couldn't be dead. Not Lily. She was too
strong. Too vital. He loved her.

He lay there in the snow and mud, breathing as if he'd
just run a mile, staring at the violent night sky, and cursed
fate for being so cruel.

He didn't hear the jeep approach. Barely felt the strong
hands that lifted him onto the stretcher. All he could think
about was Lily.

Robert fought the hands pressing him down. "Got
to…find her," he said.

"It's okay, mate," a British voice said. "I'm a medic
with the Allied Medical Forces. We're going to get you out
of here. Looks like you've got a bit of a problem with that
leg. Try to relax, all right?"

Robert tried to tell the medic that he didn't want to leave.
That he couldn't leave without Lily, but his thoughts were
jumbled, his voice weak. "There's a woman," he said. "In
the pub. Jesus."

The young man in the red jumpsuit looked over his
shoulder at the crumpled building. There was knowledge

in his eyes when he looked at Robert. "There aren't any survivors in there, chap."

"No..."

The young man glanced at Robert's leg and muttered a curse. "I need some morphine over here!"

"No!" Robert shoved at the hands pinning him. "I've got to find her. For God's sake..."

"Easy, mate, we're going to take care of you."

The needle bit into his arm. Robert fought the drug, but it dragged at him. He stared at the flames and smoke and debris while he slowly came apart inside. "Lily," he whispered.

And then the drug sent him to a place where he couldn't feel anything at all.

Chapter 1

Twenty-one months later
Somewhere in Virginia

Doctor Robert Davidson left his BMW in the parking lot and took the redbrick path toward the building at the rear of the complex. It was a path he'd walked plenty of times in the last year and a half. A path he'd never imagined he would take. But even though he'd been reluctant at first, he walked it with a great sense of pride. Of duty. Of respect.

Just that morning Robert had been summoned by Samuel Hatch, director of the top-secret division of the CIA known only as ARIES. The call had come just before 5:00 a.m. Like all of Hatch's transmissions, it had been brief and to the point, with few details. Hatch needed an agent with Robert's expertise and credentials. He would be deployed immediately. Long-term assignment. High-level security clearance. Top-secret mission.

The drive from Robert's home outside Washington D.C. had taken just over two hours. Stiff from the long drive, he ignored the tinge of pain in his thigh as he passed several low-rise buildings where ivy flourished on the redbrick exterior. From the outside, the center looked like an Ivy League college financed by trust funds and old money. Robert knew differently. Behind the genteel facade lay one of the American government's most top-secret facilities in the world. With emphasis on foreign intelligence, biomedical research, genetic engineering and high-tech gadgetry, the ARIES boys and girls played with toys the CIA didn't even dream of. Toys that, in the eyes of the rest of the world, hadn't yet been invented. The ARIES agents, scientists and researchers had the best of everything. Money was never a problem because when it came to ARIES, Uncle Sam had bottomless pockets.

Robert told himself he wasn't nervous as he swiped his security card through the reader, then punched in his six-digit PIN number. He didn't get nervous. Once a man had had his world shaken the way he had twenty-one months ago, it took a lot more than a cryptic call in the middle of the night to shake him.

The steel-core door slid open to a small, windowless room with a tile floor and three white walls. Dead ahead, an elevator door dominated the fourth wall. In the center of the room, black inlaid tile formed a thick line on the floor. Robert stepped up to the line, then looked into the lens of the camera glaring at him and waited for the identification scan to begin. An instant later, a green light flickered, letting him know the retinal scan was complete. The elevator door swished open, and he stepped inside. Frowning at the panel mounted next to the door, he set his palm against the glass and waited while his palm and fingerprints were scanned and the images run through the ARIES personal identification database. Like every other piece of equipment at the ARIES center, the security system was light-years ahead of its time and utterly fail-safe.

Once the green light flashed to tell him his prints had been scanned and approved, Robert pressed the button to the underground level, and the elevator rushed him toward ARIES's inner sanctum and Samuel Hatch's private office a hundred feet below ground.

He assured himself a second time that it wasn't nerves gnawing at his gut. For one thing, Robert didn't believe in premonitions. Still, he couldn't deny he had a feeling about this assignment. Hatch didn't call on his ARIES agents for anything but the most difficult of tasks. He wondered what the good director was going to ask him to do this time.

The elevator doors whooshed open. Robert stepped into a large room filled with low-rise cubicles, about half of them occupied by men and women hunched over computers or speaking into communication headsets. He spotted Carla Juarez, who waved, flashed a dazzling smile, then turned her wheelchair and headed in his direction. Robert watched her approach and smiled for the first time that day. He liked Carla. She was young and pretty with a lovely sense of humor. Up until a year ago she'd been a field operative. Then she'd taken a bullet in her back during a deep cover operation in Eastern Europe. The injury had left her partially paralyzed. She'd been through hell in the last year— something he identified with even though they'd never discussed anything so personal. But unlike Robert, Carla had never grown bitter.

"Hey, Dr. Davidson, how's it going?" she asked.

Because he didn't want to answer that truthfully, Robert put on a grin and lied through his teeth. "Couldn't be better."

She rolled her eyes. "For an agent, you're not a very good liar."

"Thanks." Leaning forward, he pressed a kiss to her cheek. "I think."

"Pin bothering you?"

Subconsciously, he brushed his hand over his left thigh. "Must be a front coming in," he said shortly, not because he was annoyed but because it embarrassed him to complain about his leg to a woman with a severed spinal cord.

"Takes time," she said breezily. "Been able to run yet?"

"I'm up to two miles." It hurt like hell, but he ran. He'd be damned if he was going to spend the rest of his life letting the residual damage from a shattered femur keep him idle. "Played basketball a couple of weeks ago."

"Ethan told me he beat your butt."

"I guess that makes him a better liar than me."

"And a sore loser." She smiled. "Hatch is expecting you."

"Thanks." Robert opened the door to find Samuel Hatch standing at the back of his office looking at a tiny, withered plant.

He looked over his shoulder at Robert and scowled. "Damn strawberry plant is going to die on me," he muttered.

"They need sunlight."

"Security had a cow when I suggested I get an office with a view."

Robert stepped closer and glanced at the plant, wondering why a man like Hatch was so concerned with a scraggly little plant no one cared about. "They like sandy soil," he offered. "Or maybe some cow manure."

At Hatch's questioning look, he added, "I worked in a nursery part-time during high school."

"I'll see if procurement can get me a plant light and some cow poop, then."

Hatch left the plant and seated himself behind his desk. Robert guessed him to be about sixty years of age, though he could pass for forty-five. He was bald on top but kept the rest of his gray hair cropped short. He was of medium height and slightly rumpled in appearance. Part soldier, part scientist, he was fit for his age and glowing with health. He would have been ordinary-looking if not for the sharp intelligence that burned like gemstones in his green eyes.

Robert took the adjacent chair and waited for the briefing to begin.

"How's the leg?" Hatch asked, pulling a file from his drawer and setting it on the desk between them.

Robert shifted uncomfortably in the chair, wondering how the other man would react if he answered truthfully. "No problems."

"You running?"

"Twice a week. Two miles."

"Good. I like my agents in shape." Hatch opened the file. "I need you to go to Rebelia."

For a moment, Robert wasn't sure he'd heard him right. Then the meaning behind the single word struck him like a rude slap. Dread curdled in his stomach. He stared at the older man, aware that his heart rate had spiked, that a cold sweat had broken out on the back of his neck.

"I know how you feel about Rebelia, Robert, but—"

"I don't think you do—"

"Dr. Alex Morrow is still missing." Hatch cut him off. "I want my operative back."

Robert had never met Morrow, but he'd heard of his work as a environmental biologist within the ARIES network. The man was brilliant. A legend in a few circles. "I knew he was missing. I thought you'd send someone else."

Hatch looked at him with those sharp green eyes. "You know Rebelia."

Robert shifted uneasily in his chair, wishing he'd never heard of that godforsaken country, trying hard to control the pounding of his heart—and the bitterness at the back of his throat.

"I need you, Robert. You know Rebelia and her people better than any man in the division," Hatch said. "You know the customs. The language, the regional dialects. You have contacts—"

"Hatch, with all due respect I haven't been in the country for almost two years."

"Save the excuses, Robert." A hint of ice laced Hatch's voice. "I'm not asking."

Clamping his jaws together, Robert looked at his hands, then at Hatch. "Rebelia is still pretty volatile these days."

"You can handle it." Hatch's eyes narrowed, sharpened. "Can't you?"

After an interminable moment, Robert nodded. He could handle it. But he sure as hell didn't like it. Not because of the civil war, but because of the ghosts.

"All right," he said. "I'm in. What do you need?"

"Your mission is twofold. Your first priority is to set up a base of operations for what will be the third leg of the mission. While you're there I want you to find out everything you can about Bruno DeBruzkya."

The sweat on Robert's neck turned to ice at the mention of DeBruzkya. He could feel the muscles bunching with tension. "You mean aside from his being a ruthless son of a bitch?"

"Intelligence tells us he's been stealing gems."

"I know about the gems."

"Then I'll recap what we know so far. We have substantial evidence telling us that he's behind at least four heists. The Stedt Museum in London. The Legvold collection in Stockholm. A private collector in Frankfurt.''

''The Gala Summit.'' Robert had been there as part of the surveillance team. He knew what had gone down. And he knew Hatch had nearly lost one of his agents. ''Do you have any intelligence as to why he's amassing gems.''

''Could be any number of things. Maybe he's financing weapons. Maybe something worse. I want to know.''

Robert didn't even want to think about what a sinister man like DeBruzkya could do with weapons of mass destruction.

Hatch frowned at him. ''We need to know what he's up to. The gems are secondary, but some information would be nice at this point.''

Robert's nerves coiled a notch tighter. He stared at Hatch, wondering if the other man knew how much he hated DeBruzkya. If Hatch knew Robert held the dictator responsible not only for an injury that had left him permanently maimed, but for the death of a woman he'd once loved more than life itself. He knew that wasn't the most objective mind-set for a field agent about to embark on a deep-cover mission, but Robert never claimed to be a good agent.

''What's my cover?'' he asked.

Hatch handed him a slender manila folder with the name PHOENIX typed in bold letters on the tab. ''Your papers are inside. French passport. Medical degree. You're part of a team of medical doctors traveling to Rebelia from Paris to administer medical aid to sick and injured children. Your meeting point is in a small village outside Rajalla. It's all there in the file in French. Your initial contact will meet you at a pub on the outskirts of the city and take you to your source, who will give you enough information on DeBruzkya for you to get started.''

Robert took the file and paged through it, seeing that, as usual, Samuel Hatch and his team had been very thorough. "I guess I'll need to brush up on my French."

"And your Rebelian dialects. All communication will be via the ARIES satellite. I've got new encoding set up. Your code name is PHOENIX."

"When do I leave?"

Hatch glanced at his watch. "Two hours. I've got a jet waiting at Annapolis that will take you to La Guardia. From there you'll take the Concorde to Paris then hop on the train to Rajalla."

Robert slid the folder into his briefcase and rose. "All right."

Hatch stood, regarding him with intelligent green eyes that invariably gave the impression he could read not only one's body language but thoughts, as well. "Watch yourself." He extended his hand. "You know what DeBruzkya is capable of."

"I can handle DeBruzkya." As he shook the other man's hand, Robert knew the real question was whether or not he could handle the ghosts.

At eight the next evening Robert sat in a greasy booth in an obscure little pub called Ludwig's and nursed a stein of watered-down beer. The pub was crowded with weekend revelers. The booze was cheap, the cigarette smoke was thick and talk was of the old days and revolution.

Robert sipped his beer, wishing he were anywhere but this dank little bar in a country he wished to God he'd never set foot in. He'd been in Rebelia less than two hours, and already she dominated his thoughts. The last hours they'd spent together, making love on the narrow bed in her room above the pub. The fight they'd had over her refusal to leave with him. The violence of her death. The black months that followed.

He knew thinking of her wasn't going to do a damn thing for his frame of mind or his mission. But he'd never learned how to block thoughts of her. Damn it, of all the places Hatch could have shipped him to, why did it have to be this hellhole? It wasn't like the world was lacking hellholes. Any one of a dozen or so would have done just fine.

Restless, he finished his beer and motioned for the bartender to bring another. He wasn't enjoying it, but he didn't have anything else to do until his contact arrived. He'd already set up base camp, renting a small apartment above a market in a seedy section of town, where he'd installed the tiny communications satellite dish and left a backup short wave radio per Hatch's instructions. He knew he should keep a clear head, but for the first time in a long time, Robert didn't want a clear head. Sometimes all that clarity made life a hell of a lot more difficult.

"Sir?"

Robert looked up from his beer to see a young man with black hair and a matching mustache grinning at him, and he took a long sip of beer. "Get lost."

"I'm Jacques."

Robert watched him closely, zeroing in on his restless hands and nervous fidget and went with the predesignated script. "What's your sign, Jacques?"

The other man didn't blink. "ARIES, sir."

"If you're an ARIES, what does that make me?"

"PHOENIX."

The code words confirmed that this young man with the engaging smile and vivid blue eyes was, indeed, his contact. Robert extended his hand. "I was starting to think you weren't going to show."

"The soldiers set up a roadblock, sir. They're angry at the rebels again. I had to wait them out."

"Hopefully, they're not feeling trigger-happy this evening. I don't feel like getting shot at." Robert rubbed the dull ache in his thigh.

"Yes, sir."

"And cut out the sir crap."

"Yes, s—" Jacques flushed. "What do I call you?"

"My close friends call me PHOENIX." Rising, Robert dug five Rebelian dollars out of his pocket and left them on the table. "Let's go."

The young man glanced toward a narrow door at the rear of the bar. "This way."

Looking once over his shoulder, Robert followed Jacques past the bar and out the back door into a narrow alley. Two men clad in ragged coats and dangerous scowls stood against the crumbling brick building smoking Rebelian cigarettes. They eyed Robert with a combination of hostility and suspicion. Robert stared back, keenly aware that if something went wrong he was on his own, outnumbered three to one and without a sidearm to boot.

"Hey, you the American?"

Robert glanced at the tall man with a bald head and full beard and mustache. His nerves jumped when the man reached into his coat pocket. A dozen scenarios rushed through his mind. For an instant he considered reaching for the switchblade strapped to his calf, but he knew if the other man had a gun there was no way he'd get to it in time. Adrenaline cut a path through his gut when the man produced a small, lethal-looking pistol.

Never taking his eyes from the pistol, he raised his hands and took a step back. "What the hell is this?" he growled.

Turning the pistol so the butt faced Robert, the bald man

laughed outright, then passed the pistol to him. "You Americans are so jumpy."

The three men broke into hearty laughter. Robert wasn't amused and snarled a very American profanity as he accepted the pistol and tucked it into the waistband of his jeans.

"You're a real comedian," he said.

"Thank you."

Resisting the urge to roll his eyes, Robert said, "If you're finished joking around, how about if you take me to my contact?"

The bald man scratched the top of his head and glanced at the other two men. He spoke in rapid Rebelian. Robert was only able to catch every other word or so, but what he was able to decipher gave him a bad feeling in the pit of his stomach.

"Your contact is a very important person within the rebel movement," said Jacques.

"Somehow I already figured that out." Robert stared at him, waiting, wondering what the hell these three men were up to. "Take me to him."

"The only way I can do that is to blindfold you."

"Look, either you trust me or you don't," Robert snapped.

The three men exchanged looks again. The bald man spoke first. "This has nothing to do with trust."

"Then why the blindfold?"

"Because if the soldiers capture you, they will torture you until you reveal the location of our headquarters. We can't risk that. The blindfold is for your own protection, my friend."

Because of the threat of hostile soldiers, the journey to the rebel stronghold was made on foot. Blindfolded, Robert walked behind Jacques with the bald man and his cohort bringing up the rear. A mile into the walk, his left thigh began to throb. Robert had learned to deal with the pain, mostly by directing his thoughts elsewhere. He was a firm believer in the mind-over-matter philosophy and had decided a long time ago that the injury was not going to limit his physical capabilities. Of course, the injury didn't always cooperate.

The cold rain wasn't helping matters. But Robert used the cold and wet to keep his mind off the pain. Still, after three miles, his limp became so pronounced that the bald man paused and touched him on the shoulder. "Do you need to stop and rest, American?"

The blindfold pressed soggily against his eyes. Robert smelled wet foliage and damp earth and guessed they were probably deep in the forests to the north of Rajalla. Cold rain dripped down the collar of his jacket, and the material pressed wetly against his back. His leg ached with every beat of his heart. But because stopping wasn't going to help any of those things, he shook his head. "Let's keep moving."

"It's not much farther."

He concentrated on his mission objectives as he walked, formulating questions for his Rebelian contact. He wanted a run down on DeBruzkya. Rumors about an American who had been captured. Or gems. He tried hard to keep his mind on the business at hand, but his thoughts went repeatedly to a woman with iridescent hazel eyes.

"You can take off the blindfold."

Thankful to be rid of the soggy material, Robert stopped and stripped it off. They were in the midst of a forest thick with tall trees and low-growing brush. Ahead, he could just make out the jagged peaks of the mountains and knew they were heading north. Blinking to clear his eyes, he spotted a faint path that wove between the trees to a small cottage nestled beneath the thick canopy of Rebelian pines. Yellow light shone in the windows. Smoke chugged from a stone chimney, and the smell of wood smoke hung in the air.

"Your contact is inside." Smiling, Jacques reached over and squeezed his shoulder. "We're glad to have you here, American."

Meeting his gaze, Robert saw the sincerity behind the words, the truth in the other man's eyes, and nodded. "We believe in freedom in America," he said.

Bowing slightly, Jacques backed away. "Your contact knows how to reach me if you need anything."

Robert stood in the rain and watched the three men disappear down the trail, then looked through the trees at the cottage. The sight was surreal in the utter darkness, like something out of an old fairy tale. A pretty cottage surrounded by a beautiful forest and the backdrop of breathtaking mountains. He wasn't sure why, but the sight made him think about Lily. She would have liked it here.

"Don't go there, buddy," he said, cursing the ghosts that refused to give him peace even after so many months.

He pulled the old revolver from the waistband of his jeans, checked the cylinder and found it loaded. Hoping his contact knew English, he shoved the revolver into the waistband of his jeans, and started toward the cottage.

His heart pounded hard and fast as he stepped onto the stone porch and knocked on the door. Instinctively, he stood to one side, just in case whomever was on the inside had a nervous trigger finger and decided to shoot first and ask questions later. He saw a shadow move inside the window, and his nerves zinged. Resting his right hand lightly on the butt of the pistol, he knocked again.

The door swung open. Recognition sparked like a hot wire and sent a surge of shock to his brain. Robert stumbled back. His first fleeting thought was that he was seeing his first ghost.

Lily.

He stared at her, aware of his heart pounding in his chest. He tried to utter her name, but his brain was so overwhelmed, he couldn't speak. All he could think was that he'd seen her die. That it was an absolute impossibility for Lillian Scott to be standing there in a thick cotton sweater and faded blue jeans staring at him as if he were the one who'd come back from the dead instead of her.

A thousand words tangled inside Robert, but he choked on every one of them as if they were shards of glass. Emotions snapped through him like thunderbolts, shocking his body with their awesome power. He stared at the woman standing in the doorway, aware of his heart raging in his chest, the dull roar of blood rushing through his veins.

He couldn't believe Lily was alive. But it was her; he knew it as surely as he saw the flash of recognition in her hazel eyes. There was no other woman like her. No other who could affect him like this. He would know her anywhere and under any circumstance. He would know her in the dark, just by the feel of her, the scent of her. The energy surrounding her.

Robert stared, speechless and shocked to his bones. Her hair was longer, but still as radiant as burnished copper. She had the same flawless skin, as fragile as fine German porcelain. Only now there was a tiny scar that ran from her left eyebrow to the hairline at her temple.

"Lily," he whispered after an infinite moment.

"Robert. My God. I didn't..." She blinked, as if trying to wake herself from a dream. "How did you..."

Neither of them seemed capable of completing a sentence. Slowly, he once again became aware of his surroundings. The ping of rain against the tin roof. The crackle of a fire in the hearth. The smell of bread and wood smoke and woman. His leg ached dully, the way it always did when he overexerted himself, but he barely noticed the pain. And for the first time since receiving the injury, he was glad for the distraction.

"C-come in," she said.

When he only continued to stare at her, she stepped back. "You're getting wet."

"I'm already wet." But Robert knew the weather no longer rated on his list of concerns.

His heart raced with his pulse as he stepped into the cottage. Warmth and a startling sense of comfort he didn't quite trust embraced him. He looked around, seeing immediately that whomever lived here had somehow managed to turn a ramshackle hovel into a home.

"What are you doing here?" she asked.

Robert watched as she crossed to the fire and tossed another log into the flames. Before he even realized he was watching her, his eyes swept over her, taking in every detail. She'd lost weight, but the curves he'd once known intimately still defined her shape. Even through the thick cotton sweater she wore, he could see the outline of her full breasts. Her jeans were snug enough so that he could see the gentle roundness of her hips. And in those fleeting seconds her beauty made him remember all the things he'd tried so desperately to forget in the twenty-one months since he'd last seen her.

Robert cut the thought short with practiced precision. He wasn't exactly sure what was going on but knew he couldn't dwell on it. He couldn't let himself think of her in those terms. Not when he'd worked so hard to get her out of his system.

"I could ask you the same question," he said.

"I—I live here." She glanced at him over her shoulder

as she walked into a small kitchen area. "Were you looking for me?"

"No," he said quickly and held his ground at the door. "I was supposed to meet someone here."

He watched her pour Rebelian black tea into two mismatched cups. She looked cool on the outside, maybe even a little tough, but her hands were shaking, and for the first time he realized she was merely hiding her shock better than he was.

She carried both cups to the wooden chairs in front of the hearth. "Your contact?"

That she knew about his contact shocked him all over again. Lily didn't know he was an ARIES operative. No one did, aside from his counterparts and other ARIES personnel. There was no way in hell he would ever tell her. The less she knew about him, the safer she would be.

Because he wasn't quite sure how to respond, he didn't answer. Instead, he followed her to the hearth, keenly aware of her scent, that her essence filled not only the room, but the entire house. "I'm doing some missionary work for the French government."

She looked at him oddly, a student perplexed by a particularly difficult math equation. "I was supposed to meet someone here tonight, as well."

A sinking sensation swamped his gut. And suddenly he knew this was no coincidence. "Jacques brought me here."

Her knowing eyes met his. "Jacques is…with me. He's part of the movement."

With me. Of all the words that stuck in his brain, he hated it that it was those two. He stared at her, torn between turning around and walking out and forgetting this had ever happened, and shaking her until she told him how it was that she was alive and he'd spent the last twenty-one months dying a slow death because he'd thought her gone.

"There's got to be some kind of mistake," he said.

"There's no mistake." She handed him one of the cups. "I don't have any sugar. That's one of the many things we no longer have in Rebelia."

Amazed that she could be thinking about sugar when his world had just been rocked off its foundation, he took the cup and sipped the strong, dark tea, trying desperately to rally his brain into a functioning mode.

"I just can't believe it's you," she said, sipping her tea. "This has been planned for months. We need your help."

"I'm here for information," he said. "Not to help you."

Holding her cup between her slender hands, she looked at him through the rising steam. "I'm your contact. And if you want information from me, you're going to have to earn it."

Chapter 2

Having spent the last two years in a country decimated by civil war, hunger and indiscriminate violence, Lily thought she had endured every kind of shock a human being could endure. She'd seen things she couldn't fathom. Things she refused to think of once the lights were out and she was alone in her bed. A few minutes earlier, she'd thought she could handle just about anything fate saw fit to throw her way.

She'd been wrong.

Not even the horrors of war had prepared her for seeing Robert again. She simply couldn't believe he was standing in her living room, as warm and alive as the last time she'd seen him. The night she'd hurt him terribly and then watched as he'd been cut down by shrapnel.

God in heaven, how was she going to handle this? How was she going to tell him everything that had happened since he'd left? Things that would change both their lives forever. The questions gnawed at her like voracious little beasts. Questions that terrified her more than the threat of any bomb or soldier's bayonet or stray bullet. Questions she had absolutely no idea how to answer.

Standing next to the hearth, Robert regarded her with hard, suspicious eyes. He may look the same, she mused, but the last months had changed him. Made him hard. Maybe even bitter. She considered the bitterness in her own heart and wondered if the last months had been as hard for him as they had been for her. She didn't see how.

Still, the steely gaze that swept the length of her remained starkly familiar. The pull was still there, too, she realized, and a shiver rippled through her hard enough to make her hands shake. She endured his scrutiny with stoic silence, hoping he couldn't hear the deafening rush of blood through her veins or see her shake.

Refusing to be cowed, Lily stared at him, trying to keep her thoughts on the business at hand and failing miserably. He offered a commanding presence that unnerved her as much as the sight of any enemy soldier. Broad shoulders. Lean hips. Legs slightly bowed with muscle. He seemed taller than she remembered even though she knew that was an impossibility. He had the most fascinating face of any man she'd ever seen. Intelligence and a subtle cunning burned bright and hot behind piercing blue eyes. Laugh lines cupped a mouth that was much more harsh than it had been when she'd known him. A five-o'clock shadow darkened a square jaw that lent him a hostile countenance. Even from three feet away she could smell him, an out-of-doors scent that reminded her of mountains and rain—and a time when he'd ruled her senses as surely as he'd held her heart in the palm of his hand.

Lily cut the thought short with brutal precision. Now wasn't the time to remember how well she'd once known this man.

"You can't possibly be my contact," he said after an excruciating minute.

"I am." Having lost her appetite for the tea, she took it to the sink and dumped it.

"Lily, for God's sake, I thought you were dead."

For a while, Lily had thought she'd been dead, too, only to realize that sometimes it was much more painful to be alive. The old pain roiled inside her as the memories shifted restlessly. Memories she'd refused to think of because the pain was too great. Memories that had eaten at her from the inside out for nearly two years. If it hadn't been for Jack, she wasn't sure she would have survived. Sweet, precious Jack had given her hope when the last of her hope had been all but ripped from her heart.

Gathering her frazzled nerves and the tangled remnants of her composure, she turned to face him. "As you can see, I'm very much alive."

"I can see that. But…my God, how—"

"I was injured." Self-conscious, she touched the scar at her temple and tried not to remember that her physical injuries had not been the worst of what she'd endured.

He stared at her with those hard eyes, and she knew the shock of seeing her was giving way to the need for an explanation. A explanation she had absolutely no idea how to relay. She'd consoled herself with anger in the weeks she'd been held captive, tried hard to convince herself that Robert had abandoned her. Some days she'd even believed it. Days when it was easier to be angry than it was to hurt.

"Why didn't you contact me?" he asked incredulously. "Why didn't you let me know you were alive?"

Because she hadn't the slightest clue how to answer him without opening a Pandora's box of pain that would change both of their lives irrevocably, she turned to rinse the cup. Stacking it neatly on the rack, she crossed to the fire to warm her hands, aware that Robert had trailed her.

"I can't discuss that right now," she said.

He stared at her, his expression incredulous and angry. "I deserve an explanation, damn it. We were…together.'

Pulse pounding like a jackhammer, she stared at him. "It's in the past, Robert. Let it go. I've moved on. Maybe you should have, too."

Robert felt as if he'd been slapped. "I want to know what happened."

"No, you don't." Because she couldn't bear to look at him and think of those terrible days, she walked into the small living area and motioned for him to take one of two chairs in front of the hearth.

Never taking his eyes from her, he started for the farthest chair, but had to cross in front of her to reach it. Feeling as if she'd suddenly strayed too close to a rogue tiger in a flimsy cage, she backed up a step, trying not to notice the way he winced when he sat down.

"You're limping," she said, watching him closely.

"It's an old injury."

She wondered which were worse, the injuries that left scars on flesh or the ones that left an indelible mark on the psyche and shattered the heart. "If you want to get into some dry clothes, I can hang yours near the fire."

He looked at the sweater and jeans that clung damply to his frame. "I've got a change of clothes in the duffel."

"You can change in the back. There's a room for you."

Robert grabbed his duffel and slung it over his shoulder. Lily rose and walked through the kitchen to the small room that had been added to the cottage as a pantry many years ago, back when people had had food. With wood plank floors and shelves holding a meager supply of canned vegetables and fruits, it was barely large enough for the cot, let alone a man of Robert's size. But it was all she had and it was going to have to do.

He stepped into the room and set his duffel on the narrow cot. The mirror above the sink caught his stare, and their eyes met, held.

Lily felt the contact like the blast of a mortar. Looking quickly away, she stepped back. "There's no door, but Jacques put up this curtain to give you some privacy."

"This is fine."

"I'll just…be in the living room."

"I'll be there in a minute."

She wasn't sure why she hesitated. Maybe because there was so much more she needed to say. Maybe because she wasn't quite sure if he was a figment of her imagination. But she couldn't stop looking at him. By the time she realized what she was doing, it was too late for her to escape.

Never taking his eyes from hers, Robert reached for the hem of his sweater and pulled it over his head. Lily's breath stalled in her lungs as his magnificent chest loomed into view. She saw a thatch of dark hair. The ripple of muscle beneath taut flesh. Vivid blue eyes that discerned a hell of a lot more than they revealed. The sight of him shook her, and for a moment she couldn't move. She'd faced a lot of terrible things in the years she'd been in Rebelia, but oddly none of those things had unnerved her as much as the sight of Dr. Robert Davidson taking off his shirt.

"Maybe you want to stay while I change pants, too," he said.

Feeling a hot blush burn her cheeks, she yanked the muslin curtain closed and fled.

Lily's heart was still beating heavily against her breast a few minutes later when Robert walked into the living area and found her at the hearth.

"Where do you want me to put my clothes?" he asked.

She turned to find him standing right behind her, his wet clothes in a bundle. He'd put on a flannel shirt over a black T-shirt. The faded jeans he wore fit him loosely, but there was no denying the sinew of his legs or the bulge of his manhood beneath.

Barely sparing him a glance, she took the clothes from him. Pulling a ring set into the wall over the hearth, she stretched the thin cord to the opposite wall and secured it to a small hook. Once the line was taut, she set about draping his jeans, shirt and jacket over the cord. She could feel his eyes on her as she worked, but she didn't dare turn to face him. She had to get herself calmed down first.

"How is it that you're here?" he asked when she'd finished.

Because she didn't feel capable of explaining something so complex at the moment, she hedged. "I could ask you the same question."

"All right. I'm working with a group of French doctors on a humanitarian—"

She swung to face him. "That doesn't explain why you're here. In my house. I wasn't expecting an American."

"Exactly who were you expecting?"

"Someone…who needed information. For the cause."

"The freedom movement?"

"That's right."

He shrugged. "You got me."

A vague sense of uneasiness rippled through her. Robert Davidson might be a smart man, he might even be brilliant, but he'd never been a good liar. "I don't understand what part you're playing in this."

"Maybe you don't need to know. Maybe I just want you to talk to me about what you know. About what you've been hearing."

"Why are you here?"

"Let's just say I'm not here for the weather." He rolled his shoulder. "I want information."

"What kind of information?"

"You're involved with the freedom movement." He shrugged. "Maybe you know something that could be useful."

"Like what?"

He hit her with a direct stare. "What do you know about Bruno DeBruzkya?"

Another ripple of uneasiness went through her, only stronger this time and she fought a slow rise of panic.

When she didn't answer, he smiled, but it was a cold, hard smile. "Okay. If you don't want to talk about De-Bruzkya, we can always go back to him." He looked around the room. "Maybe you could start by telling me what you're doing here. Why you're living here. Like this."

The question shouldn't have startled her. She'd known he would eventually begin asking more personal questions. Risking a look at him, she found him watching her intently and felt his stare all the way to her bones.

"That's not a difficult question, is it?" he asked.

No, she thought. He wasn't asking the difficult questions yet. But she knew they were coming. And she had absolutely no idea how to answer any of them.

"I'm involved with the freedom movement. I get food and medical supplies to the sick children. The orphans. I raise money, collect food and toys and try to give them hope, let them know someone in the world cares."

"You still working?"

"I wrote for the *Rebelian Times Press* for a while."

"And now?"

"A few months ago DeBruzkya took control of the media, and I just couldn't do it any longer."

"Censorship," Robert said with distaste.

Lily nodded, feeling the same distaste all the way to her bones. "I kept writing. About the war. About the people. The children. They've all got stories to tell. Some of them are quite amazing." She grimaced. "I didn't have an income, but by then the economy was so bad it didn't really matter. I sent pieces to the *Guardian* in London and the *New York Times*. One thing led to another, and before I knew it I had started a sort of underground newspaper."

He cut her a sharp look. "Jesus, Lily..."

"The *Rebellion* is printed weekly. For some people, it's the only way they can find out what's going on in their own country that isn't fabricated by the government or part of DeBruzkya's propaganda."

He stared at her intently. "DeBruzkya doesn't tolerate journalists who print the truth. He's murdered them in the past. Damn it, Lily, he's brutal—"

''He doesn't know about the *Rebellion*.''

''Lily, for God's sake, how can you be so naive?''

''I may be a lot of things,'' she snapped, ''but naive isn't one of them.''

Rising abruptly, Robert limped to the fire. Setting his hand against the mantel, he leaned and stared into the flames, the muscles in his jaws working angrily. ''De-Bruzkya is ruthless. If he wants to find you, he'll stop at nothing until he does.''

The words chilled her, but Lily didn't let herself react. She might be afraid on occasion, but she refused to live her life in fear. She refused to let it make her decisions for her. ''I've been careful. I write under a pseudonym. He doesn't know I'm an American. He doesn't know where I live.''

''I don't understand how you can believe that, unless you're into denial.''

''I'm not denying anything.''

''He's a dangerous son of a bitch, Lily. Especially to the people who've crossed him.''

''I haven't crossed him.''

He cut her a hard look. ''I'd say running an underground newspaper in the midst of his dirty little war qualifies as crossing him. Information in the wrong hands can be a dangerous thing to a dictator.''

''It would be a thousand times worse if I sat back and did nothing.''

For the first time the layers of anger thinned enough for her to see the raw pain beneath, and she knew his concern for her was real. The realization touched her, and she felt her emotions shift dangerously.

''Why do you do it?'' he asked quietly.

For the lost ones, she thought. ''Because I have to.''

He contemplated her like an angry dog that had just been swiped by a unassuming feline. Lily stared back, wondering how he would react if he knew everything.

And as she gazed into the electric blue of his eyes, the endless months they'd been apart melted away like steel in a smelter. The pang of longing was so powerful that for a moment she couldn't catch her breath. The urge to go to him pulled at her like a dangerous tide. A riptide easing a hapless swimmer into a treacherous sea.

But because she knew he represented a very real danger to her—because she represented an even bigger threat to him—Lily banished the thoughts. She could never think of Robert in those terms again. Going to him, touching him, getting too close were things she couldn't allow herself to do. Giving in to the feelings coiling inside her might just get them both killed.

A cry from the bedroom at the rear of the cottage jolted her. She felt Robert's questioning stare on her, but she didn't dare meet his gaze. In her peripheral vision she saw him glance toward the rear of the cottage, and a shudder ran the length of her. For a instant, she stood there, frozen with indecision, a hundred emotions pulling her in a hundred different directions.

"Is there a child here?" he asked.

Trying in vain not to shake, Lily rose from the chair. "That's...Jack."

"Jack? Who is Jack?"

She started toward the bedroom, keenly aware that Robert was following her and that she didn't have the slightest idea how she was going to explain a one-year-old baby to a man who had every right to know.

Lily closed her eyes. "Jack is...my son."

Behind her, she heard Robert stop dead in his tracks, but she didn't slow down. She didn't turn to look at him. She wasn't sure what her eyes would reveal if she did. She'd never been able to lie—not to Robert. She wouldn't lie now—even if the truth was more brutal than any lie she could have fabricated.

Jack is my son.

The words reverberated like the echo of a killing shot inside Robert's head. He stood in the semidarkness of the hall and watched Lily disappear into a small bedroom at the rear of the cottage, his head reeling.

Lily had a child. He couldn't believe it. Couldn't believe she'd moved on so easily while he'd spent the last twenty-one months crippled by the past. The thought angered him, shook him more than he wanted to admit. He tried to blame his reaction on exhaustion and stress and the shock of seeing her again after believing her dead for so long. But he knew there was more to it than that. Knew it went a hell of a lot deeper than any of those things.

Movement down the hall yanked him from his dark reverie. He looked up to see Lily holding a small bundle wrapped in a blanket. A blue blanket. He wondered how, in a country as devastated as Rebelia, she'd managed to find a blue blanket for her baby boy.

He stared at her, then the child, trying desperately not to think about what her having a child meant.

I've moved on. You should have, too.

The full meaning of the words penetrated his brain. Evidently, she had, indeed, moved on. Judging from the size of the baby, she hadn't waited too long after Robert had left to do so. He wondered who the father was and tried like hell to ignore the knot of jealousy that tightened in his gut. He knew it was stupid to feel that way. His relationship with Lily had been over for a long time. Any feelings he'd once had for her had been replaced by bitterness.

The bitterness surged forth now with such force that Robert could taste its acrid flavor at the back of his throat. He watched her approach, then pass him without acknowledging him. Feeling angry and out of place, he trailed her to the living room, then paused to watch her spread a blanket on the sofa and lay the child down to change him.

"He's your...*son?*" he asked.

She didn't look at him but continued tending the baby. "Yes."

Robert felt the affirmation like a physical punch. Lily

had a son. He couldn't believe it. His brain simply refused to absorb the information. "How old is he?"

She did look at him then, but her hazel eyes were cool. "About nine months."

Mentally he calculated the months, felt a hot cauldron of anger begin to boil. No, she hadn't waited very long at all.

"His name is Jack," she added.

"Jack." He repeated the name, thinking of the young man who'd brought him here. His name was also Jacques, but he'd had a French accent and pronounced it differently. Robert wondered if Jacques was this child's father.

Robert thought of the endless months of grief. The kind of black grief that ate at a man's soul and changed who he was. He thought of all the surgeries that had been required to repair the shattered bone in his thigh. The ensuing months of rehabilitation. The knowledge that he would never be the same. He thought of the secret hope he'd held in his heart that Lily would show up alive and smiling and ready to spend the rest of her life with him. God, he'd been such a fool.

It infuriated him that while he'd been going through all those things, she'd taken up with another man—and had a son with him.

Anger and jealousy melded into a single, ugly emotion and snarled inside him like a rabid beast. He wanted to lash out at her. The words were poised on his tongue, sharp as a knife and ready to cut. But he knew better than to let that beast out of its cage. Knew it would take him apart if he let it.

With the mission foremost in his mind, he couldn't let that happen.

Relieved that Lily was busy tending to the baby, Robert closed his eyes, willing away the emotions swamping him. She'd moved on. He had to accept it. She was alive. That was the important thing. It would have to be enough.

"He's been ill," she said, fastening old-fashioned diaper pins at Jack's pudgy hips. "I've taken him to the doctor in the village, but Dr. Salov hasn't been able to give me a diagnosis.''

Robert's attention snapped to Lily. ''The baby has been sick?'' For an instant, angry male and concerned doctor clashed. Then his physician's mind clicked into place. ''What are the symptoms?''

Lily lifted the child, then pressed a kiss to his forehead. ''The symptoms haven't been consistent, but several times I've noticed that his fingers and toes are blue. Sometimes he's cold to the touch. He had a low-grade fever last week, but it went away after a couple of days.'' She looked at the child in her arms, worry creasing her brows. ''Sometimes he's…lethargic. He sleeps a little too much. Some days he doesn't eat enough.''

Robert glanced at the child and for the first time got a good look at him. Jack was a beautiful baby with vivid blue eyes that were alert and intelligent. He had thick brown hair with a cowlick at his crown and the face of an angel come down from the heavens. Robert had never been partial to babies. But the sight of Lily's baby awed and amazed him nonetheless.

''Nice looking kid,'' he said.

''Thanks.'' Robert saw the quick flash of pride in her eyes and the smile she couldn't quite hide. ''He's everything to me.''

''Do you mind if I examine him?''

She cast him a startled look but made no move to hand over the baby.

''Lily, for God's sake, what do you think I'm going to do? Throw him out the window? Come on. I'm a doctor. Let me examine him and see if I find anything out of the ordinary.''

''All right.'' She glanced toward the rear of the cottage. ''I can put him down on the bed in the bedroom,'' she said and turned to carry Jack down the hall.

Snagging his medical bag off the floor, Robert followed, entering the bedroom just in time to see Lily lay Jack on the bed. He knew he should be paying attention to the child and not the bed, but he couldn't help but notice it was little more than a twin-size mattress set up on a homemade wooden pedestal. Hardly big enough for Lily, let alone Jack's father. The thought of her sharing that bed with another man disturbed him a hell of a lot more than he wanted to admit, and another wave of jealousy seared him.

As if realizing his thoughts, Lily said, "I thought you'd have more room if I laid him on the bed."

"This is fine," he snapped.

She unwrapped the blanket, and Robert found himself staring at a perfect baby boy wearing pajamas with little blue ducks and tiny booties that had been made to look like traditional Rebelian shoes. And he found himself smiling despite the knot of tension at the back of his neck. "What's up, doc?" he said in his best Bugs Bunny voice.

Jack kicked out his legs in delight. "Gah!"

"That's what I thought," Robert said.

Lily leaned forward. "What is it?"

"A Bugs Bunny fan," he said deadpan.

She didn't quite laugh, but he heard her release the breath she'd been holding and figured the level of tension wasn't going to get any lower.

"Let's have a look at you." Struggling hard to keep his mind on the business at hand, Robert dug into his medical bag for his stethoscope and thermometer and quickly examined the baby. All the while Jack cooed and kicked his feet in quiet protest.

"Temperature is slightly elevated," Robert said.

Lily pressed her hand to her breast and looked worriedly at her son. "He's got a fever? What does that mean?"

Robert held up his hand to silence her. "Heartbeat is regular and strong. Pulse is good." Using his penlight, he checked the baby's eyes and ears, then moved on to do a quick check of his extremities. The blue tone of his fingers and toes worried him. Taking one of Jack's fingers between his thumb and forefinger, Robert pressed and watched the tiny pad turn white. When he released it, the blood returned slowly. A little too slowly in Robert's opinion.

"Okay, big guy. I think that'll do it."

Leaning forward, Lily pulled on his pajamas then carried him to the crib. "Why is his temperature elevated?" she asked over her shoulder as she laid him in the crib.

Robert walked to the crib and looked at Jack in time to hear him giggle and was surprised to find himself smiling. He didn't have much to smile about at the moment, but there was something contagious about the sound of a baby's laughter. "I don't know. The fever isn't high, certainly not anything to worry about at this point. I can give him a dose of acetaminophen to take it down."

"All right."

"He appears to be just fine at the moment, but I'd like to run a couple of blood tests."

Lily turned on him, her eyes huge and concerned. "Blood tests? Why? What did you find?"

"I didn't find anything definitive, but just to be safe I'd like to rule out a few things."

Never taking her eyes from his, she came around the crib, a mother lion facing off with a big male who'd just threatened her cub. "Don't give me some vague doctorlike answer, damn it. What are you looking for?"

Robert didn't want to worry her needlessly, but he had to tell her what he thought, regardless of how difficult the truth might be.

"I'm not looking for anything specific at this point," he said. "But from the cursory exam I performed, I can see that his circulation isn't quite normal. I don't think it's anything serious at this point, but it definitely warrants a few nonobtrusive tests."

"Circulation? Oh, my God." She pressed a hand to her breast. "What could it be?"

He shrugged. "It could be something as benign as a slight case of anemia. Any number of things that aren't too serious—"

"But…it could be serious?"

He hated to be the one to put that sharp-edged worry in her eyes, but he didn't see any way around it. "I don't know, Lily. That's why I'd like to run some blood tests. Just stay calm. This is nothing to get worked up about, okay?"

Biting her lip, she looked over her shoulder at the baby cooing in the crib. "He's everything to me," she said. "I could never bear it if something happened to him."

"Nothing's going to happen to him," he said firmly. "These are routine tests. Chances are the pediatrician will prescribe some vitamins with iron, and Jack will be just fine."

She didn't look convinced, but at least she no longer looked as if she were going to jump out of her skin. He supposed they'd both learned that fate didn't always bestow a kind outcome.

The instincts he'd developed in the course of his experience as a doctor told him to reach out and touch her, just to reassure her that her child was going to be fine. But Robert didn't dare touch her. Deep down inside he knew it wasn't the physician who wanted to touch her, but the man who'd never gotten her out of his system.

"I'd like to take him to the hospital in Rajalla where there's a pediatric unit and laboratory facilities," he said.

Lily visibly paled, but masked it by quickly turning away. Noticing that her hands were shaking, Robert watched her closely and wondered about her level of anxiety at the mention of the hospital in Rajalla. "Is there a problem with Rajalla?"

"No. Of course not." She looked directly at him and smiled, but Robert saw the shimmer of nerves beneath the surface. "It's just that the city has…changed since you were last there."

Rajalla was the capital city of Rebelia. Robert had spent a good bit of time there and remembered it as a pretty, bustling metropolis with several sleek skyscrapers, ancient stone churches, a bazaar where local farmers and artisans sold stone-baked bread and Rebelian stained glass, and some of the most beautiful parks in all of Europe.

Robert had researched Rajalla carefully before leaving the United States. He knew DeBruzkya's soldiers had invaded the city. He knew those soldiers had destroyed many of the buildings, including several historical cathedrals. He knew the once-healthy economy had slumped, that people had fled to the nearby country of Holzberg to become refugees.

But he was getting some odd vibes from Lily and wanted to hear her view. "How has it changed?"

She moved away from the crib as if what she were about to say was somehow harmful to her son. "DeBruzkya is in control of the entire city now. There are armed soldiers everywhere, including the hospital."

"The soldiers don't know who you are, do they?"

The hairs at his nape prickled when she didn't answer.

"DeBruzkya himself has spent a fair amount of time at the hospital," she said. "His sister is pregnant. The general is fanatical about his sister's unborn child because that child will become his only heir."

"Does DeBruzkya know who you are?" he asked.

Lily turned to look at him, her expression troubled and stubborn at once. And suddenly Robert got a very bad feeling in the pit of his stomach.

"Does he know who you are?" he repeated.

"He knows my face."

Robert cursed.

"He doesn't know I'm with the freedom fighters," she said quickly.

"Does he know what you do?"

She stared at him, a hunted animal trapped in the crosshairs of a high powered rifle. "No."

He scrubbed a hand over his jaw. "I can't believe you would do something so incredibly foolhardy."

"Robert, I can handle this. I know what I'm do—"

"You're so far over your head you don't know up from down," he growled.

"I'm not afraid of him," she snapped.

He shot her a hard look. "You're too damn smart not to be afraid."

She evidently didn't have anything to say to that, so she turned away. Robert contemplated her in profile, liking what he saw even though he was dangerously furious.

He wanted to believe he was just being paranoid, but his instincts were telling him there was a hell lot more to the situation than what she was letting on.

Lily was lying to him. She was hiding something important. Something dangerous. And for the first time in his life Robert found himself hoping his instincts were wrong.

Chapter 3

Lily's knees trembled as she walked down the narrow hall toward the main room of the cottage. Robert had only been there an hour, and already she was a wreck. She honestly didn't know how she was going to get through this. It was bad enough having Robert in the cottage, dredging up all the old emotions. But it was infinitely worse knowing Jack could be seriously ill. She'd suffered so many losses in her life. She didn't think she could bear it if something happened to her precious child.

In the last hour it seemed as if every nerve in her body had been stripped bare and exposed. Every new bit of information had those nerves jumping like a bad tooth prodded with a sharp instrument. Her entire world had been rocked off its foundation when she'd seen Robert standing on her porch, glaring at her with those cool blue eyes.

Because she couldn't seem to get herself settled down, Lily took a few minutes to stack some logs on the grate in the hearth. When the fire was blazing and she finally ran out of things to do, she turned to face Robert. He'd taken one of two chairs and was staring at her intently, as if she were a puzzle that had just befuddled him.

"Stop looking at me that way," she snapped.

"I'm just trying to figure out what you've gotten yourself into since I left."

"I haven't gotten myself into anything."

"Yeah, I guess you blindfold all your visitors."

"That's just a precaution. In case you haven't noticed there's a civil war going on."

"I've noticed," he shot back. "I've noticed a lot of things since I've been here, and I've yet to get a straight answer out of you about any of them."

She tried to laugh but didn't quite manage.

"What the hell are you up to, Lily?"

"I don't know what you're talking about."

"The bits and pieces I'm getting from you don't fit," he said. "Why don't you tell me the whole story?"

She glared at him. "And what story would that be?"

"The one that explains what you're still doing in this godforsaken country with an innocent child in tow."

Because she was much more comfortable with anger than any of the other emotions boiling inside her, she held on to it with the desperation of a drowning woman hanging on to a float. "I got caught up in the movement," she snapped. "Is that mysterious enough for you?"

"You were involved with the rebels before...I left the first time. Tell me something I don't already know."

Letting out a shuddery breath, she sank into the second chair and looked into the fire. "Nothing has changed."

"Everything has changed, damn it. Don't lie to me."

Her eyes met his, and within their depths he saw the memories, felt them in his heart the way he had a thousand times in the months since he'd last seen her. A young doctor and an American journalist in a strange land surrounded by ugliness and danger. Two people longing for their homeland, but bound by their love of freedom and a responsibility to help those unable to help themselves. Robert and

Lily had spent their days doing what they could to breathe life into a country dying a slow death of oppression. By day, Robert inoculated children, treating the innocent for disease and malnutrition and neglect. Lily wrote her articles, sending them to newspapers in London, New York and Frankfurt, and visited the orphans, the children whose parents had been killed in the war. The children no one cared about.

By night, Lily and Robert met in a smoky little pub, exchanging stories, decompressing, laughing on the outside because inside they felt like crying. For a few short hours they escaped the war, talking about all the things they wanted to do with their lives, their hopes and dreams and plans for the future. Surrounded by despair and destruction and hopelessness, they found peace and their own tiny slice of paradise. They fell in love in that dank little pub. The most unlikely of places that led them to something extraordinary and breathtaking....

Lily shoved the memories away with brutal precision, the way she'd done a thousand times in the last twenty-one months, but she wasn't fast enough to keep them from cutting her. Instead of giving in to the hot burn of tears, or memories that had been seared into her brain like a brand, she took a deep breath and looked at Robert.

"Things were looking hopeless for the freedom fighters," she began. "There had been so many good men killed. Families devastated by grief. All because they wanted to be free. DeBruzkya was putting out a lot of propaganda, telling the world how he was going to turn the country around. He's a very charismatic man. A politician and dynamic speaker capable of rallying huge numbers of people and making them believe him. Facts were hard to come by. People wanted to believe him. They want to believe in the goodness of people. They wanted desperately to believe that he would rebuild their nation. They didn't have a clue about his firing squads or that he didn't have the slightest intention of turning Rebelia into a democracy.''

Realizing her hands had turned suddenly icy, she held them to the fire and continued. ''Most people were so involved with just trying to survive, they didn't know what was going on with the revolution. But having spent time with the freedom fighters, I knew exactly what was happening. I saw what DeBruzkya was doing. And I knew the single most powerful thing I could do was tell the truth to the people.'' She shrugged. ''I began putting out a monthly newsletter. At first it was just a way for me to get my thoughts down on paper and exchange ideas with others. But over the months that newsletter slowly evolved into a sort of underground newspaper.''

Sitting a few feet away, Robert listened intently. He didn't look happy about what she was telling him. But Lily wasn't going to let his disapproval influence her one way or another.

''My newspaper is called the *Rebellion*,'' she said. ''I put it out weekly, updating people on where to find medicine for their children, where DeBruzkya's soldiers have been, where the bombing is expected to take place, where to find food, what the freedom fighters have been doing to save their country, where the secret rallies are being held. People want to be free. They want to know if the soldiers are going to come to their village.''

''How is the newspaper distributed?''

''Mostly through e-mail, but many don't have access to computers, so several young men who aren't yet old enough to fight, but still want to be involved, deliver the newspaper.''

Robert cursed mildly. ''You know DeBruzkya will kill you if he finds out what you're doing.''

She withheld the shiver that crept up her spine. Lily knew better than anyone what the general was capable of. ''That's why I'm concerned about taking Jack to the hospital. If DeBruzkya spots me…''

"Jack needs a blood test. If we can't do it at the hospital in Rajalla, then we've got to go elsewhere."

"The other hospitals have been destroyed."

Robert swore under his breath.

"I'll just have to...be careful. Robert, I can do it. I'm good at being careful."

Robert cut her a hard look. "How well does DeBruzkya know your face?"

Lily stared at him, not wanting to answer because she knew he would overreact.

For several long minutes, the only sounds came from the rain pinging against the tin roof and the crackle of the fire. When the silence became unbearable, she rose and crossed to the kitchen. There, she removed a dusty bottle of French cognac and poured a small portion into two snifters.

In the living room, she handed one to Robert. "I think you're going to need this."

He accepted the snifter, swirled the golden liquid within. "That sounds distinctly ominous."

"It is." She took the chair and sipped the amber liquid, let it burn away some of the nerves. "Before Jack was born, I...met with General DeBruzkya. Several times. Under false pretenses."

For an instant she thought Robert was going to come out of his chair. "You *what?*"

She glanced toward the bedroom. "Quiet, or you'll wake Jack."

"Why didn't you tell me?"

"Because I knew you'd react like this."

"What were you thinking, meeting with DeBruzkya? Lily, are you *crazy?*"

"You've heard the term keep your friends close, keep your enemies closer...."

"I don't think that means snuggling up with a viper."

She would have smiled if the situation hadn't been so dire. God, she missed American sarcasm. Robert's dry humor had always made her laugh, even when things were bleak. She missed that, too. She didn't want to admit it, but she missed a lot of things about this man. "I interviewed the general under the pretenses of my writing his autobiography."

Robert shook his head. "Lily…"

"He has an ego."

"He's also a sociopath. I can't believe you would put yourself at risk like that."

"I was careful. We always met him in public places. The bistro over on Balboa Avenue near the bazaar. A café near the disco. We had a picnic at the park over on Salazar."

"You met with him *three times?*" he asked incredulously. "Lily, what could you possibly have been thinking?"

"Something I should have been thinking about all along."

"Yeah? What's that? Suicide?"

"I'm going to expose DeBruzkya to the world for what he is."

Robert glared at her. "Oh, so you're going to take him down single-handedly, huh?"

"If I have to."

"Why don't you leave that to the trained agents and the freedom fighters? Lily, damn it, this isn't your war."

"I'm in the perfect position to do this."

"Why?"

She changed tactics. "Because DeBruzkya is committing terrible human rights abuses. I've seen it, Robert. The malnourished children. Entire villages wiped out. Men and women and children." She thought of the little girl she'd met at one of the orphanages, and to her horror, her voice broke with the last word. "I can't stand by and do nothing."

"You haven't changed a bit, have you?" he growled. "You're still as hardheaded as ever."

"I may be hardheaded, but I know when I'm in a position to make a difference."

"So Lillian Scott can bring down the infamous Bruno DeBruzkya when the people of Rebelia and the American CIA can't. That's rich as hell!"

"I know his weak spot."

"Oh, yeah?" Smiling unpleasantly, he leaned forward and challenged her with a killing look. "So what is it? You got some kind of secret weapon stashed in your kitchen? Military resources we haven't yet discussed? Soldiers training in the backyard? A knife in your sock? What? What's your secret weapon, Lily?"

She met his gaze in kind. "Me."

The single word echoed like a clap of thunder. Robert squashed down temper and tried not to think about how little of this was under his control. "What the bloody hell are you talking about?"

Pulling her legs beneath her in a protective gesture, Lily met his gaze. "General DeBruzkya is…intrigued by the idea of my writing his autobiography."

"So, he's an egomaniac."

"Among other things."

"What the hell is that supposed to mean?" But Robert had read the general's profile; Hatch had included it in the file, and it read like a horror novel. The anger burning inside him shifted and tangled with a thin thread of fear and ran straight to his gut. "Jesus, Lily. Don't tell me you've—" Robert struggled for the right words "—let him believe there's something between you."

"Not exactly."

"What the hell does that mean?"

She blew out a breath. "Ever since I interviewed him months ago, he's been asking people about me, trying to find out where I live. He's invited me to his palace for dinner several times, but I've always found an excuse not to go. He's asked me several times about the autobiography. He's obsessed with the idea. He wants to go down in history as being one of the greatest leaders of all time."

"Lily, for God's sake…"

"I know what I'm doing."

"What if he connects you to the *Rebellion*?"

"I anticipated that, and there's no way he can connect me to the newspaper."

"DeBruzkya isn't stupid. He's cunning and smart and connected."

"So am I."

"Don't make the mistake of underestimating him."

"I'd appreciate it if you didn't underestimate me, either."

Frustration snarled through him that she was being so hardheaded about this. Once upon a time her courage and determination had drawn him, and he'd loved her for it. Now, he figured he'd be lucky if those two things didn't get her killed.

"I can't believe you've gotten yourself into such a dangerous, impossible situation." Cursing, he rose and paced to the fireplace to stare into the flames. "You're playing a dangerous game, Lily."

"I'm in a position to make a difference."

"You're in a position to get yourself killed!"

"I can handle the general."

Robert knew she was cool under fire. He'd been in some intense situations with her; she didn't lose her head easily. Still, the fact that she thought fast on her feet didn't make her a match for DeBruzkya's brutality. Robert knew all too well what the general was capable of. His file on De-Bruzkya contained not only a psychological profile of the general, but photographs of atrocities most people couldn't fathom. DeBruzkya was a monster who'd fooled hundreds of thousands of people and brought an entire country to its knees. If he found out a woman he trusted—a woman he was interested in romantically—was putting out a black market newspaper there was no doubt he would react swiftly and violently.

Robert's stomach roiled at the thought. He glanced at

Lily and felt nauseous. He'd seen her die twenty-one months ago. Even though there was no longer anything between them save for a few memories and a truckload of bitterness, he didn't want to see her hurt or killed. By God, not on his watch.

"What about Jack?" he asked, playing his ace. "What's going to happen to him if you end up getting yourself shot?"

"I don't plan on getting myself shot any time soon, so you can cut out the scare tactic crap."

She stuck out her chin, but not before he saw the minute ripple that went through her when he'd mentioned Jack. And Robert knew he'd struck the nerve he'd been aiming for. He hadn't enjoyed seeing her go pale. But he damn sure wasn't sorry for making her think twice about what she was doing. And he'd be damned if he was going to keep his mouth shut and play nice while she walked into the sunset with a madman.

"You may be a good journalist, but you don't have the training for something like this, Lily."

He saw the walls go up in her eyes. He'd seen that look a hundred times in the months he'd known her, and he knew she was shutting him out. Damn her for being so stubborn.

"I'm not going to change my mind," she said.

"I'm not going to condone a suicide mission."

The low rumble of thunder punctuated the words with an ominous finality that raised gooseflesh on his arms.

Shaking her head in impatience, she rose. "It's late. I need to get some sleep."

Robert knew it wasn't a good idea to touch her. Not when he was angry and frustrated and still reeling from the shock of seeing her alive. But he crossed the short distance between them anyway. Her eyes widened when he stepped into her personal space, but her surprise wasn't enough to stop him. "We're not finished talking about this," he said.

"You know I won't change my mind."

"And you know I won't give up."

"Touché."

"We're going to talk about the other thing, too, Lily."

She paled a little, then stepped back as if suddenly realizing she needed to put space between herself and something dangerous. "I can't talk about that," she said.

"I can't ignore it."

"You don't know everything, Robert. Don't push."

He tried to bank the swift rise of anger, but it was much too powerful and slammed into him like a rogue wave. He glared at her, feeling more than he wanted, remembering more than he should, wanting something he knew he could never have. "You're brave enough to face off with De-Bruzkya, but when it comes to us you turn tail and run."

"I don't want to talk about it," she returned evenly.

"I deserve an explanation."

She hesitated for an interminable moment, her eyes large and startled. He waited for an answer, but he knew it wouldn't come. She wasn't going to talk to him. Not now. Maybe not ever. Still, he waited. For what, he hadn't the slightest idea. She stared, and he knew she was waiting for the same elusive thing.

"I have to go check on Jack." She turned away, but stopped halfway to the hall, her head tilted slightly toward him, her back ramrod straight.

Even in profile she was lovely. It unnerved him a little to realize that after all the months of pain he was still attracted to her.

Robert couldn't take his eyes off her and cursed himself for letting what should have been a quick and painless briefing turn into something a hell of a lot more personal. He'd only been in the cottage an hour and already she was messing with his head, making him remember things he was better off forgetting, making him want things he was a fool for considering.

But he was only a man. A man who'd been alone for a long time. And so he drank in the sight of her silky red hair and slender shoulders and felt the heady pull of lust. He studied the fragile lines of her profile, the mouth that had lied to him so easily, the same mouth that could drive him insane with need.

Her hair was pulled into a ponytail, revealing the delicate line of her jaw. There was worry in her eyes, but those amazing hazel eyes could still suck the breath right out of a man's lungs, even if there was an ocean of anger standing between them.

Abruptly, she turned to face him. Their eyes met, her hazel clashing against the blue of his. Robert felt the impact like a fighter jet flying low and plowing into him at Mach 1. The back of his neck heated when she licked her lips, and he felt another stir of lust low in his groin. He tried hard not to remember how many times he'd kissed that mouth, how many times she'd kissed him back, how good every single one of those kisses had been. But he did and his body responded with a vengeance that stunned him.

Cursing himself for letting the moment stretch, he stepped back. "I'm going to turn in," he said woodenly and started for the little room off the kitchen.

He heard her moving behind him, but he didn't stop. The last thing he wanted was close proximity. Damn it, the last thing he wanted to do was spend the next few days lusting after a woman who'd made her feelings for him crystal clear. A woman who'd shattered his heart and then moved on to another man before the wounds she'd left behind had even had a chance to scab over.

The tiny room was in dismal condition, but clean. Robert was still searching for the light switch when Lily came in with a candle.

"I'm sorry, but there's no electricity back here."

"Terrific." He took the candle from her, careful not to let his fingers brush against hers. Turning, he set the candle on the small counter next to the sink.

"I'm sorry I can't offer you more."

"This is fine." He risked a look at her. "I'm not here to enjoy myself."

Kneeling, she transferred canning jars from one shelf to another, giving him some room.

"I can do that," he said.

Ignoring him, she continued working until she'd cleared one of the shelves. "There's a shower in the main bathroom off the hall. There's usually hot water in the morning." She looked away from him, wiped her hands on her jeans. "If you need anything else…"

Before he could stop himself, he reached out and touched her shoulder. "What I need are answers."

He felt a tremor run the length of her. Then she turned away. He let his hand drop. She brushed by him without answering, without meeting his gaze. Robert watched her move down the hall, feeling petty and pathetic and frustrated as hell.

"What the hell are you doing?" he muttered to himself and dropped his duffel onto the narrow cot. Trying not to think too hard about the answer, he pulled out the battery-powered satellite phone and palm-size computer and set the antenna up on the shelf Lily had cleared. He hit several buttons on the computer, and the liquid crystal display screen glowed ethereally in the candlelight. He waited for the satellite signal to go through, then slipped the tiny padded microphone into his ear and listened to the grid coordinates beep. He typed in his identification number and password, then waited for a mechanical female voice to ask him a pre-designated question for both voice recognition and the correct answer.

"Operation please," the mechanical voice asked.

"PHOENIX," he said.

A click sounded, and then Samuel Hatch's voice came on the line. "Good to hear from you, PHOENIX. I trust you arrived at your destination safe and sound."

"I did."

"Any trouble getting to your contact?"

Robert closed his eyes and tried not to think about Lily. "No problems." He set the tiny camera on the shelf so he and Hatch would have video as well as audio. Having both was not only a convenience, but a security measure to prevent agents from communicating while under duress.

"Have you had a chance to question your contact?"

"Not thoroughly. I arrived pretty late. But I do know that there is information to be had on my target."

"Okay. Good. Anything we can use?"

He sighed, trying not to think about Lily. "Probably."

"What about Dr. Morrow?"

"I'll delve into that tomorrow."

"And the gems?"

"I should be able to find out more tomorrow."

"Good." Hatch paused as if studying him. "Everything else okay? You look...tired."

"Long day, Hatch. Everything is fine." Robert looked at the camera, wondering if he looked as strung out as he felt.

"You now have a sidearm for personal protection?"

"That's correct."

"Good. Then we're set. Keep in touch, and be careful. If you get into trouble, you know there's a doctor at the hospital who can help."

"Roman Orloff. I know."

"Good."

"My contact has a sick child," he said abruptly. "At some point I'm going to talk to Orloff to see about running some tests."

"I don't see a problem with that. It fits nicely with your cover."

Robert scrubbed a hand over his jaw, feeling the stubble, knowing he wasn't going to do anything about it until morning.

"PHOENIX?"

He glanced at the screen to see a concerned expression on Hatch's face and realized belatedly his body language might be relaying more about his frame of mind than he was comfortable with.

"Take care of yourself. I mean it. If things get dangerous, put out the call and we'll send someone in. You got that?"

"Loud and clear."

The display blinked, then disconnected. Robert stared at the blank screen for a moment, then folded the tiny computer and slid it into its case. He washed his face in the sink, then blew out the candle and stepped out of his jeans. Rain pinged against the roof as he lay down on the lumpy mattress and pulled the blanket over his hips. The pillow smelled of grass and laundry detergent. The combination reminded him of Lily.

Lacing his hands behind his head, he stared at the dancing shadows on the ceiling and tried to turn off his brain. But his mind continued to reel with all the things he'd learned in the last hours. And even though exhaustion swept through him in shimmering waves, he knew he wouldn't sleep. The old ache in his thigh had come to life, but tonight the pain was more like an old friend compared to all the other things going through his head.

Turning onto his side, he punched the pillow and tried not to think of the woman sleeping at the other end of the cottage. But he did. He thought of her the same way he'd thought of her every night for the last twenty-one months. He lay in the darkness and watched the water slide down the window and berated himself for thinking of her at all, for wanting a woman who'd moved on to another man. A woman who'd hurt him terribly. A woman he hadn't been able to forgive. Damn her.

Damn his own foolish heart.

And damn the son of a bitch she'd fallen in love with.

Chapter 4

Robert awoke abruptly to the sensation of small, sticky fingers touching his face. He was a split second away from pulling out the revolver Jacques had given him when his sleep-dazed mind pinpointed the source.

Jack.

Opening one eye, he found himself staring into a pudgy face with petal-soft skin, thick hair that was sticking up at the crown and blue eyes filled with the kind of deep innocence that belonged only to the very young. Eye to eye, Robert blinked at the child, trying hard not to think of the dream he'd been having about his mother. A dream that had been anything but innocent.

Jack stood before him on wobbly legs, wearing blue duck pajamas, Rebelian slippers and an ornery grin. He had what looked like flour on his chin. Something pink and sticky was smeared around his bow mouth.

"Gah!" Flour-covered fingers reached out, prodding Robert's nose. Tugging on his ear. His lips.

Not quite sure how to escape short of jumping up and

running out the rear door, Robert endured the contact. He'd never had an aversion to children. Hell, he liked kids—as long as he could walk away at the end of the day.

"Gah!"

"Morning to you, too," he said as he sat up.

The little room didn't look quite so dank this morning. Sunshine streamed in through the window above the sink. A breeze ruffled bright yellow curtains. He could hear music coming from somewhere else in the house. Good old-fashioned American rock and roll, if he wasn't mistaken. The sound of it boosted his spirits almost as much as the smell of something baking, filling the air with cinnamon and spice.

Little Jack stretched his arms upward and reached for Robert's face again, but Robert turned his head. "Where's your mommy, tough guy?" Licking his lips, he tasted strawberry jelly. Terrific.

Lily came through the door a moment later looking like a harried mother. A wooden spoon in one hand, a towel in the other, she spotted Jack and shot Robert an apologetic smile. "Sorry. He's fast," she said, scooping the baby into her arms.

Robert sat on the cot and stared at her, speechless and a little stunned that anyone could look so damn good so damn early in the morning. She was wearing a pair of faded jeans with an oversize sweatshirt and a turtleneck beneath it. She had flour on her cheek and a powdery little handprint on her backside. A very nicely shaped backside, at that. She'd pulled her wavy red hair into a ponytail, but several strands had fought free to curl around her face. Robert thought about the dream he'd been having about her and wondered how Jacques would feel if he knew the American staying in his house was ogling the mother of his child in very inappropriate ways.

"We didn't mean to wake you so early," she said. "Jack's an early riser."

"It's okay. We were just, uh, getting acquainted," Robert said.

Jack squirmed in her arms, stretching his arms toward Robert. "Gah!"

Glancing at her son, Lily chuckled. "I think he likes you."

Robert glanced at the squirming baby, relieved that she had a good grip on him. "I have that effect on babies."

Pressing a quick kiss to a fat cheek, she hefted her son and turned toward the adjoining kitchen. At the door, she stopped and looked at Robert over her shoulder. "Would you like something to eat?"

"Whatever you're having will be fine," he said, careful to keep the threadbare blanket in his lap or else betray the state in which the dream had left him.

"Oatmeal okay?"

"Fine."

One side of her mouth curved upward. "You have flour on your chin."

He rubbed his hand over his chin. "Something smells good."

"I'm making bread. An old Rebelian recipe with cinnamon and yeast."

"Sounds good."

"They are."

"Mind if I use your shower?"

"Sure. Down the hall. On the right. I left a towel for you on the vanity. We've had electricity all morning, so there should be plenty of hot water."

Robert watched her leave the room, all too aware that she still had one of the most shapely derrieres he'd ever laid eyes on. As he rose and headed toward the shower, he didn't think he was going to make use of the hot water.

For the first time since moving into the cottage six months earlier, Lily wished it were bigger. She'd never felt that way before, when it had just been her and Jack. But

Robert had a way of filling up a room. It seemed as if she couldn't turn around without bumping into him, without touching him, without making eye contact. With the high-wire tension zinging between them like erratic electricity, she figured she'd be lucky to walk away from this encounter without getting burned.

She still couldn't quite believe Robert was back, larger than life and full of questions she had absolutely no desire to answer. Worse, she couldn't believe he was staying in her house. Of all the terrible things she could have faced in Rebelia, this was the one scenario she'd never anticipated.

She might still be attracted to him. She might even have feelings for him buried deep in the recesses of her heart. But there was no way she could ever give in to them. Letting him go all those months ago had been the most difficult thing she'd ever had to do. Hurting him had shattered her into a thousand pieces. Pieces she was still trying to put back together.

Lily told herself she hadn't had a choice. Losing a giant piece of her heart had been a price she'd been willing to pay. A sacrifice she'd been willing to make. No matter how much she wanted to tell him the truth, she knew that was the one thing she could never do. To open her heart to him now would put him in grave danger, would put Jack in danger. She might have learned to live without Robert in the last months, but she would never be able to live with herself knowing his blood was on her hands.

She had Jack to think about now. Her son was all that mattered. They'd gotten along just fine without Robert up until now and would continue to do so long after he left.

After settling Jack into his homemade high chair, Lily started some water boiling on the stove, then turned to her son. ''You have a piece of toast to finish, big guy.''

''Toh!'' Jack squealed in delight.

''That's right. Toast.'' Smiling, she picked up the soggy

bread and put it in a tiny outstretched hand. "Here you go."

"Toh! Gah!" Little Jack kicked his chubby legs and clutched the flaccid toast with fat fingers.

"Okay, big bite," she said and he chomped down on the bread with tiny, hit-or-miss teeth.

The kettle began to whistle. When Lily turned to pour water over oatmeal, she saw the toast sail across the small kitchen and smack into a lean, denim-clad leg. She looked up to see Robert standing in the doorway, felt her breath leave her lungs in a single, quick rush.

Oh, my, the man was something to look at.

"Kid has a hell of an arm. You ever consider putting him in little league?"

Horrified, she glanced at the jelly dribbling down his thigh. "Do you want me to get that?"

"You've got your hands full. If you'll just point me in the direction of a towel."

"There, by the sink."

"Right."

He walked to the sink, snagged the towel and began wiping at the jelly. His dark brown hair was still wet from a shower and combed straight back revealing thick, arched brows and a high forehead. The jeans he wore hugged lean hips and muscular thighs and...well, she wouldn't think about the rest. The flannel shirt he'd been buttoning when he walked into the room had fallen open to reveal a dark thatch of hair and a lot more muscle than she remembered. For an instant, she could only stare and try not to remember what it had felt like to run her fingers over that muscled chest and those flat nipples.

When she looked up he was staring at her. The air between them shifted and thickened. Jack's incessant baby talk faded to a pleasant hum. Lily knew she was staring, but she couldn't seem to stop. Good Lord, she'd forgotten just how good Robert Davidson looked. And she'd definitely forgotten the effect he had on her.

Keenly aware of the blood suffusing her cheeks, she turned to the stove and twisted off the single burner to the off position. Behind her, she could hear Robert talking to Jack—something about the Cincinnati Reds—but she didn't dare turn around. Not when her heart was pinging in her chest like beads in a baby's rattle.

She couldn't believe her composure had crumpled at the mere sight of him. She'd had nerves of steel when it came to dealing with Bruno DeBruzkya. But one look at Robert Davidson's chest and those nerves melted like chocolate.

"Okay, slugger, whatcha got there?"

As much as she wanted to turn around and watch Robert with her son, Lily didn't dare. She wasn't sure what the sight of them together would do to her, what it would do to her heart.

For a full minute she stared straight ahead, listening, longing for something elusive, yet as vital as the air she breathed. When the curiosity got to be too much, she tilted her head slightly and stole a peek at man and baby. Out of the corner of her eye, she saw Jack pounding his spoon against his high chair tray. Robert was squatting in front of him, making silly faces. He said something in a voice that sounded amazingly like Bugs Bunny, and Jack giggled.

The sound of her son's laughter tore a hole clean through her heart. The pain was so sharp she had to close her eyes. Taking a deep, calming breath, she finished making the oatmeal and struggled to get herself under control. She couldn't afford to let Robert know her feelings. One wrong word to him, and he would discover her secret. She knew he wasn't the kind of man to let something like that go. He would want to do the honorable thing. Dear God, she couldn't let that happen. Not when doing the honorable thing could end up getting him killed.

"Something smells good."

"Oatmeal." Realizing she was stirring the oatmeal into glue, she set the spoon aside and turned to face Robert. Amusement rippled through her when she found him and her son embroiled in a game of catch with the kitchen towel. Of course, Jack was now a lot more interested in the towel than his breakfast.

"He's a pretty good catcher, too," Robert said.

"Scouts will be out looking for him soon." Smiling, she eased the towel from Jack's chubby fingers. "But right now he needs to eat his breakfast."

Robert turned a sympathetic look at Jack. "Sorry, pal."

Jack squealed and reached for the towel. "Gah!"

"Yeah, I know, I know," Robert said. "Oatmeal before that no-hitter."

Lily watched them and swore she wasn't going to let the moment get to her. "We don't have any sugar here in Rebelia, so I added a little cinnamon."

"That's fine." Watching her carefully, he took the bowl from her and began to eat.

Shaken more than she wanted to admit, Lily started toward Jack. The mangled piece of toast sat on the counter, so she snagged the baby's bottle of goat's milk and set to work releasing him from the high chair.

"He's already trying to talk," Robert said.

Lily closed her eyes and told herself her son's first word wasn't something she'd fantasized about sharing with Robert. "He said 'toast' this morning."

"Right before he chucked it across the room."

"You should have seen the hard-boiled egg yesterday morning."

"Line drive, huh?"

"Home run."

Smiling in spite of herself, she pressed a kiss to Jack's forehead, wishing her nerves would settle. She pulled him from the chair then held him close for a moment, taking in his sweet baby scent. For an instant she found herself wishing he would stay little forever so she could hold him just like this and keep him safe.

Aware that Robert was watching them, she carried Jack

to the sink, wetted a fresh towel and wiped at the ring of jelly around his mouth.

"Whenever you can work in some time with me, I'd like to talk to you," he said.

Her pulse spiked. "Robert—"

"About DeBruzkya," he clarified.

"Oh." She flushed, realizing she'd misunderstood and overreacted. "Let me put Jack down for a nap."

Lily carried her son to her bedroom at the rear of the cottage and laid him in the crib. When he fussed, she offered him the bottle of milk. "Oh, you're a fussy one this morning, aren't you?"

She held the bottle while he suckled. For several long minutes he watched her with innocent blue eyes. When his lids grew heavy, she propped the bottle on a pillow and began to gently rock his crib. Humming an old Rebelian lullaby, she lost herself in the beauty of watching her son sleep. Such a small moment in time and yet so profound. The sight of him safe and warm in his crib touched her as nothing else in the world could. And she loved him so much it hurt just to look at him.

"Sleep tight, sweet baby," she whispered.

Bending, she pulled the blankets up to his pudgy chin, then set the bottle on the dresser. Taking a deep breath, she left the bedroom, leaving the door open so she would hear him if he woke. She found Robert standing at the window in the living area, staring out at the winter-dead forest. The earlier sunshine had given way to clouds, and the cottage had grown chilly. He looked at her when she entered the room, but he didn't smile. Lily felt the rise of tension like a physical touch.

"It was getting colder, so I closed the window in the kitchen," he said.

"Thank you. It was nice this morning, but it looks like rain for this afternoon."

"I'd forgotten how late spring comes to Rebelia," he said.

''It still freezes at night sometimes. Two weeks ago we had snow.'' She hadn't meant to mention snow. It had been snowing that last night….

For an instant, he looked like he wanted to say more, but the moment passed and he remained silent. ''What do you know about Bruno DeBruzkya?''

She walked to the hearth and put another log on the fire. ''Why are you so interested in DeBruzkya?'' she said, trying to sound nonchalant.

''I can't tell you that.'' He shot her a sober look.

Mystified by his cryptic answer, she tried to read his expression, realized she couldn't, even though at one time she'd been very good at it.

''I think you know me well enough to know I'm one of the good guys,'' he added.

That was the one thing she knew with utter certainty.

Aware that her pulse was racing, that her thoughts were keeping perfect time, Lily walked into the kitchen and knelt in the corner near the stove. Pulling up a corner of the stained linoleum, she peeled it back, revealing a secret door set into the wooden planks beneath. She extracted a small lockbox, then replaced the trap door and linoleum. ''The soldiers have never been here, but I have to be prepared if they show up.''

''What's in the box?''

''All of my notes on the freedom movement. Copies of the *Rebellion*. Information I've accumulated on DeBruzkya. Documentation on some of the things he's done. Some of the data is handwritten. Some of it is on disk, some on videotape. I've even taken some photographs.''

''Stuff he wouldn't want anyone getting their hands on,'' Robert commented.

''Proof that he's killing people and has been systematically destroying this beautiful country for nearly two years.''

''Lily, you're playing a dangerous game.''

All she could think was that this hadn't been a game to

her for a very long time. She crossed to the hearth, set the lockbox on the floor and opened it. She handed Robert the latest copy of the *Rebellion* then busied herself booting up her laptop and arranging some of her handwritten notes.

"This is written in Rebelian," he said.

"You know Rebelian."

"Yeah, but I'm rusty." He looked sheepish. "I don't want to miss anything important. Do you think you could hit on some of the highlights for me?"

For a moment she wanted to tell him no. She didn't want to work too closely with him. The less time she spent with him the better off she and Jack would be. The better off Robert would be.

She nodded. "All right."

He skimmed the newsletter-style paper in his hand. "Do you trust the people you work with not to sell you out?"

"I'm very selective about who I deal with."

"I'm sure DeBruzkya would pay a nice bounty for the head of the editor of an underground newspaper."

She repressed a shiver. "None of the people I work with would sell me out."

"Lily—" Robert's voice was softer than before "—the cause is a good one but you're taking a huge risk."

She thought of everything she'd seen in the years she'd been in Rebelia. Everything that had been done to her, to the people she'd known and cared for, the children no one cared about. She shook her head. "There's a lot at stake. An entire country. Her people, her children—"

"At what cost to you?"

That was a question she couldn't answer. "Jack and I are fine. Nobody knows we're here. I mean, even you were blindfolded when Jacques brought you here. We're safe and happy—"

"If DeBruzkya captured Jacques and shoved spikes under his fingernails, he'd sell you out."

"Stop it," she snapped. "You're trying to frighten me."

"I'm trying to save your life."

His quick anger surprised her, and for a moment she didn't know how to respond. Her own temper stirred when she realized his anger had little to do with her newspaper and everything to do with the way they'd left things twenty-one months ago. Why couldn't he just let the past go? He didn't know what had happened to her. He didn't know what could happen if she told him too much. If she let herself feel too much.

"I don't expect you to understand," she said.

"Good, because your staying here with that child is a little beyond my realm of understanding."

"Don't lecture me about Jack."

"How does his father feel about your keeping him in the same house where you run an underground newspaper? In your fervor to save the children and keep the freedom movement alive have you even bothered to think about the safety of your own son?"

Fury swept over her with such force that the words tangled on her tongue. "How dare you imply that I'm endangering my son."

"What would you call it?"

"I'd call it an impossible situation that I'm dealing with the best way I can."

Rising abruptly, he paced to the window and stared again at the forest. "It didn't take you very long to find someone else, did it, Lily?" he asked without looking at her.

The words struck her like a breath-stealing punch, and for several seconds she could do nothing but concentrate on getting oxygen into her lungs. "I can't talk about that."

"You can't talk about it, or you won't?"

"I don't owe you an explanation. I don't owe you anything."

"Of course not," he said nastily. "I was only your lover."

She felt the words like a bullet, piercing flesh and bone and slamming into her heart to shatter it like a piece of crystal. "Stop it, Robert. What happened between us...was a long time ago. A lifetime ago. A lot has happened since then.''

"Like what?"

When she didn't answer, he turned to her, struck her with a look cold enough to freeze hell. "Who's Jack's father, Lily?"

Her heart pinged hard against her ribs, then began to race.

"Did you know him when you were seeing me? Were you seeing him behind my back? Is that why you refused to leave?"

She stared at him, speechless and hurting and on the verge of panic. "That's a petty and hateful thing to say."

"I want to know. I deserve an answer."

"Don't do this."

"Don't do what? Ask for the truth?" He crossed the room but stopped two feet away from her, as if he didn't trust himself not to strike out at her if he got too close. "Is it Jacques?"

"Jacques?" If she hadn't been so shaken she might have laughed. But she didn't because the moment was breaking her heart. Instead, she said nothing more, and watched as the realization entered his expression. And it killed her inside to let him believe a lie.

Face dark with anger, he turned and stalked to the window. Lily looked at the lockbox, at all the information she'd accumulated on a man she'd dedicated her life to destroying, and for the first time since this nightmare had begun wondered if that goal was worth the sacrifices.

She risked a look at Robert. She couldn't ever remember seeing him look so desolate. Not Robert Davidson the doctor. The gentle man who healed the wounded. But something had changed inside him since the last time she'd seen him. A bitterness that had made him hard. He looked isolated and alone and dangerous as hell standing there, staring sightlessly out the window. What had happened to the gentle man she'd once known? The man who'd held her and laughed with her and made love to her as if she were the only woman in the world?

I destroyed him, she thought, and turned to flee to her room before he could see the tears.

Chapter 5

Robert found the bottle of cognac in the kitchen. He didn't know where she kept the snifters, so he poured two fingers into a teacup and slammed it back in two bitter gulps. He'd never been much of a drinker, had certainly never acquired a taste for cognac, but his temper was pumping pure adrenaline, and if he didn't get himself calmed down or find some kind of an outlet he was going to break something.

Hoping the alcohol would dull the sharp edge of fury pumping through him, he poured a second time then put the bottle away and carried the cup into the living area.

He knew better than to let any of this get to him. Damn it, he wasn't a jealous man. Had never been possessive or obsessive or particularly neurotic when it came to women. He'd always considered himself above that kind of imbecilic behavior. He was an enlightened man and worked through his problems with reason and civility and intellect. But the more primal side of him knew that if Jacques came through the door at that moment, Robert would take a great deal of satisfaction in decking him with all the diplomacy of an alley drunk.

He took another drink, grimacing against the bite of alcohol on his tongue. He knew what the problem was and he hated it almost as much as he hated the idea of Jacques taking over where he'd left off twenty-one months ago. Robert wasn't merely jealous. No, this was much worse than simple jealousy. He still had feelings for her. Deep, irrevocable feelings that came from a place inside him he couldn't control. It was as simple and terrible as that. And he knew with every beat of his heart that there wasn't a damn thing he could do about it except move on.

Easier said than done when the woman had him tied up in knots. Here he was on one of the most important missions of his career, consoling himself with cognac because he couldn't keep his emotions in check, when he should be questioning her about DeBruzkya and Dr. Morrow. How pathetic was that?

"Drinking isn't going to help anything."

Robert looked up to find Lily standing in the doorway looking breathtaking and troubled and so beautiful he wanted to reach out and touch her just to make sure she was real. "Maybe not, but it's damn sure going to make me feel better."

"I can't do this, Robert."

He didn't want to know what *this* was, so he remained silent, knowing she was probably going to tell him, anyway.

The alcohol was beginning to fuzz his brain. And for the first time since he'd taken that first drink he wasn't so sure it was a good idea. Suddenly he needed his intellect, and it wasn't anywhere to be found. "You can't deal with me because you don't have the guts to tell me the truth."

"Don't lecture me about guts."

"Then talk to me, damn it. Tell me why you let me think you were dead for twenty-one months. Tell me why you had a son with another man. Tell me why we're not together right now, Lily.''

She crossed to him. For a moment he thought she was going to poke him in the chest with her finger, but she didn't. ''I can't get involved with you. I don't *want* to get involved with you. There's no way we can just pick up where we left off. Is that clear enough for you?''

She was standing so close he could smell the clean scent of her hair. A hint of the forest. The warmth of sunshine. And the sweet scent of mountain air rolled into a single, intoxicating aroma. The combination was beginning to make him feel woozy. ''I got you loud and clear,'' he managed to speak.

''I expect you to respect my feelings while you're in my home. If you can't do that, then I'm going to have to ask you to leave. Are you getting this?''

Her eyes were luminous in the soft light coming in through the kitchen window. Robert stared at her, shocked that he could want her even as she trounced him with that sharp mouth of hers. Frustration coiled and burned in his gut like barbed wire being pulled ever tighter. The voice of reason called out for him to turn and walk away before he did something stupid, but the need to touch her was much more powerful.

She winced when he raised his hand and brushed a lock of hair from her face. Her eyes widened. Her full lips parted as if she were about to protest, but she didn't. Robert looked at her, aware of the color riding high in her cheeks. That her pupils were dilated. He stared, knowing those things weren't the reactions of a woman who wanted a man to stay away.

''If you want me to stay away from you I suggest you stop looking at me that way,'' he growled.

''I—I don't know what you mean.''

''You're sending out mixed signals like a Las Vegas marquee.''

''I'm ticked off.''

"Yeah, and maybe I'm the only one who has the guts to acknowledge what's really going on."

"You're out of line," she snapped.

"You're damn straight I am." He started to brush his fingers over her lips, but she slapped his hand away.

"You know better than to drink alcohol," she said.

Robert didn't think his reaction to her had a damn thing to do with the alcohol he'd consumed, though she was right in that he'd never been able to handle much in the way of drinking. When he was in high school, he'd been diagnosed with a rare blood disease he'd inherited from his father. One of the effects of the disease was that his body couldn't break down alcohol. He was able to drink in moderation, but the effects were magnified. Lily had teased him about it when they'd been together.

"I know better than to do a lot of things, but I do them anyway." He shrugged. "Here I am."

"I'm still wondering about your motives."

"I thought that was obvious."

"I might believe you if the pieces fit." She shook her head. "They don't."

Scowling, Robert walked into the kitchen and dumped the remaining cognac down the drain. Since Lily didn't know about his being an agent for ARIES, maybe it wasn't such a bad idea to let her think his motives were of a more personal nature.

Cursing under his breath, he rinsed the glass then set it to drain and walked into the living area. "Talk to me about DeBruzkya." He didn't miss the irony in that the most dangerous subject they could possibly discuss was the only safe topic to breach.

She glanced at him from the chair where she was sitting, her expression perplexed and perhaps a little suspicious. "What do you want to know?"

"Everything. Anything you can tell me."

The lockbox lay open on the floor in front of her. Lily slipped from the chair and knelt. She lifted a well-used folder and a brown envelope, then held both out for Robert. "This is everything I've been able to document in the last couple of years."

Taking the chair next to hers, Robert took the folder, and opened it and skimmed the contents. "You've been busy."

"So has DeBruzkya."

He picked up a photo, set it down quickly. "Not the kind of stuff he would want the rest of the world to know about."

Frowning, she gestured toward the file. "There are some things going on that I don't understand."

"Like what?"

"From the information I've been able to gather, he's suddenly become very interested in acquiring gemstones."

The hairs at the back of Robert's neck prickled. "Gemstones? How do you know?"

"Come on, Robert. I'm a journalist. I dig up information for a living."

"So what did you dig up?"

"There have been a series of robberies," she said.

"They've been in the news at home," he said easily. "They've taken place in several countries. The Stedt Museum in London—"

"The Legvold collection in Stockholm. Van Werten in Frankfurt," Lily finished.

"DeBruzkya is behind the robberies?" he asked.

"During one of our interview sessions, he told me about his interest in acquiring gemstones. I made a note but didn't think anything about it. Then a few months later I heard about the robberies. I did a little digging, and sure enough, some of his top lieutenants were out of the country during each of the robberies. Later, I learned he'd acquired several of the gems for his collection. I know him well enough to assume it wasn't by conventional means."

Thunder rumbled outside. Robert saw her shiver but fought the urge to move closer to her. Lily reached behind the chair, pulled out a threadbare quilt and draped it over her shoulders.

"Two people were nearly killed last week when he hit the Gala Summit in D.C.," he said. "One of them was a good friend of mine."

"I read about it," she said. "I'm sorry. I hope your friend is all right."

He thought of Ethan and Kelly and almost smiled. "He's doing just fine."

"DeBruzkya is getting bolder and bolder."

"He's out of control."

"Is that why you're here?" She shot him a canny look.

Robert stared at her. "I'm here to inoculate children against disease. That's all you need to know."

She didn't look convinced, but he didn't push it. "What troubles me most about this is that DeBruzkya doesn't seem like the kind of man who would be interested in gemstones."

"True. He's more of a weapons of mass destruction kind of guy." Robert frowned at the thought. "Even if he's amassing these gems to finance his dirty little war, it doesn't seem like his style."

"There's another bizarre twist that might help put the pieces together for you."

"I can't wait to hear it," he said dryly.

"Have you ever heard of the Gem of Power?" she asked.

"I've heard enough to know it's an old Rebelian legend that no one believes, including me."

"Quite a few people do believe in this legend, particularly some of the older peasants from the southern mining region. The legend has been around for hundreds of years." Leaning back in the chair, she brought her knees up to her chest and hugged them to her. "The last time I met with DeBruzkya, he mentioned this Gem of Power. I thought it was odd at the time, but now I'm not so sure it was odd at all."

"DeBruzkya doesn't strike me as a superstitious man."

''Me, neither, but for some reason he appears to believe in this particular legend.''

''You're kidding?''

She shook her head. ''He started talking about it one day when we were having espresso at a café in Rajalla. At first I didn't know where he was going with it. I'd been so involved with the freedom movement here that I hadn't kept up with world events, so I didn't know about the gem thefts.''

''What do the thefts have to do with an old legend?'' Robert asked.

''I'm not sure, but I swear, Robert, that day I met with DeBruzkya and he talked about the legend, I think he believed it. I could see the fanaticism in his eyes.'' The memory of fervor with which he told the legend made her shiver, and she pulled the quilt more tightly about her shoulders. ''He was creeping me out.''

''What's the legend about?''

''Something like 'he who owns the stone will have the power to rule the world.'''

''Sounds good in theory, if you're a nutcase. I don't think DeBruzkya is a nutcase. Dangerous, definitely, but not a nut.''

''Maybe he's going to use it to play upon the superstitions of the Rebelian people. You know, to control them.''

''Could be. He's a control freak, but I don't see how he could believe a legend would give him any kind of meaningful leverage.'' He scrubbed a hand over his jaw. ''What's the story behind the legend?''

''I've heard it told in slightly different ways in different circles. The way DeBruzkya told it, the legend started some four hundred years ago when a Rebelian ruler had a huge stone set for his bride. Shortly after the birth of their first child, a son, she died after a long and terrible illness. Four generations of royal brides died the same way. Their deaths started to give the stone a bad rap as being cursed. The fifth-generation bride was a bit more shrewd than the others and decided she wasn't going to be the next in line. She covertly sold the stone to a rich merchant who wanted to murder his wife. At that point, the stone disappeared into the Rebelian population. No one knows where it is.''

"What kind of stone?" he asked.

"No one knows."

"How does that fit with the claim of power to rule the world?"

Lily shrugged. "Maybe the stone enables its owner to commit the perfect murder."

"Most times it takes more than one murder to rule a country."

Mass murder, she thought and shivered.

"That's quite a legend." Robert said.

"Makes you wonder about the guy asking for your hand." Lily wasn't superstitious, but she couldn't keep the gooseflesh from raising on her arms. She listened to the rain ping against the tin roof and thought about the legend and tried not to let it trouble her.

"You put on a good front, Lily. But it's pretty clear to me that you're more afraid than you're letting on."

The statement jolted her, and for a moment she wasn't sure how to answer. She didn't like admitting to being afraid—it made her feel somehow diminished—but she didn't think Robert would believe a lie. "Only a fool wouldn't be afraid of a man like DeBruzkya."

"How did you get close to him?"

"I let him think he was in control of the situation. That he could use me to get what he wanted."

"To write his autobiography?"

She nodded. "I led him to believe I was a hungry young writer with big plans for my career. His ego made it easy to deceive him. All I had to do was let him think I was going to tell the world that he is not the evil man the mainstream media have portrayed him to be, but a misunderstood leader with a brilliant mind and ambitious ideas for his country and the rest of Europe."

"Ego," Robert muttered.

"That makes him predictable."

"To a degree." He rubbed his left thigh. "Do you know where his headquarters is located?"

"It's supposed to be secret, but during one of our meetings he hinted that it's in the mountains to the north."

"Rugged country," Robert said. "Hartz Forest area?"

She nodded, debating whether to tell him the rest. She knew he wouldn't approve, but then she'd done a lot of things in the last twenty-one months he wouldn't approve of. She suspected there was something more going on with him than he was letting on, but for the life of her she couldn't figure out what it was. She supposed both of them were keeping their fair share of secrets.

"One evening after one of our meetings, I followed him," she said.

Quick anger flickered in his eyes. "You *what?*"

"I said I fol—"

"I heard you the first time," he snapped. "What I want to know is how you could do something so foolhardy."

Annoyed that he would raise his voice to her over risking her life for something she believed in vehemently, she rose abruptly. "If I were a man you'd be slapping me on the back and telling me how brave I was."

"Or maybe I'd deck you. Do you have any idea how dangerous that was?"

"Of course I do."

"And of course you did it anyway, didn't you? For God's sake, Lily, if the soldiers had found you—"

"They didn't."

Leaning forward, Robert put his elbows on his knees and stared at his boots. "Damn it."

"This is exactly what I'm talking about. If you can't deal with me as an equal—"

"What I can't deal with is your taking stupid risks—"

"There's nothing stupid about trying to stop a madman." She started to turn away, but he stopped her.

"Sit down," he growled.

Lily stood her ground.

Scrubbing his hands over his face, he looked at her. "Please," he said. "I'd like to finish this."

Slowly, she sank into the chair.

"Where's the headquarters?" he asked.

"It's the old Veisweimar Castle."

Robert's head snapped up at the mention of the old castle. "That place is barely standing."

"Not anymore. It's a fortress replete with luxury suites, gargoyles and a moat."

"A moat?"

She nodded. "DeBruzkya brought in heavy machinery and had a moat dug.

"Have you been inside?"

She shook her head. "No. I've only seen it from a distance, but DeBruzkya bragged about it in great detail."

"What else do you know?"

"I know he hired a small army of stonemasons to build a wall around the entire grounds. An interior design firm from Paris installed four luxury suites." Lily had seen the structure that one and only time, and it had left quite an impression on her mind. Since, she'd dug up everything she could get her hands on and read about it. The Veisweimar Castle was a behemoth structure built in medieval times. A century later it fell to ruin, then became a prison during the nineteenth century where prisoners were routinely tortured and executed.

"What kind of security has he got?" Robert asked.

"DeBruzkya's fanatical about security. There were too many armed soldiers for me to get close, but I got within a hundred yards of the outer perimeter. From what I could tell he's got a hundred or so armed soldiers guarding the place. Then there's the moat, of course."

"Alligators?"

She glanced at Robert, surprised to see that he'd made a joke. "I don't think so," she said.

"Good, I hate big slimy lizards with fangs."

Despite the seriousness of the subject she smiled. It was an odd moment for humor, but she knew that during prolonged periods of high stress, humor could be a powerful tool against despair. As a doctor, Robert would know that. She wondered if he was using humor for her benefit or his.

"The outer wall is topped with concrete," she said. "Shards of glass and concertina wire were imbedded in the concrete."

"Guess he doesn't want his neighbors popping over unexpectedly."

"I don't know him well. I mean, on a personal level. But from talking with him and others who know him, I was able to put together a sort of psychological profile." She slid a sheet of paper from a manila folder. "From all appearances he's a paranoid sociopath suffering from delusions of grandeur."

Scowling, Robert took the paper and skimmed it. "Nice."

"I wouldn't recommend pissing him off."

Shaking his head, Robert cursed. "What the hell kind of crazy bastard are we dealing with?"

"A very dangerous one."

Lily jumped when a crack of thunder shook the walls. She knew Robert was watching her, but she didn't meet his gaze. She didn't want him to know how jumpy this was making her.

"Have you ever heard anyone mention an American doctor by the name of Alex Morrow?" he asked after a moment.

Lily repeated the name, knowing it was familiar, but for the life of her she couldn't remember where she'd heard it. "I'm not sure. Who is he?"

"He's an environmental geologist. An American who disappeared during a conference in Holzberg."

"He's a friend of yours?"

Robert nodded. "I need to find him."

She'd been wondering about his motivations for showing up, for having so many questions about DeBruzkya, and realized a piece of the puzzle had fallen neatly into place. But she also knew Morrow wasn't the only reason Robert was here. "You think DeBruzkya is involved in Morrow's disappearance?"

"I think he's involved up to his bald head and beady eyes." Crossing his ankle over his knee, he absently began to massage his thigh.

Lily watched for a moment, remembering his limp, and felt a tug of guilt. She wondered how badly he'd been injured on that last terrible night. She wondered if he'd been able to forgive her.

"Do you need something for the pain?" she asked.

His gaze jerked to hers. For an instant she saw surprise in its vivid blue depths, then his eyes hardened and cooled, like molten steel plunged into ice water. "I'm fine."

"I couldn't help but notice your limp yesterday."

As if realizing he'd been massaging his thigh, he released it and leaned back in the chair. "It's a long walk from Rajalla to your cottage."

"What happened, Robert?"

His expression darkened. He glanced toward the window, then at her. "I thought you didn't want to talk about that night."

"I just…" She struggled with words she couldn't quite get right. "I don't. I just…I'm sorry you were hurt."

His gaze burned into hers. "So am I."

She felt the heat of his stare as surely as she felt her heart roll over and begin to pound against her breast. Outside, the storm hurled rain and small hailstones against the tin roof. Even though it was still early, the windows had gone dark.

"I took a hit from some shrapnel." He looked away, and she wondered if, for an instant, he was back at the pub, hurting and angry because she'd refused to leave with him. She wondered if he blamed her. If he hated her.

"Were you badly injured?" she asked.

"Compound fracture of the femur. A few bone fragments. But there wasn't any arterial damage." He shrugged, looking distinctly uncomfortable. "A titanium pin, a few bolts, and I'm almost new."

"My God." The night flashed horribly in her mind's eye, the images hitting her with the same force as the bombs striking the ground. Some nights she could still feel the hot breath of the explosion. The smell of singed hair. The pain of her burns. "That could have been fatal."

"That's one of the advantages of being a doctor. You get into a tight spot in the field and you can treat yourself." He grinned, but the grin was tight and plastic, and she instinctively knew the injury had been much worse than he was letting on.

"Some British medics picked me up," he said. "They shot me up with morphine and put me on a plane to Paris. It took a couple of surgeries, but the surgeon was able to save the leg."

"Does it still bother you much?"

He offered a wan smile. "Only when I have to hike six miles blindfolded in the rain."

Hurting for him, trying not to imagine what he'd gone through, she looked down, realizing her knuckles were white. "I'm sorry you had to go through that. It must have been terrible."

"It was a long time ago."

"You don't forget something like that."

For several minutes, they sat in silence and listened to the rain. Then he asked, "What about you?"

She glanced up, found his eyes already on her, asking questions she had no desire to answer. She'd known by bringing up that night that she would be opening the door to a subject that was best left closed and locked down tight. Lily didn't want to talk about what had happened to her that night. She knew it wasn't fair, but they'd both been around enough to know life wasn't always fair. She'd been around enough to know some things were best left unremembered—even if she couldn't forget.

"I need to check on Jack," she said.

She started to rise, but he reached out and grasped her forearm. "Quid pro quo," he said.

"It doesn't work that way." She'd meant for the words to come out strong, but they came out as nothing more than a whisper.

He must have read something in her eyes, because he suddenly released her. "I'm not going to let this go."

"Yes, you are," she said, but her heart was pounding when she walked away.

Chapter 6

Jack had never been much of a crier. Normally he was a content baby with a sweet personality and easygoing temperament. But over the last couple of months, it seemed that he'd been cranky more often than not. He wasn't sleeping as well. Some days he was finicky with his food.

At 2:00 a.m. Lily turned on the tiny lamp next to her bed, slipped into her robe, went to the crib and gathered her son into her arms. "Mommy's here, sweetheart."

But Jack wasn't having any sweet talk. His little body strained with each wail. His skin felt clammy and damp against hers even though the cottage was cool. Concerned, Lily held him snugly against her, caressing the back of his head and murmuring a mother's sweet nothings. She tried using the pacifier she kept on hand for emergencies, but he refused it. Cradling him in her arms, she paced the room several times, rocking him, talking to him, stroking him. But he didn't stop crying.

It was the third time in as many hours that she'd been up with him. The longer she listened to him cry, the more certain she became that something was wrong. She wasn't exactly sure how she knew, but she did. The pitch of his cry wasn't quite right. It seemed almost frantic. Usually, he stopped crying immediately upon being picked up. Tonight, he hadn't even slowed down.

"Shh. It's okay, big guy," she cooed. "Are you sick? Do you have a tummy ache?"

Knowing a mother's nervousness could be easily transmitted to a child, she tried to keep her tone light. But she heard the sharp edge of concern in her voice. She felt that same concern all the way down to her bones. As much as she didn't want to admit it, she feared he might be seriously sick.

She carried him to her bed and laid him down, sliding her finger into his diaper. Dry. It was the second time she'd checked it. And the second time she'd found it dry. Earlier, she'd warmed a bottle of goat's milk. He'd refused it an hour ago. Surely he must be hungry now. But when she put the nipple to his lips, he turned his head and cried even louder.

Because she couldn't stand to see him lying on the bed and crying, she scooped him into her arms. Cradling him gently, she hummed a meaningless nursery rhyme and began to pace the room. But Jack didn't stop crying.

"What's wrong, sweetheart?" she murmured. "Mommy's here, sweet baby."

She carried him to the ancient rocker beside her bed, she pulled the quilt over both of them and began to rock, the way she had when he was a newborn. Rocking usually quieted him when nothing else would. Even when he'd had a painful bout with colic, rocking had usually lulled him to sleep. They'd spent some long and uncomfortable nights together in this rocker. Then one of the Rebelian women in the village had suggested goat's milk instead of cow milk. The colic had ceased immediately, and she'd been giving him goat's milk ever since.

After five minutes of rocking, Jack's cries became even

more frantic. Lily had been trying to ignore the quiver of worry hovering in her gut. Surely he was just being fussy because he was teething, wasn't he? All babies were fussy when those first couple of teeth cut through their tender gums, weren't they? But when she laid Jack on the bed and saw that his lips were darker than usual and the tips of his little fingers were blue, worry shot up the scale into full-fledged fear.

"Okay, sweetheart," she said, scooping him into her arms. "Let's go get Robert."

"I'm right here."

Lily jolted at the sound of his voice. She looked up to see Robert standing in the doorway of her bedroom wearing nothing more than a pair of faded jeans and a sour look. His hair was sticking up. Black stubble darkened his jaw. He didn't look very doctorly, but she was glad to see him nonetheless.

"Something's wrong," she said. "I can't seem to get him calmed down." She laid Jack on the bed, concern rippling through her when his little body went taut with another high-pitched wail. "He's never cried like this. Even as a newborn he was a very calm and happy baby. But the last couple of months he's been…fussy."

Robert walked to the bed and looked at the baby.

"I thought he needed changing, but he wasn't wet. I warmed some milk for him, but he refused to take it."

"Does he usually take a bottle at night?" he asked.

She nodded. "Goat's milk, because he had a bout with colic."

"Did he take any milk tonight?"

"No." She looked at her child, felt the worry tighten like a chain around her chest. "His coloring is…off. His lips seem darker."

Bending, Robert lifted one of Jack's fingers and gently squeezed the tip.

"What is it?" she asked.

"Just checking circulation. His refill rate is slow."

"What does that mean?" Lily pressed a hand to her chest. "My God. Is it serious?"

"Probably not. But I think it's smarter to err on the side of caution." Robert looked at her. "I don't think we should wait much longer before taking him to the hospital."

"Then it *is* serious." Her heart stuttered and threatened to stop. "My God—"

"Just take it easy, Lily. I don't think anything at this point. With a child this age, it could be any number of things."

"But why is he crying like that? Is he in pain?"

"Look, I've got some acetaminophen in my bag. Let me dose him. That should help him get to sleep."

Lily looked at her precious child and set her hand against his forehead. "I love him so much, Robert. I couldn't bear it if—"

"Nothing's going to happen to him," he said firmly. "Just stay calm for me, all right?"

"Okay." She took a deep breath. "I'm just…scared."

"I know you are." He looked into her eyes. "Everything is going to be all right."

The way he said it left no room for doubt. And for that she was incredibly grateful. "Okay," she said, feeling calmer.

"Good girl."

For an instant she thought he would offer comfort. Comfort she badly needed at that moment. Instead, he turned and started down the hall. She knew he was going to get his medical bag, but she felt his departure far too acutely. She turned to her son, felt her heart swell within her chest. Jack represented all the goodness in a world that wasn't always good. He represented hope for a future that was many times uncertain. He gave her joy when there was none to be had. If anything happened to him, she didn't think she could go on. "Everything's going to be all right, sweetheart," she said.

Lily had never been the kind of mother to overreact.

Even when she'd been a new mother and hadn't known a thing about babies, she'd taken all Jack's ailments pretty much in stride. This time was different, however. She didn't know how, but she *knew* there was something wrong with her baby. Something serious that was beyond her experience. Maybe beyond Robert's. As she stared at her son, the thought brought a hot rush of tears to her eyes, and her heart simply broke.

"Lily."

Quickly wiping away the tears, she turned to face him.

"I know one of the doctors at the hospital in Rajalla. Dr. Roman Orloff. We can trust him. He'll run the tests without alerting DeBruzkya or his soldiers."

"All I care about is getting Jack well."

She watched as he administered a small dose of acetaminophen. Jack had never been a good medicine taker and resisted, but Robert handled him with the gentle firmness of a man who'd administered medicine many times. She knew it was silly, but seeing Robert with Jack eased the fear clenching her chest.

"That should take down his temperature and help him rest," he said.

Lily walked over to stand beside him, and they both stared at Jack for a moment.

"I'd like to run a couple of preliminary clotting tests tonight if it's all right with you," Robert said after a moment.

"You can run tests here?"

"I've got the equipment to measure red and white blood cell counts and platelets. I can put some cells on a slide, scan it and send the scan via my satellite phone to the lab. The rest will have to be done at the hospital."

"Sounds pretty high-tech."

"It is."

She nodded. "Let's do it."

"I'll need your permission to take a blood sample."

"You've got it." She glanced at Jack. He had stopped

crying, but he looked pale and listless, and that broke her heart. "How will you get the sample?"

"A quick prick on his heel."

"Poor little guy."

Robert smiled, but she knew it was only to reassure her. "He's going to be fine," he said.

And for the first time since he'd shown up at her door, she was grateful he was there.

In his small room off the kitchen, Robert inserted the slide into the scanner, locked it down to keep the resolution from bleeding and, using his palm-size computer, adjusted the magnification. He tried to concentrate on getting a perfect scan, but he knew the odds were against it under field conditions. If he weren't so damn distracted...

He knew better than to think of Jack and Lily on a personal level. He told himself he would have done this even if mother and child were strangers he'd met on the street. He was a doctor, after all. That's what he did. He would have made sure they received proper medical care no matter who they were.

Only this woman and her child weren't strangers. Robert had felt that the instant he'd set foot in the cottage, the instant he laid eyes on that child. Jack may not be his son, but he felt a connection nonetheless. And if he wasn't careful, he was going to find himself getting a little too close for comfort. A grave mistake considering the circumstances. Not only were he and Lily finished, but he had a mission to carry out.

He couldn't let this woman and her child interfere with finding Alex Morrow and collecting information on Bruno DeBruzkya. Damn it, he and Lily were through. Had been for almost two years. She had a child and a life that didn't include him. She'd moved on. Robert needed to do the same.

Cursing under his breath, he clicked the mouse to open the software and scanned the cells on the slide. Once the cells had been scanned, he saved the image and information to the tiny disk, then sent both files to the satellite hub, which patched them directly through to ARIES headquarters. He'd instructed Hatch to forward the scan to the laboratory on site, along with an order for the tests he wanted run. He'd been able to skirt most of Hatch's questions about whose blood they were testing. Hatch hadn't pressed, but Robert knew he'd eventually have to come clean. He didn't relish the idea of explaining to his boss that he was holed up with a woman he'd spent the last twenty-one months trying to get out of his system.

"How long will it be?"

He looked up from his tiny computer to find Lily standing in the doorway. Because the sight of her invariably triggered inappropriate thoughts, he looked at the computer and stared blindly at the screen. "We should have preliminary results in a few minutes. Dr. Orloff is expecting us."

"Good."

After shutting down the computer, he rose and started toward her. "How's Jack?"

"He's finally asleep." She hugged herself as if against a chill. "I think he's exhausted."

Because it was too early to make any kind of definitive diagnosis, Robert hadn't yet admitted to Lily that he was, indeed, concerned about her son. His symptoms were consistent with several types of anemia that, though rare, were most often diagnosed in children under two years of age. He wanted to reassure her, but at this point he knew those reassurances could turn out to be false. It made him feel lousy that he couldn't even offer her that.

"If he needs any kind of medication that isn't available in Rajalla, I can have some sent to you from Paris or Frankfurt," he said.

She nodded. "Thank you."

Robert could see the strain in her eyes, the fear hovering just beneath her calm facade. Even though she was doing a pretty good job of masking it, he sensed the tension ra-

diating through her. Shadows of fatigue marred the porcelain skin beneath her eyes. He wondered how well she
would hold up if it turned out to be something serious. He
hoped like hell it wasn't.

"You haven't had any sleep," he said. "Why don't you
lie down? I'll wake you when the results come back."

"No." She shook her head. "There's no way I could
sleep without knowing—"

"Lily, these tests are only preliminary. They may not tell
us anything."

"I can't sleep knowing he's sick. That he could be seriously ill. For God's sake, Robert, he's the reason I get
out of bed every day." Her voice broke with the last word.
"I can't let anything happen to him. He's so little and sweet
and helpless...."

"It's not going to do either of you any good if you worry
yourself sick."

"I have a bad feeling about this," she whispered.

"It may turn out to be something as simple as anemia.
That's very treatable. I can prescribe some vitamins. A shot
of B-12. A change in diet, maybe. And he'll be good as
new."

She shook her head. "He's so weak he couldn't even
squeeze my finger. That's a game we play. Kind of like
peekaboo. He wanted to play, I could see it in his eyes.
But he couldn't because he was too weak." She blinked
back tears. "That breaks my heart."

Robert sensed her emotions unraveling and felt a quiver
of uneasiness in his gut. "It's going to be all right," he
said.

"You don't know that."

He wanted badly to reassure her but knew that would be
a dangerous move at this point. She was vulnerable. Hell,
maybe he was, too. Instead, he held his ground and watched
her break.

Turning away from him, she lowered her head and put
her face in her hands. She didn't make a sound, but Robert

could see that her shoulders were shaking. Lily had never been an overly emotional woman. She was calm and rational and not prone to outbursts. He supposed that was why watching her break was so damn hard.

Damn it, he hadn't wanted this to happen. He didn't want to be in this position. So he stood there, feeling helpless and lousy because he couldn't reassure her, because he didn't trust himself to touch her, because he wanted her and knew it was wrong.

"Lily…"

She cut him off by holding up a trembling hand. "Just give me a minute." But she didn't stop crying. She didn't raise her head. And she didn't look at him. She just stood there and silently cried. A silence that was as loud as any keening.

When he couldn't stand it anymore, Robert reached for her. "Come here," he said.

"I'm okay."

"Yeah, I can tell by the way you're shaking." Putting his arm gently around her shoulders, he pulled her against him.

She stiffened, then raised shimmering hazel eyes to his. "You don't have to do this."

"Yes, I do," he said and put his arms around her.

She felt incredibly small cocooned within his arms. The sensation of her against him shocked him with pleasure, and he couldn't help but marvel at how perfect the fit was. He could feel the tremors rising inside her, but she didn't make a sound. He held her and tried not to think about how it was affecting him. But her scent rose to titillate him. The essence of clean hair and mountain air and woman. He rested his head against hers and breathed in deeply, felt an uncomfortable stir deep in his gut that didn't have a damn thing to do with physical sensation.

Robert knew he was playing with fire. He knew he should let her go and take a long, cold shower. But the feel of her against him overpowered logic.

''Tell me he's going to be all right,'' she whispered.

Closing his eyes, Robert caressed the back of her head. ''We're going to do everything we can, okay?''

A sigh shuddered out of her. A sound so filled with soul-wrenching emotion that he tightened his arms around her and wished fervently that he could take away her worry. He ran his hands over her shoulders and down her back, telling himself it was a gesture of comfort. But he was all too aware of her body pressed against his. Her scent filling his lungs. The knowledge of the physical ecstasy they'd once shared. She wasn't wearing a bra, and he could feel the soft brush of her breasts against his chest. His body stirred in response, the hot rush of blood to his groin making his sex heavy and uncomfortable. He started to shift away, but for the first time he realized her arms were around him, too.

''Just…hold me for a moment,'' she said.

He didn't move away, but he didn't get any closer, either. The short span from his hips to hers was hellish for him, but he couldn't close the distance without making his state of arousal evident. She was upset and had a sick child to deal with, for God's sake. As far as he knew she had someone else in her life. What kind of man was he—what kind of *doctor*—wanting her when she was at her most vulnerable?

''You're going to be all right,'' he said after a moment.

Pulling away slightly, she looked at him with ravaged eyes. ''Tell me Jack's going to be all right,'' she said fiercely.

Robert knew better than to make false promises. But there was no way he could look into her luminous eyes and let her hurt. ''He's going to be all right.''

Her face was only a few short inches from his. So close he could see the wet streaks of tears on her cheeks. The thrum of her pulse at her throat. The uncertainty in her eyes. She looked frightened and vulnerable and incredibly beautiful at once. He was keenly aware of her arms around him.

She moved against him, and every nerve in his body zinged with pleasure. If she could feel his arousal against her, she made no indication, made no move to pull away. Robert wasn't sure if that was good or bad, just very, very dangerous.

A cry from the rear bedroom jolted him. As if suddenly realizing the precariousness of the situation, Lily blinked at him and loosened her arms. "I...need to check on Jack."

Robert released her and stepped back, but he felt her departure like a piece of his own flesh being ripped away. For an interminable moment, neither of them moved. Electricity snapped in the small space between them. He felt the tingle with a thousand nerve endings, felt the pull of her, like the undertow of a powerful river threatening to pull him into murky depths and drown him.

Without a word, she turned and fled the room.

Robert stood staring after her for a long time, trying hard to ignore the rapid-fire beat of his heart and the slow ache of sexual frustration in his groin. Cursing under his breath, he turned to the palm computer lying on the cot. He stared at the screen unseeing for a moment while his body and his brain reconciled what had just happened. He knew he was treading on thin ice. Lily Scott was the last woman in the world he should be having sexual feelings for. For God's sake, she'd had a child with another man. She'd let him believe she was dead for twenty-one months. But Robert could no longer deny that something powerful lingered between them. The only question that remained was whether either of them were crazy enough to do anything about it.

The computer beeped. Robert glanced at the tiny screen to see the incoming communication light flicker. He pulled out the satellite phone, quickly set up the dish antenna, hit several keys and the liquid crystal display screen glowed. He waited impatiently for the satellite signal to go through. When the green light flickered, he slipped the tiny microphone into his ear and listened to the grid coordinates beep.

He typed in his identification number and password, then waited for voice recognition.

Hatch's image appeared on the screen.

"What have you got?" Robert asked, surprised by the level of tension in his voice.

If Hatch noticed he made no indication. "One of the technicians called a few minutes ago with some prelim results. He wants me to patch you through."

"Roger that."

"Everything else okay?"

"Fine."

The lights blinked with a flash of lightning, then the room went dark. "Damn it," Robert muttered.

"I'm hoping that's a storm that just took out your lights and not DeBruzkya's fireworks," Hatch said.

"It's the storm."

"Okay, then. Patching you through."

Robert stared hard at the other man's image and felt the hairs at his nape prickle. It wasn't like Hatch not to ask him about the mission. Not to ask him why the hell he was running blood tests on a child when he should be interrogating his contact about DeBruzkya. Robert hadn't done squat, and yet Hatch hadn't even asked for an update. What the hell was going on?

Robert started to speak, but the click of the transfer cut him off. He waited impatiently through a series of clicks as he was patched through to the ARIES biomedical research facility. An instant later a male voice came over the line. "Dr. Davidson?"

"What have you got?"

A man with red hair and freckles wearing a white lab coat materialized on the screen. "We got some of the preliminary test results back on the blood sample image."

Robert pulled up a blank screen with which to type in notes. "Go," he said impatiently.

"It shows that this child has a very serious blood disease."

Robert's hands froze on the keyboard, a terrible uneasiness crawling along the back of his neck. "What disease?"

"Juvenile onset hereditary hemoedema."

The words hit him like a punch. Shocking and brutal and damningly familiar. Robert stared at the man's image on the screen, aware that his heart was pounding, that his brain was trying desperately not to jump to conclusions—and failing miserably. "Are you sure?" he heard himself say.

"There's no mistake." The other man paused. "With hereditary hemoedema the blood lacks a certain protein—"

"I know what it is," he growled.

"If the child is showing symptoms, then you know the long-term prognosis is much improved if he gets a bone marrow transplant from a matching donor."

Matching donor.

He closed his eyes.

"Dr. Davidson?"

Robert disconnected and stood staring at the blank screen, his thoughts running a hundred miles an hour. He knew all about hereditary hemoedema. Hell, he was an *expert* on the disease. He'd inherited it from his father and had been dealing with it since he was fourteen years old. And he knew it could only mean one thing when it came to that innocent child sleeping in the bedroom down the hall.

"Hell." His voice sounded strange in the utter silence of the room. His chest felt tight, and for a moment, he couldn't take a breath.

He thought about Jack. A little boy with hereditary juvenile onset hemoedema. A little boy with *his* eyes. *His* genes. *His* disease.

God in heaven. Jack was *his* son.

The reality of the situation shattered him. Why hadn't he realized this before? The truth had been right under his nose. How could he have been so blind?

Knowing there was only one way to find out, Robert started for Lily's bedroom.

Chapter 7

Lily carried the cup of tea from the kitchen toward her bedroom, where Jack was sleeping. The hall was pitch-black. But she'd long since grown used to the blackouts. The darkness didn't bother her. She felt as if she'd been living in darkness for a very long time.

She was midway down the hall when a flash of lightning illuminated Robert's silhouette standing in the doorway of her room. The sight of him startled her. She stopped, felt the kick of adrenaline in her blood. In the instant his face had been illuminated, she'd seen something in his eyes. Something dangerous and primal and as unpredictable as the storm.

Her heart rolled into a hard staccato. Another flash of lightning revealed that Robert was moving toward her at a determined clip, his gaze hard, his jaw taut. She knew it was ridiculous, but for the first time in her life she was afraid of him. She felt the fear crawling inside her. Adrenaline burned in her muscles like acid. The urge to flee was strong, but his stare held her suspended, like an insect in amber.

She stepped back. It unnerved her that she couldn't see him. Something had changed in the minutes since they'd talked. She was sure of it. She could feel the volatile zing of his thoughts in the air between them.

She heard herself utter his name, but her voice came out as little more than a whisper. She couldn't see him, but she heard the steady progression of his footfalls. She could feel him getting closer, the raw energy pouring off him in electric waves.

Her back encountered the wall, and she realized belatedly she'd taken several steps back. Her brain raced for explanations for his silent approach, but none of them fit. Lightning flashed outside her bedroom window. He'd stopped several feet away from her and stood there, unmoving, as if he were made of stone.

"Why are you looking at me like that?" she asked.

For a moment the only sound came from the wind tearing around the cottage. Thunder crashed, and she jumped. A strobe of lightning illuminated his face. And in the depths of his eyes she saw...devastation. She saw the fury of a man who'd been betrayed. A man who'd been lied to. A man she'd hurt terribly.

A man who knew the truth.

"How old is he," he snarled.

"I—I told you. N-nine months."

"You're lying, damn it."

"No."

"He's mine."

His words vibrated through her brain like the chiseled point of a jackhammer. They pounded her until she couldn't think, couldn't breathe. The cup of tea slipped from her hand. It hit the floor and shattered. Hot tea spewed onto her bare ankles, but she barely felt the scald. Vaguely, she thought of the glass and made a mental note to clean it as soon as possible.

"He's a year old, isn't he, Lily?"

"Yes," she whispered.

"You kept him from me."

"Robert—"

"I want to know why, damn it. And I want to know *right now!*"

But the only information her brain seemed capable of processing was that he'd discovered her secret. The one secret she'd sworn to keep no matter what the cost to her.

"It's n-not what you think," she managed after a moment.

"You don't know what I think."

She struggled to calm her racing mind. "H-how did you know?"

"The blood test." His jaw flexed. "But it should have been obvious from the beginning. You must think I'm a pretty big fool."

"That's not the way it was."

"You took something precious from me." He started toward her.

She raised her hands as if to fend him off, but knew they wouldn't stop him. "Please, Robert. Just…calm down."

"I want an explanation," he snarled.

"I—I tried to contact you."

"You didn't try very hard." He stopped scant inches from her. So close she could feel the warmth of his breath on her face. She heard a heartbeat, but for the life of her she couldn't tell if it was hers or his. But it was beating so fast she felt certain it would explode. Or maybe they'd both just go up in flames.

"You lied to me," he said, slamming his open hand against the wall next to her with the last word.

A jab of real fear sent her back hard against the wall. The urge to run was strong, but Lily had never been a coward. She had to face this. Had to face him. Had to face what she'd done. "I'm sorry," she said.

"That's not good enough," he said between clenched teeth.

Lily stared at him, aware of her breath rushing raggedly from her throat. "Please, don't. Not like this."

"Don't do what? Ask for the truth?"

She felt trapped, like a rabbit in the crosshairs of a high-powered rifle. "You won't like it."

"Maybe I like being lied to even less. Did that ever cross your mind?" Leaning dangerously close to her, he put his hands on the wall on either side of her. "Why did you keep my son from me? Why didn't you tell me you were alive?"

"I couldn't," she choked.

"Do you have any idea what it did to me thinking you were dead?"

"I'm sorry."

"Sorry won't cut it, damn it!"

"Robert—"

"You ripped my heart out, Lily. You knew what losing you would do to me, but you did it anyway, didn't you?" He ground his teeth with the last word. "Damn you."

She'd never seen him so angry, so cold, so utterly merciless. All the things that had happened in the last twenty-one months jumbled in her brain. Her being injured. Jack's birth. Her dangerous meetings with DeBruzkya. She wanted to answer him. Robert was a rational man. Surely he would understand why she hadn't wanted to put him at risk.

But he was so close, she couldn't think. Her mind couldn't form a single coherent thought. She gasped with a sudden thunderclap. Robert's hands went to either side of her face, and every nerve in her body jumped. His palms were cool and slightly rough against her cheeks. He wasn't exceptionally tall, barely six feet, but he seemed to tower over her, and she had to crane her neck to maintain eye contact.

"I want to know why you lied to me," he said.

Lily tried to slide to one side. She had to get away from him, from the questions. From the truth she didn't want to face. But he trapped her with his body. "You owe me the truth," he said.

"I can't," she whispered.

He leaned into her with the full weight of his body. The contact shocked her. She could feel the hard ridge of him against her belly, shocking her senses and kindling a flame that had burned tiny and hot for almost two years. "I don't want this."

"That's not what your eyes are telling me."

"Stop before this goes too far."

"Too late," he said, and lowered his mouth to hers.

The kiss struck her as if a lightning bolt had stabbed down through the roof and run the length of her body. She felt herself go rigid. Long denied needs coiled and snapped inside her like lit fuses doused with gunpowder. She tried desperately to deny the desire her intellect had struggled so hard to forget. But the truth of the moment seared her, and she was lost. To reason. To sanity.

But her body remembered. Every hard plane. Every solid ridge of muscle. Every brush of hard against soft. She remembered the heady jitter of nerves at his touch. The promise of more. The anticipation of knowing she would get it.

All the while his mouth worked black magic on hers. A combination of gentle and fierce that made her legs weak and beckoned her to make a mistake. Lily felt herself begin to unravel, like yarn ripped from a spool to tangle and shred. Her senses flickered. Common sense fluttered away. Vaguely she was aware of her arms going around his shoulders. His name on her lips. The truth bursting in her heart.

Making a sound low in his throat, he slipped his tongue between her lips. The sudden taste of him shocked her with pleasure. She opened to him, delving into the warm silkiness of his mouth with her tongue. He murmured something in her ear, but she couldn't make out the words over the pounding of blood in her veins. She'd forgotten what it was like to be kissed like this. To be swept away and lost in a man's arms. In Robert's arms. The rightness of it fractured her control.

She arched against him, her hands skimming over his shoulders where rock hard muscles bunched and trembled with restrained power. His hands swept down her back, pausing at her hips and holding her in place while he moved against her. The flood of arousal mingled with urgency and coursed hotly through her, a lava flow barreling down a mountain to devour everything in its path.

And not even the knowledge that she was making a mistake could stop her. She kissed him with wild abandon, poured endless months of heartbreak and loneliness into it. She let herself feel all the things she had refused to feel, refused to remember, all the things she had denied for what seemed like eternity.

She shuddered when his hands brushed over her breasts. She'd forgotten how powerful desire could be. How he could make her breasts ache for his touch. She arced, giving him full access. His hands possessed her, molding her flesh. She cried out when he brushed his fingertips over her sensitized nipples, but he swallowed the sound with another kiss. She writhed in his arms, wild for his touch, frantic to ease the fire burning within her.

He made love to her mouth, drugging her and making her forget about all the reasons they shouldn't be doing this. He kissed her neck, her collarbone, the point of her shoulder. She smothered a cry when he raised her sweater and took her nipple into his mouth. She felt herself go wet between her legs. Her vision blurred when he began to suckle. She cupped the back of his head, guiding him, wanting him closer, wanting him inside her. She could feel the pounding of blood in her womb, tiny waves moving through her. Reaching down, she ran her fingers along the length of his arousal. A steel rod trapped within his jeans. Her hand went to his zipper, but he grasped her wrist and stopped her.

For an instant confusion swirled, then she felt him working the snap of her jeans. Lowering the zipper. She burned and ached and felt if he didn't touch her soon she would die with wanting. The world tilted beneath her feel when his hands met the crisp curls at her V. Whispering his name, Lily opened to him. Shifting closer, he separated her folds and dipped two fingers inside her.

The intimacy of the contact shattered her. White light exploded behind her lids, as violent and shocking as the lightning and thunder outside. She cried out his name when he began to stroke her. Deeply, knowing exactly where to touch, how much pressure to use, when to tease, when to satisfy. A minute part of her brain knew she should stop this before things got out of control. But the rest of her knew things had already passed that point, and she could do nothing but hang on for the ride.

The waves built inside her, a relentless tide spilling onto a jagged shore. She rode the peaks, letting their power tumble her end over end until she didn't know up from down. All the while he stroked her, deeply and firmly, driving her to a fever pitch, up and over the edge into a freefall.

She didn't want the moment to end. The preciousness of it clenched her heart. She closed her eyes against the flood of emotion. Physical and emotional sensation melded into a single profound ache and shimmered inside her, like a diamond melting beneath a thousand suns. Tears burned behind her lids, yet her body sang with a joy that couldn't be contained. She heard his name on her lips. A name she'd whispered a thousand times in the last months as she'd cried in the dark and denied what she knew to be true.

He captured her mouth, and she drank in the essence of him like a woman dying of thirst. She heard a sound, and only then did she realized a sob had escaped her.

Robert pulled back, his expression concerned. "I…didn't mean to hurt you."

Embarrassed that her emotions had spiraled out of control, Lily started to turn away, but he stopped her by touching her face gently.

"I didn't mean to make you cry." Shifting slightly, he brushed the damp hair from her face, then caught a tear with the pad of his thumb. "Lily."

"It's okay," she said, feeling awkward and silly and completely overwhelmed by what had just happened. "I'm just...that was...too much for me to handle."

"I'm sorry."

"No, it's my fault. I shouldn't have let that happen."

"I didn't give you much choice."

"I didn't exactly say no."

Robert looked away. Lily's cheeks burned with the memory of everything they'd done and the wanton way she'd reacted to his kiss. She wasn't a prude, but she didn't give up control easily. Robert was the only person she'd ever met who could do that to her. He'd always possessed the unique ability to destroy her inhibitions and make her lose control. Not only physically, but emotionally. She supposed that's why things had always been so intense between them. There was no middle ground when it came to her and Robert. It was all or nothing. Win or lose. Heaven or hell.

And now he knew her secret.

The thought sent a spear of panic skidding up her spine. Oh, what had she been *thinking* letting things get out of hand like that? She hadn't been thinking at all. That was the problem. That had always been the problem with Robert. One touch, and her intellect crumpled and turned to dust.

Lily didn't know what to do. He'd just proven to her that she was vulnerable to him. Far more vulnerable than she'd ever imagined. If she wasn't careful, he would lure her into making another mistake. A mistake that could end up costing both of them far more than their hearts.

Robert stared hard at her, keenly aware that he was still fully aroused and dangerously furious. He could still feel the wetness from her on his fingers, the hot pulse of blood in his groin. He didn't understand how she could have done this to him. How she could have done this to them. To that innocent child sleeping down the hall.

He was a father.

The thought staggered him. He told himself he should have seen it coming. The timing had been right. Jack was small for his age, but he was sick, and Robert should have known. Instead, he'd taken her at her word and assumed Jacques was Jack's father. Why hadn't he suspected? Robert had never been one to run away from the truth or his responsibilities. But maybe this particular truth wasn't something he was ready to face.

He had a one-year-old son. A little boy with a sweet smile and vivid blue eyes and a serious blood disease.

"Hell," he muttered.

Because he couldn't bear to stand so close to her and want her and at the same time be so furious he wanted to shake her, Robert stepped back. For the first time in his life he didn't trust himself to do the right thing. "I want answers, and I want them now," he ground out.

"Not here." Leaning against the wall, she worked frantically to fasten her jeans. "I've got to get this glass picked up."

He took another step back, cursing the burn of lust in his groin. He might be angry with her, but it didn't seem to be affecting his attraction to her. A dangerous combination for a man who'd just broken his number-one rule and lost control.

Turning away from her, he stalked to the living room. The fire had burned down to embers so he added a couple of logs. Because he wasn't yet ready to sit down, he went to the kitchen, put water in the kettle and set it over a burner. He wanted coffee, but she didn't appear to have any so he figured he'd have to settle for tea. Damn it, he was starting to hate tea.

He'd just poured two steaming cups when Lily walked into the kitchen. Robert glanced at her, felt his gut tighten at the sight of her, then quickly looked at his tea. "How is he?" he asked.

"Sleeping." She picked up her cup. "He drank some of the milk."

"Good. That will help him keep his strength up." He carried his cup to the living room. Because he was too restless to sit, he set it on the small table between the two chairs and walked over to stare into the fire. He was aware of her moving behind him, setting down her tea and taking one of the chairs. He could still smell the sweet scent of her. Still see the way she'd looked at him when he'd kissed her and stroked her to climax…

Robert crushed the image with a single blow. He couldn't think of that now. Instead, he turned to her, felt the beauty of her impact him, and he prayed she didn't notice. He didn't want her to know she had that kind of power. He didn't trust her not to use it against him.

"He has juvenile hereditary hemoedema," he said.

Lily reacted as if he'd slapped her. The blood drained from her face. She pressed a hand to her stomach. The urge to go to her, to comfort her was strong, but Robert didn't dare. Not at a time like this. Not when he knew touching her wouldn't stop with simple comforting.

"Is it serious?" she asked.

"I've had it since I was fourteen."

"Is that why he's been sick? Why his fingers are blue?" He nodded.

"What do we do? I mean, can it be treated? Can we help him?"

He took a step closer. "The disease is incurable, but it's not life-threatening if he gets the proper care."

"Incurable." She looked ill. "Oh, God."

"He's going to be all right."

"How can you know—"

"I'm a doctor, Lily. I've got the same disease." He didn't think this was the time to tell her it was the same disease that had killed his father and brother. That losing those two people to hemoedema was the main reason he'd become a doctor.

"How do we treat it?" she asked.

"Eventually, he'll need a bone marrow transplant."

For an instant tears shimmered in her eyes, but she blinked them back. "Then I want to have him treated right away."

"Not in Rebelia. Paris, maybe. Or London—" *Or the clinic in D.C.*

"But he's sick now. I can't bear to see him so ill. Surely there's something we can do now, isn't there?"

"A transfusion will help."

"But my blood type isn't—"

"Mine is."

Lowering her head, she put her face in her hands and let out a long, shuddery breath. For a moment the only other sounds were the rain pinging against the roof and the crackle of the fire. When she'd gained control of her emotions she raised her head and looked at him. "Thank you."

Because he couldn't accept her gratitude for something he would have taken his last breath to do, he didn't answer. Instead, he stood with his back to the fire, watching her, trying not to think about how simple things had once been between them and how complex they were now.

"Tell me what I have to do," she said.

"I'll set something up with Dr. Orloff in Rajalla."

"All right."

"I want some answers, Lily," he said. "Damn it, I want them now."

She curled more deeply into the chair. Robert knew it was a protective gesture. He hated that she felt she needed to protect herself from him. But he wanted the truth. All of it.

"You were pregnant with Jack when I left Rebelia," he prompted.

"I didn't know it at the time, of course, but yes, I was pregnant."

"Why didn't you contact me?"

"There are a lot of reasons." She looked down at her tea. "All of them are…complicated."

"I'm real good at complicated, Lily. What I'm not good at is being lied to."

"I'm sorry I hurt you."

Tension shot through him at the apology. He knew she was expecting him to say it was okay, but he couldn't. It wasn't okay. Not by a long shot. So he didn't say anything at all.

Her eyes were ravaged when they met his. "If it's any consolation, I didn't realize you thought I'd been killed."

"What happened?"

"I was knocked unconscious and received a serious concussion when the building was destroyed. I had a broken clavicle. My shoulder and part of my arm were burned."

"How did you get out?"

"I didn't." She looked away. "The soldiers found me the next morning."

He felt the words like a whiplash across his belly. He imagined her lying among rubble, alone and badly injured, only to be discovered by hostile soldiers. "DeBruzkya's men?"

She nodded. "I was conscious by then, but I was trapped beneath the rubble. I was weak and dehydrated." A breath shuddered out of her. "At first the soldiers were cruel. They wouldn't help me. They just stood there, smoking cigarettes and laughing. Taunting me." She closed her eyes as if remembering, and the pain on her face was so vivid he had to look away.

"I didn't know if they were going to kill me or help me," she said. "I was lapsing in and out of lucidity. Then two young soldiers came with a stretcher and pulled me from the rubble."

"Did they help you?" He didn't want to think of how vulnerable or frightened she must have felt, being at the mercy of DeBruzkya's soldiers. The dictator wasn't known for merciful treatment of prisoners.

She risked a look at Robert, but she couldn't meet his gaze. "They were decent for the most part. One of the older soldiers...touched me inappropriately. I couldn't think of how to stop them, so I told them I knew DeBruzkya. The man in command stopped the others before things went too far."

"My God, Lily."

"They eventually took me to the hospital in Rajalla. A few days later, DeBruzkya showed up."

Robert couldn't stop looking at her, couldn't imagine this fragile woman injured at and the hands of enemy soldiers or a brutal man like DeBruzkya. "Why?"

She shrugged. "I wasn't sure at first. I was very frightened. I mean, he's been known to murder rebels on the spot. But to my surprise, he was very...human. He wished me well and told the doctors to make sure I was well taken care of. He sat with me several times, and we just... talked."

"About what?"

"I had interviewed him about a year and a half ago for a series of articles I was working on, so we had been introduced before."

"And you knew how to play him."

She nodded. "That was when I told him I wanted to write his autobiography."

The hairs at the back of Robert's neck prickled. "What did he say?"

"He loved the idea immediately."

"Lily..."

"We met several times in the coming weeks—"

"You really *are* crazy."

"I always insisted we meet in public places. The café in Rajalla. The royal palace. He bought me dinner once."

Because his heart was thrumming, Robert rose and paced to the hearth. The fire didn't need another log, but he put one on anyway. He needed to move. Damn it, he couldn't handle the thought of her manipulating such a dangerous, brutal man.

"One of the first things I realized about him is that he likes to talk. About himself. I've known things about him for months."

"Like what?"

"He told me about the Gem of Power. I got the impression he wanted me to believe he actually believed in the legend. Of course, I didn't, but I let him think so."

"What else?"

"In a nutshell, he wants to rule all of Europe. And he feels very misunderstood."

"That tends to happen to psychopaths."

"He's fanatical to be sure." She paused as if searching for the correct words. "But he's also very…charismatic. Not often, but when he wants something, he can be very persuasive."

Robert cut her a sharp look. "What did he want from you?"

"The autobiography."

He stared hard at her, knowing that wasn't all, feeling it all the way to his bones. His hackles rose at the thought of her getting herself into such a dangerous situation all alone. "What else, Lily?"

Her eyes widened for an instant, then skittered away. She shrugged. "That's it."

Robert sensed there was more going on between her and Bruno DeBruzkya than she was telling him, but evidently she wasn't ready to talk about it. He wasn't sure he was ready to hear it. And he wondered how far she had been willing to go to get what she wanted.

"I contacted the American government several times looking for you, but I kept getting lost in the shuffle. But now you're suddenly here…."

"I'm here on a humanitarian mission," he said. "You know that."

She didn't say anything, and a little swirl of uneasiness went through him at the thought of her knowing more than she should. "You put yourself in terrible danger." Not only herself, he thought, but her child. *His* child.

"I knew I was in over my head, but the opportunity was too good to let pass."

"You were pregnant…"

She nodded.

"Then you put our child in danger, too." *Our child.* The words shocked him. Shocked him so badly he wasn't sure he would ever get used to them. "You had no right to do that."

"If I hadn't asked for DeBruzkya that day, the soldiers would have raped me. They probably would have killed me to cover their crime."

Robert felt the words like a dull knife twisting in his gut. He turned away and closed his eyes, not wanting to imagine such an atrocity. She'd been badly injured and pregnant. But he knew DeBruzkya's soldiers wouldn't have cared. If she hadn't dropped DeBruzkya's name, they would have been on her like a pack of dogs on a piece of meat. The thought made bile rise in the back of his throat.

"I didn't have a choice but to do what I did," she said.

The words spun him around. "You could have left with me that day when I asked."

"I still had work to do here. I couldn't walk away."

Because he didn't want to rehash an old argument they would never agree on—because he hadn't forgiven her for what she'd done—he rose abruptly.

"Robert—"

"Don't." He turned on her. "You made your choice, Lily. That speaks louder than anything you can say now. I got your message loud and clear." For several long seconds neither of them spoke, then Robert sighed, too tired to argue further. "How far is the hospital from here?"

"About six miles."

"Do you have transportation?"

Grimacing, she shook her head. "We'll have to walk."

He cursed, calculating how long it would take them to hike through six miles of heavy woods with a sick one-year-old child in tow. He wondered how well his leg would hold up. "We'll leave at first light."

"We'll have to wait until dark to leave."

"Soldiers?"

She nodded. "It's not safe to travel by day."

An uncomfortable thought lodged in his brain. "Is DeBruzkya looking for you, Lily?" he asked.

She stared at him, her eyes wide and cautious and so lovely he wanted to step right into her gaze and lose himself forever. But her silence quickly reminded him just how dangerous that kind of thinking was.

"For God's sake." Lowering his head, he pinched the bridge of his nose between his thumb and forefinger. "He's looking for you. That's why you haven't been able to take Jack to the hospital."

She nodded.

"That's why you haven't been able to leave the country."

"He has soldiers at the airport. Patrols all along the border. I couldn't risk it with Jack."

Raising his head, he stared hard at her, wondering if the situation could get any worse. "Exactly why is he looking for you?"

"Because he's a very bad man," she whispered.

For the first time Robert saw the true depth of her fear of DeBruzkya in her eyes. The kind of fear a woman like Lily should never have to feel. The kind of fear no human being should have to feel toward another.

"This is personal for him," he said.

When she didn't respond, he snapped at her. "He's obsessed with you, isn't he?"

Sighing, she looked at the floor.

"How in God's name could you let things go this far?"

"I didn't see it coming. I thought I could do it. Then I

realized I was pregnant and all my priorities changed. I dropped out of sight. I thought he would forget about me. Forget about that stupid autobiography. Robert, I didn't think he would come after me. But he's…obsessive and crazy.''

"Crazy like a rogue lion.''

"That's why I can't let you step into the center of this,'' she said.

He jerked his gaze to hers. "No, that's your job, isn't it?''

"Come on, Robert. I know you're up to something.''

"I'm here to inoculate the children.''

She took a step toward him, raising her hand as if to touch him. "Don't mess with DeBruzkya.''

Because he wasn't sure what he would do if she touched him, Robert raised his hand, stopping her. "Don't let your imagination get the best of you.''

"All these questions about DeBruzkya. What am I supposed to think?''

He stared at her for a moment, trying in vain to ignore the storm of emotions cutting through him with the same violence and pain as the shrapnel had twenty-one months ago. The urge to go to her, to gather her into his arms, to kiss her and keep her safe was overpowering. But Robert resisted. He knew where it would lead, and it was a path he didn't want to take.

Turning away from her, he headed toward the kitchen. He heard her call his name, but he didn't stop. His legs were shaking when he crossed to the tiny porcelain sink. His hands shook when he set his cup down. Standing at the window, he stared out at the dying storm and the first fragile rays of sunlight coming through the treetops and tried not to think about how profoundly his life had been changed.

Chapter 8

General Bruno DeBruzkya sat behind the wide span of glossy mahogany desk and stared at the frayed photograph on the leather blotter in front of him. A woman with striking hazel eyes and skin as fine as German porcelain smiled back at him. A woman he'd thought of far too often in the months since he'd last seen her.

Lillian Scott.

She reminded him of a flower. Soft and fragrant and as colorful as the mountain columbine that grew in the highlands of the Hartz Forest. He was thinking of her every day now—far too often for a man leading a country in a time of civil war. But war could be a lonely time for a man. Especially a man of his political and social stature. And so on the rare occasions when he was alone, or in the dark of night when a man's needs came calling, he thought of her. The afternoon spent at the café in Rajalla. The rainy morning at the bistro on Balboa Avenue near the bazaar where they'd drank strong Rebelian espresso and laughed at inconsequential things.

Bruno wasn't prone to sentimentalities or maudlin affairs. He was a hard man who'd led an even harder life in a world that could be brutal. In his fifty-five years, he'd seen things that would terrify most men. He'd done things that would shock even the most hardened soldiers. Bruno didn't get emotionally entangled with women. When his needs became a distraction he took care of them discreetly and without fanfare at the brothel on the east side of town. He'd known Inga for nearly ten years. But lately, the sex and meaningless small talk weren't enough.

There came a time in a man's life when he began to think about the future. About getting old. About leaving his legacy to one of his own blood. A wife. A family. An heir to carry on the work he'd begun. That he had a nephew on the way should have been enough. But it wasn't. Bruno wanted more. He wanted a son.

Lillian Scott might be an American journalist—there was no love lost between Bruno DeBruzkya and the Americans—but, she would make the perfect wife. She was young and lovely with the kind of spirit that had always appealed to him. She would make the perfect mother to the sons she would bear him. While she may not love him, she would quickly learn to respect him. That was all Bruno asked. As long as she shared his bed and bore his children, he would give her everything.

He'd dreamed of her again last night. A disturbing dream that had left him aroused and wanting when he'd wakened. Bruno didn't like wanting. Worse, he didn't like wanting something and knowing he may never get it. Wanting had been his constant companion as a child. He'd learned to despise it; he still despised it.

The memory of his childhood made him grimace. Even though those days were long gone, he would never forget what it had been like to be a skinny boy with an empty stomach and not a hope in the world of ever making something of himself. He'd grown up in a small village in the Hartz Forest. His family hadn't had enough money to send him to school, so he'd never gotten a formal education. But he'd liked to read—history mostly—and had filled his days with tales of Napoleon and Hitler and Stalin. Tired of being poor and reliant and hopeless, certain he was destined for greatness, he'd lied about his age and joined the Rebelian Army when he was only sixteen.

It was in the military that Bruno DeBruzkya found his calling. He might have lacked a formal education, but his intelligence and natural charisma more than made up for it. He learned at a very young age how to influence people, how to manipulate them, how to make them do what he wanted. For the few who refused to bow to his wishes, he didn't have any compunction about removing them.

Bruno was very good at eliminating obstacles.

In the following years, he rose quickly through the ranks of the army, eventually gaining favor with King Luna. The king even invited him into the royal palace in nearby Rajalla where they dined on lamb, fresh vegetables from the queen's garden and sweet German wine. King Luna had talked about his hopes for the Rebelian Empire, and all the things a talented young man like Bruno could do to help make that future a reality.

Outwardly, Bruno had nodded with excitement. But inwardly, he'd laughed. What an old fool! King Luna was soft and incompetent and completely unworthy of taking Rebelia into the twenty-first century. Rebelia deserved more than what an old man with a soft head could offer. Two days after having dinner with King Luna, Bruno and his soldiers rushed the palace and slaughtered the royal family in their sleep.

At first, the Rebelian people had rebelled against Bruno's ideals and his new style of leadership. To prevent civil war, he'd taken over the newspaper and started a powerful propaganda campaign. He imprisoned the few who dared to speak out against his regime. He controlled the rest by withholding food or medical supplies—or simply by destroying their homes and businesses.

In an effort to win the hearts and minds of his people, Bruno gave public speeches at the town square. Eventually, some of the people began to listen; some even began to believe. Be patient, he told them; good things come to those who wait. Stand behind him and he would lead Rebelia to a greatness the likes of which the country had never seen. And to those courageous few who believed, he'd given food and medicine and hope.

But after two years of being in power, civil war had broken out. Bands of rebels roamed the countryside, holing up like rats in the forests and villages surrounding the city, speaking out against his leadership. Stupid peasants. What did they know about running a country? Not a damn thing. He'd been so close to taking his nation to the next level, to taking the next step. If only the rebels hadn't interfered.

Restless and angry and disturbingly uncertain, Bruno reached for the crystal tumbler of cognac and sipped, marveling at the slow, rich burn at the back of his throat. He picked up the photograph and studied the lovely lines of her face. Even though the war wasn't quite going as he had planned, he was going to have to make time for Lillian Scott. He wasn't getting any younger, after all. All he had to do was find her.

Never taking his eyes from the photo, he drew on the Cuban cigar, savoring the rich tobacco, then tapped the ashes into the brass tray next to his blotter. Lillian stared back at him with those incredible eyes. Eyes that burned with intelligence and a woman's secret passions. She was by far the most beautiful woman he'd ever met. Not only was she quick-witted and engaging, but she shared his ideals. Such a rarity in a world rampant with sheep. Lillian Scott was no sheep. She was a wolf. Like him. He'd sensed her power from the start. He only wished he'd had the foresight to have appreciated its rarity.

The uneasy realization that he may never see her again caused an odd flutter of panic in his chest. For the hundredth time he berated himself for having let her slip away. She was such a prize. How could he let that happen?

It seemed just yesterday he'd found her, broken and burned and at the mercy of his soldiers. His men had been ready to pounce on her like wolves on an injured lamb. But if Bruno admired any trait in a human being, whether it be man or woman or American, it was guts. Even injured and bleeding and in pain, she'd stood up to his soldiers, ready to fight them to the death.

To think of how close his soldiers had come to killing her—or worse—made him shudder. He smiled at the memory of how he'd saved her from such a terrible fate. He wasn't sure why he'd done it at the time. Maybe the way she'd looked at him. Not pleadingly, the way some had. No, Lillian Scott would never beg. She looked at him as if to say she'd see him in hell before she'd let anyone lay a hand on her. She'd been baffled when he'd ordered her taken to the hospital in Rajalla. She hadn't realized just how much he prized her kind of courage.

Leaning forward slightly, he pressed his finger to the photograph. "Where are you, my flower?" he whispered into the silence of his private chambers.

She smiled at him. An angel with a dazzling smile and the kind of body that could blind even the most cautious of men. Bruno considered himself very cautious.

He pressed the intercom button on the phone and summoned Colonel Hansel Sokolov, his right-hand man and the closest thing to a confidant he would ever have.

An instant later, a firm knock sounded and Sokolov entered, greeting him with a formal salute. "General!"

"At ease," DeBruzkya said.

"Sir." Sokolov approached his desk.

"I have two orders this afternoon that will take precedence over all else."

"Yes, sir!"

"I want our forest patrols increased. All rebels are to be brought to headquarters and interrogated. If they are found with contraband, particularly any literature speaking out against my regime, they are to be taken to a judge, convicted of treason and executed.''

Uncertainty flickered in Sokolov's eyes an instant before he shouted, ''Yes, sir!''

''And I would like to place a bounty on the young American woman we imprisoned for a time last year.''

''A bounty?'' Sokolov's brows knitted. ''An American? Sir?''

''Lillian Scott. She is an American journalist. I'm offering one hundred thousand American dollars to any man, woman or child who brings her to me.''

''But, sir, for civilians?''

''You have your orders. I suggest you make these two things a priority. Are we clear?''

''Very clear, General.'' Sokolov saluted.

''That will be all.''

DeBruzkya watched the other man leave, realizing that giving the order had lifted his spirits. Leaning back in his chair, he drew on the cigar and let the rich smoke swirl around his tongue. With a bounty of one hundred thousand American dollars on her head, it wouldn't take long to find her.

He glanced at the photograph and felt the familiar coil of need. Oh, yes. He would find her. When he did, he would convince her to write his autobiography just as she'd promised all those months ago. And when she was finished, if she didn't agree to become his bride, to bear his children until he had the son he wanted, he would simply kill her.

Twilight hovered quietly over the forest. It was a magical time when the cool winds from the mountains to the north eased into the valleys and turned the air to crystal. When the songbirds from the highland meadows sang and received answering calls from their prospective mates.

Dusk was Lily's favorite time of day. On evenings like this she liked to pack a snack of grapes, cheese and crusty bread and take Jack down to the stream for a picnic. Even though he wasn't yet old enough to eat solid food, she would spread the pretty woven blanket on the grass, and they would play simple games and laugh at silly things and for a few short hours forget about all the worries in the world. Turning to take a final look at the cottage, Lily couldn't help but wonder if those days were over for good. The thought brought a tinge of melancholy.

She slipped the straps of Jack's carrier over her shoulders, hefted his little body against her abdomen and smiled at him. "We're going to take a little hike, big guy," she said.

"Gah!" Jack cried in answer, kicking his feet out on either side of her.

Laughing outright, she craned her neck forward and touched her nose to his. He looked so happy and healthy smiling at her she wanted to laugh. Robert had given him an oral iron supplement along with a vitamin B-12 shot earlier. While Jack hadn't much liked being subjected to either of those things, his condition had improved in just a matter of hours.

"He looks good," Robert said, coming up beside her.

Lily glanced at him. "He smiled a moment ago."

"He made off with one of my boots this morning."

"I noticed. I stopped him right before he dropped it into the commode."

Robert chuckled. "I think the terrible-two phase may come a little early with him."

Lily smiled at Jack, and her heart swelled with love. "As long as he's healthy and happy. That's all I care about."

"The disease can be controlled. Researchers have made some breakthroughs in the last several years."

"He'll be able to live a normal life?"

"Aside from being sick a few times when I was young, I've led a completely normal life." His gaze lingered on hers a moment too long.

When her cheeks heated, Lily turned quickly away. Of

all the things she could have been thinking of, the kiss they'd shared the night before shouldn't have been one of them. They were about to embark on a dangerous journey, yet here she was thinking of that kiss. Damn it, she wasn't a schoolgirl. She was a grown woman with a sick child, a boatload of responsibilities and a very dangerous war raging all around her. How could she be thinking of something as inconsequential as a stolen kiss?

But Lily knew the answer. And while she may not like the route her thoughts had taken, she'd never fallen to lying to herself. There had been nothing inconsequential about that kiss. It meant something—to both of them, she was sure. Something that had absolutely nothing to do with the joining of lips and everything to do with unfinished business between a man and a woman who'd once been very much in love. A man and a woman who now shared the bond of a child.

Lily closed her eyes against the reality of that. She wasn't an impulsive woman. It wasn't like her to let a moment like that get out of control no matter how hot the kiss. But every time she looked at Robert she couldn't help but think of those fleeting moments when she'd come apart in his arms. The way his mouth had covered hers, the way his hands had moved over her body, the heat of his caress when he'd touched her intimately. The answering call of her body when she'd peaked...

Good Lord, what had she been thinking letting him touch her like that?

What had happened between them was a mistake. A moment of poor judgment run amok. The result of high emotion and hot tempers and good old-fashioned lust. While the kiss had been erotic and moving and breathtaking, she couldn't let it mean anything. She couldn't let it make her remember the feelings she'd once had for him. She couldn't let herself feel the loss of a future she'd once wanted desperately. She couldn't let her attraction to him coax her into doing something irrevocable.

"How is Jack's carrier working?"

Robert's words jerked her from her reverie. Gathering
the fragments of her composure, she tugged on the straps,
praying he didn't notice that the carrier was the last thing
on her mind. "It's comfortable." She looked at Jack and
smiled. "I think he likes it."

Robert had spent most of the day making the carrier.
He'd fashioned it from soft Rebelian wool, sewing on ad-
justable straps so that either of them could carry Jack in
front at their abdomen or as a backpack. With six miles to
cover before dawn, she figured she would be needing Robert's help at some point.

A hundred yards from the cottage the forest seemed to
swallow them. Towering pines blocked the dim light of
dusk. The path tapered to a narrow trail. Lily was aware of
Robert moving behind her. The steady tread of his hiking
boots against the earth, strong and steady, just like the man.
She found her rhythm and tried to concentrate on the trail,
on making good time. But as much as she didn't want to
talk to him, her mind was reeling with all the things they
needed to discuss. They were going to have to talk about
how they were going to handle having a child.

The thought terrified her.

Almost as much as the thought of what it could cost them
if Robert decided he wanted to be part of Jack's life.

A tremor of fear moved through her when she thought
of all the things that could happen. She knew Robert well
enough to know he would want to have a role in his son's
life. He was a good man who would never turn away from
such an important responsibility. He had every right to
know Jack. To spend time with him and guide him and
love him. Lily knew Robert would make a fabulous father
one day.

Only in this case, it could get him killed.

"Which way?"

Lily started at the sound of Robert's voice, then looked
up to see that the trail had intersected an unpaved road. She

didn't like traveling on the open road, unused as it was, but she knew if she wanted to make it to Rajalla before morning they didn't have a choice.

Next to her, Robert had removed a compass from his backpack. "Compass says we're heading east."

"We go right."

"What's to the left?"

"The road goes through a small village a few miles from here, then veers northwest into the mountains."

"Toward the Veisweimar Castle?"

Lily tried to suppress the shiver, but didn't quite manage. "Yes."

Robert tugged a palm-size electronic gadget from his pack, opened the top and punched a few buttons.

"What's that?" she asked.

"Global positioning system." He cut her a look. "In case we get lost."

"Yeah, and you're here to inoculate children," she said dryly.

Hefting his light pack, Robert started down the road. "At least the weather is cooperating."

Lily glanced over at him, trying not to notice how good he looked in the Rebelian wool sweater she'd given him. It was old and a bit tattered, but the deep blue matched his eyes perfectly. At least he wouldn't look out of place if the soldiers stopped them. They were traveling as a couple. Robert's documents identified him as a French doctor working to inoculate Rebelian children against some of the diseases that had cropped up in the last couple of years. Diseases that had once been eradicated but had been revived by poverty and malnutrition and poor living conditions.

The story they'd decided on was that their son had gotten sick and they were taking him to the hospital in Rajalla. It was a good story—and true in part—but she hoped they wouldn't have to put it to the test.

"There's an old Rebelian saying," she said after a moment.

Robert looked at her.

"Nothing changes quickly in Rebelia except the weather and the government."

He smiled, and Lily's heart gave a couple of hard taps against her rib cage. Mercy, she'd forgotten what his smile did to her. Robert Davidson had the kind of smile that would melt even the hardest of resolves.

"I don't think we can avoid talking about our situation much longer," he said after a moment.

She risked a look at him, dread twisting inside her because she knew what he would say next. She knew what he wanted. And she knew it was the one thing she could never allow.

"I'm not going to walk away from Jack," he said.

"You're not the only person involved, Robert."

"This isn't just about us anymore, Lily."

"I know that—"

"I grew up without a father," he cut in. "I don't intend to let my son grow up the same way no matter how you feel about me."

"Unless you plan to move to Rebelia permanently I don't see how—"

"Surely you don't plan to stay here."

She didn't respond.

"You have a child to raise," he said. "This hellhole of a country is no place to raise a child, especially my son."

"Don't you think I know that?" she shot back.

"Evidently, you don't or you would have gotten on a jet and hightailed it back to the United States a long time ago."

She stopped in the center of the road, aware that her heart was pounding and that her temper was riding a fast second. "I would have been stopped at the airport or the border."

"You could have called me," he snapped.

"What about the rebels, Robert? Are you willing to give

up on them? What about the orphans?'' She thought of the dozens of children she'd known over the years and had to brace against the swift slice of pain. ''There are seventeen orphanages in this country. An untold number of children have lost their parents. How can I walk away?''

''Damn it, Lily—''

''There are over a million children in Rebelia,'' she said breathlessly. ''Dozens are dying every single day. None of them should be raised under such conditions. I love Jack with all my heart. I would die for him. But I can't bring myself to leave when I know more of those children will die if I do.''

''You need to get your priorities straight,'' he said.

''How dare you suggest that I wouldn't put Jack first?''

As if sensing his mother's distress, Jack began to fuss. Lily looked down at him. ''Oh, honey, it's okay. Shh…Mommy's okay. She's just…angry.'' She frowned at Robert. ''See what you've done?''

''I didn't do anything,'' he said defensively. But he'd come over to look at their son.

Shaking inside with the remnants of temper, she worked the straps of the carrier from her shoulders. ''I know he can't understand what we're saying, but I'd appreciate it if you didn't start arguments in front of him.''

''I didn't start an argument,'' Robert growled.

''He's very perceptive.''

''He's probably hungry or wet.''

Lily dipped her finger into his diaper and frowned. Damn it, she hated it when Robert was right.

''That's what I thought,'' he said.

Annoyed, she gently worked Jack from the carrier. Robert tugged a rolled up blanket from his backpack, walked over to a clearing a few feet away and spread the blanket on the winter grass. Jack was crying in earnest, so Lily held him close and carried him to the blanket where Robert knelt.

He reached for Jack. ''Let me,'' he said.

Keenly aware that this would be the first time he held his son, Lily pressed a kiss to Jack's forehead and passed him to Robert. "If you want to change him, I'll get the bottle."

"Fine," he grumbled. But his expression softened when he took his son into his arms. "Hey, big guy. How about if we lose the diaper for a moment? Sound like a good idea to you?"

Lily watched them covertly as she dug through her backpack for the bottle. The sight of father and son together in such an ordinary situation warmed her with unexpected emotion. She stared at them, her pulse quivering, her heart swelling against her ribs. Robert held Jack expertly, but she could tell he lacked experience. He might be a doctor, but there were some things that could only be learned by doing, and holding a baby was one of them.

He unfastened the diaper pins, rolled the soiled diaper into a tight ball and slipped it into a small plastic bag. Jack flailed his arms and giggled. "I thought you'd appreciate that," Robert said.

The sight moved her a lot more than she wanted it to, certainly more than she wanted to admit. She'd dreamed of Robert holding his son but never really thought the moment would come.

"Aha gee!" Jack shouted and kicked his chubby legs.

Grinning, Robert looked at Lily. "That sounded like I'm hungry."

Jack's outburst hadn't sounded even remotely like *I'm hungry,* of course, but the thought made her laugh.

Robert looked down just in time to see the tiny fountain spray upward. *"Hey!"* he said, twisting to get out of the way.

Lily dug into her diaper bag, quickly pulled out a fresh diaper and draped it over her son. "That always happens when I change him."

Robert was busy checking his clothes for wet areas. He

looked ruffled and, Lily thought, utterly adorable. Caught up in the moment, she chuckled.

"What's so funny?" he grumbled good-naturedly.

"I don't think I've ever seen you look so surprised." She put her hand over her mouth to stifle a giggle.

"Yeah, well, who would have known he could aim like that."

The laugh trapped inside her broke free. Shaking his head, Robert burst into laughter. Their laughter echoed through the silence of the forest. It was a foreign sound in a place that had been besieged with violence and hopelessness for the last two years. But it was like music to her ears, the sound of simple human joy, the sound of hope, of life and the promise of tomorrow.

The laughter felt joyous in her throat, like chocolate ice cream on a hot day. She laughed so hard tears rolled down her cheeks. She looked at Robert in time to see him double over, and she laughed even harder. Months of stress and worry and fear broke loose inside her and were exorcised. For the first time in as long as she could remember, she felt hopeful and unburdened and indescribably free.

She looked over at Robert and saw him sit back on his heels. He was holding one of Jack's pudgy hands and laughing so hard tears were rolling down his cheeks. Lily stared at him and knew this was a moment she would never forget. No matter how things turned out, no matter what happened in the coming days and weeks and months, she would always have this moment in time, and she would forever cherish it.

Feeling foolish for making such a big thing out of a silly moment between two tired, stressed-out adults, she reached into her backpack and pulled out the baby bottle. When she turned, Robert was struggling to pin the fresh diaper.

"Now might be a good time to try that bottle," he said.

She looked at him to find him gazing steadily at her, seeing too much, she knew. "Before he gets restless," he added.

Unnerved by the way he was looking at her, she glanced down at Jack and offered him the nipple. "Okay, big guy, now's your chance if you're hungry."

Jack suckled eagerly. Lily smiled at him and felt her nerves begin to settle. "He's so cute," she said, mostly to herself. "I love to watch him take milk."

"He's a good-looking boy," Robert agreed.

Lily glanced at his diapering job and gave him credit for creativity. Because disposable diapers weren't available in Rebelia, she used cloth, which required the old-fashioned pins. Hiding her smile, she lifted Jack—and the diaper drooped to his knees.

"Oops," she said.

Robert chuckled. "So much for my diapering skills."

"Takes practice." Laying Jack on the blanket again, she handed the bottle to Robert. "Hold this for him, and I'll tighten up the diaper a little."

"Sure." He reached past her to hold the bottle steady.

Lily tried to concentrate on the task at hand, but Robert was so close she could smell his subtle scent. Feel the heat coming off him into the chill night air, touching her as surely as he'd touched her the night before.

"You're good at that," he said.

"I've had lots of practice."

"Did you breast-feed?"

She nodded. "For about six months."

"Good. I mean, that's healthy for the baby."

She could feel his eyes on her, but she didn't make eye contact. To do so now would be a dangerous prospect, to say the least. Lily might not be afraid to live alone in a war-torn country, but there was no way she was brave enough to look at Robert when she knew what she'd find in his eyes. When she knew what he would see in her eyes.

"Lily…" Gently he put his hand on her arm.

She froze, all too aware that his hand was warm and comforting against her skin. She hadn't realized how chilly the night had become until he touched her. She knew it would be a mistake to look at him. But she did, and the earth quivered beneath her. Vaguely, she heard Jack cooing. The whisper of a breeze through the naked treetops. The cry of a night bird in the distance.

Leaning close to her, Robert brushed the hair from her face. "I like hearing you laugh," he said.

Even though her heart was pounding, she forced a laugh. "Kind of a rare sound these days."

"It doesn't have to be that way."

Yes, it does, she thought, but the words refused to materialize.

"Why are you trembling?" he asked gently.

"It's cold."

"Or maybe I'm the reason." He touched the side of her face with the backs of his fingers. "I don't know if that's good or bad."

"Maybe it's best if we don't find out," she whispered.

His face was only a few dangerous inches from hers. It would be so easy to lean forward and let him kiss her again. She could tell he wanted to and felt need rushing through her with every beat of her heart. She could feel the pulse of it, hear the roar of it in her ears.

The next thing she knew she was being shoved quickly backward. "Hey!"

Her exclamation was cut short when Robert slapped a hand over her mouth. Confused, Lily gripped his wrist to wrest it away. Then out of the corner of her eye she saw the twin beams of headlights slash through the darkness. She heard the rumble of engines. Lights washed over them, playing wildly over the trees as two jeeps filled with soldiers stopped a few feet away.

"What do we do now?" she asked.

"Kiss me," Robert said.

Lily pulled back slightly. *"What?"*

"For once in your life, don't argue." Cupping the back of her head, he crushed his mouth to hers.

Chapter 9

Even with all the problems standing between them, her betrayal still fresh in his heart—and a dozen of De-Bruzkya's soldiers looking on—she felt awfully good in his arms. Robert told himself he was laying it on thick so the soldiers would believe they were a married couple and leave them alone. But the hot rush of blood to his groin refuted the lie.

"*Alteich!*"

Robert pulled away from Lily. "Stay cool and follow my lead," he whispered in her ear.

She looked bewildered and scared for an instant, then he turned his attention to the uniformed man standing in the jeep holding a spotlight on them. Determined to look the part, Robert raised his hand to block the light and squinted. "Who's there?" he asked in rapid French.

"Lieutenant Romanov with the Rebelian Army." The soldier in charge shouted something in Rebelian to his men.

Robert caught only a couple of words but ascertained they were going to check their papers. No problem, he thought. Their papers were in order. All they had to do was stay cool, and everything would be fine.

Two soldiers armed with rifles jumped down from separate jeeps and approached them. Next to him, Robert felt a tremor go through Lily. A few feet away, he could hear Jack chattering and prayed the soldiers would check their papers and leave.

The first soldier approached and shone his flashlight directly into Robert's face. Robert raised his hand to shade his eyes and used the other to dig into his backpack for the documents that had been prepared for him by ARIES. He handed his passport and certificate of travel to the soldier.

The soldier was young, still in his twenties, but his eyes seemed much older. He jerked the documents from Robert's hand, glanced at them, then spun and took them to the lieutenant.

The second soldier was built like a Rebelian ox and looked several years older. Robert glanced at him, noticing the hideous scar that ran from his right cheekbone to his chin. The soldier shone his flashlight on Lily, starting at her face, then sweeping the beam down her body. Robert still had his arm around her waist and could feel her trembling. Uneasiness and the primal need to protect what was his rose inside him in a powerful tide.

"Is there a problem?" he asked.

The soldier sneered at Robert. "Shut up." Then his eyes ran the length of Lily. He licked his lips, like a tiger about to devour a lamb.

The lieutenant jumped from the jeep with their paperwork in hand and approached them. "You're French?" he asked.

Robert nodded. "Yes."

"What part of France are you from?"

"Marseille."

"Your accent isn't southern."

"I've lived in Paris for many years."

The lieutenant walked around them while the other soldier shone his light in their faces. "Why are you in Rebelia?" he asked.

"I'm a doctor. I'm here to administer inoculations to children."

The lieutenant circled them at a leisurely pace, his hands clasped casually behind his back. But Robert saw the predatory gleam in his eyes and knew he was trying to catch him in a lie, looking for any reason to turn his soldiers loose on them.

"This is your wife?" he asked, referring to Lily.

"Yes."

"And the baby?"

Robert's heart began to pound. He was aware of the revolver he'd slipped into the waistband of his jeans pressing against the small of his back. He stared at the other man, strength for strength. "My son."

The lieutenant raised his hand and touched Lily's cheek. Anger joined the chorus of adrenaline and raw nerves and sang through Robert. Out of the corner of his eye, he saw Lily jerk away from the other man's hand and prayed she would hold her tongue.

Easy, Lily. Don't give them a reason to kill us, he thought.

"Your wife is Rebelian?" the lieutenant asked.

"French, like me," Robert answered.

A cold smile touched the other man's mouth. "She looks familiar. I could swear I've seen her before."

Lily shot him a look cold enough to freeze hell. "I've never seen you in my life," she fired off in rapid Rebelian. "I'd remember a face as ugly as yours."

The rest of the men burst into raucous laughter.

Robert squeezed her hand hard.

The lieutenant glared at his men, and they immediately fell silent. He looked at Lily, his eyes glinting in the glare of the spotlight. "Your wife doesn't seem to like soldiers," he said.

''She doesn't like anyone.'' Robert shrugged. ''Not even me.''

The men laughed again, but when the lieutenant didn't join in, they fell quickly silent.

''Women should have more respect,'' he said. ''Maybe my soldiers could teach her a lesson in respect. They've been away from their wives for a very long time.''

Cursing silently, Robert eased Lily back a step, slowly maneuvering himself more solidly between her and the men. The woods were only a few yards away. If someone started shooting he wanted her to have a straight shot at their only escape route. All she had to do was scoop up Jack and run like hell. With luck, Robert could hold the soldiers off long enough for her to get away.

''We've got a long journey ahead of us,'' Robert said. ''If you need some food or inoculations for your children, I can give them to you.''

''You got any whiskey?'' one of the men shouted in Rebelian.

The lieutenant spat something in Rebelian Robert couldn't quite translate. A beefy man with a bald head and shoulders the size of a Mack truck jumped from the jeep and approached Robert. Without warning, he drew back and rammed the rifle butt into Robert's stomach.

The air left his lungs in a rush. Pain streaked through his abdomen. Robert retched, tasted bile at the back of his throat. Vaguely, he was aware of his legs buckling. Of Lily shouting his name. He dropped to his knees, expecting another blow at the back of his head, and tried desperately to get oxygen into his lungs.

An instant later the bald man tore the backpack from his shoulders, opened the flap and dumped the contents onto the ground. Robert stared at the contents, glad he'd had the foresight to stash his high-tech equipment in the fanny pack strapped around his waist.

''You can take the inoculations,'' Robert gasped.

"They're yours. Use them for your children. There are antibiotics, too."

He felt Lily's hands on his arm. She knelt beside him, her eyes wide with fear. She reached for him, but the lieutenant pulled her roughly to her feet. "My soldiers think you need a lesson in respect."

"My son is sick," she said. "Please. W-we just want to take him to the hospital."

A cruel smile whispered across the lieutenant's face. An instant later, he grasped a handful of Lily's hair, yanked her toward him and crushed his mouth to hers. She lashed out with both fists, but he was holding her too close for her to get any leverage, and her efforts were in vain.

Raw fury sent Robert to his feet. Three of the other soldiers moved closer, their hands restless on automatic weapons. Robert knew he and Lily were outgunned and out manned ten to one. But there was no way in hell he was going to let this escalate. He'd die before he'd let that son of a bitch turn his soldiers loose on Lily. All he needed was a distraction. *Hold on, Lily,* he thought. *I'll get us out of this. Just stay cool.*

A moment later, the lieutenant released her. Lily stumbled back, breathing hard, and spat on the ground. "Bastard," she said.

The lieutenant smiled. "Ah, such disrespect." He glanced at his men. "I think there's enough of her for everyone."

The men stared at them, their faces hungry and cruel, a pack of wolves facing down a much smaller prey.

Robert leaned forward, feigning pain and clenching his stomach, all the while easing his right hand toward the fanny pack at his waist.

The lieutenant reached into a breast pocket and removed a piece of paper. Unfolding it, he handed it to Lily. "I'm afraid your little charade is over, Lillian Scott," he said.

Lily stared at the tattered sheet of paper in her hand, terror streaking through her as her face stared back at her.

Vaguely, she was aware of the paper rattling as her hands began to shake. Her legs followed suit, then suddenly her entire body was trembling violently. Never had she imagined in a thousand years that DeBruzkya would take things this far.

Heart pounding, she raised her eyes to the lieutenant. "Let my son and this man go free, and I'll go with you," she said.

"You're in no position to bargain."

She shuddered when the lieutenant's eyes swept over her, lingering on her breasts. "One hundred thousand American dollars." He licked his lips. "General DeBruzkya must want you very badly. I wonder if you're worth that much."

"You touch me, and DeBruzkya will kill you," she said.

"Maybe I just want a peek at what has the general tied up in little knots."

Lily withheld a shudder. She'd been in tough predicaments before and she'd gotten out of them alive. She would get out of this one, too. If she only had a plan...

The lieutenant brushed a strand of hair from her face. "I've always liked red hair on a woman," he whispered. "A woman like you could do a lot for the morale of my men."

Her heart was pounding so loudly she could barely hear him. But she knew what he wanted, and the thought revolted her. "My son is very sick. He needs to go to the hospital. Let both of them go and I'll...go with you."

"You're going with me anyway. Why should I bargain with you?" He looked at Robert, then at Jack. "What are they worth to you, my lamb? What will you do to protect them?"

Lily stared at him, knowing his kind and hating him. She'd met too many men like him in the years she'd been in Rebelia. Men who were cruel and violent and evil.

"They're worth everything to me," she said.

"Everything?" When she wouldn't look at him, he put

his hand beneath her chin and forced her to look at him. "Everything?"

She wasn't exactly sure what he was asking, but she knew she didn't have a choice but to agree. Just as she knew this was going to cost her. That it was going to change her life. Change all of their lives. "Yes," she said, hating the quiver in her voice.

"Good girl," he said. "Oh, yes. Good, good girl." Never taking his eyes from Lily, he snapped his fingers at one of his soldiers and motioned toward Robert. "Give him back his satchel and send him on his way."

Lily closed her eyes. Relief warred with terror. She couldn't imagine Robert walking away and leaving her but prayed that if he had to choose between her and Jack he would do the right thing and choose Jack, that he would protect the baby first and above everything else.

She gave the lieutenant the best go-to-hell look she could manage. "If you hurt them, I'll make sure DeBruzkya kills you."

She thought she saw a flash of fear in the lieutenant's eyes, but it was gone so quickly she couldn't be sure. Out of the corner of her eye she saw one of the soldiers thrust Robert's backpack at him.

"Hit the road," the soldier snarled, then turned a lascivious stare at Lily. "We have business to attend."

She wanted to look at Robert but wasn't sure what it would do to her emotions, what it would do to him, so she didn't. She heard Jack fussing when Robert picked him up off the blanket, and her heart broke. *Take good care of my son,* she thought, wondering if she would ever see him again, and felt the hot burn of tears in her eyes. She tried hard to block the thoughts, but they swirled inside her brain, cutting her like shrapnel, making her bleed until she felt she'd been bled dry.

Summoning her courage, she looked at Robert and found his eyes already upon her. He had the backpack slung over one shoulder, Jack cradled in one arm. Her heart stumbled in her chest at the sight of him with her son—their son—and regret seared through her.

She thought about the gun strapped to her thigh. She knew it wouldn't be enough in a firefight, but it might buy them some time. She would wait until Robert had Jack safely out of sight. Then she would take out the first man who touched her and deal with the consequences when the time came.

Lily couldn't believe it was going to end like this. Couldn't believe after everything she'd been through, she was going to die at the hands of DeBruzkya's soldiers. She thought of Jack, and her heart shattered.

She had to touch him one more time. Had to look into his blue eyes, kiss his tender cheek, smell his baby scent. Turning abruptly away from the lieutenant, she rushed to Robert and reached for her son. It gave her pause when Robert quickly handed him over. She held her baby close and let her tears fall. Around her the soldiers sat in their jeeps and smoked cigarettes and pretended not to watch.

"Stay cool and follow my cue," Robert whispered in French.

Lily glanced at him over the top of Jack's head. Robert stared back at her, and she thought she'd never seen a man look as dangerous as he did at that moment. The hairs at her nape prickled. And suddenly she knew he had no intention of walking away. The thought terrified her because there was no way in hell he was a match for a dozen heavily armed soldiers. What could he possibly be thinking?

She watched, puzzled, as Robert pulled one of Jack's bottles from the bag. Looking awkward and shaken, he withdrew a small prescription bottle from the fanny pack, twisted off the top and tapped several small metallic tablets that were about the size of a watch battery onto his palm.

What on earth was he doing?

The lieutenant had taken notice and was watching Robert closely. "What do you have there?"

Robert smiled sheepishly. "Ulcer," he said, rubbing the

place on his abdomen where the rifle butt had been rammed.

The lieutenant snarled in disgust. "Your life has been spared at the cost of your wife's honor. A real man would have died for her. Get out of here like the dog you are."

Robert twisted off the bottle's nipple and dropped several of the tablets—a top-secret tool, courtesy of ARIES—into the milk. Abruptly, he tossed the bottle at the lieutenant. The lieutenant caught the bottle, then stared at it with annoyance and surprise. "What the hell is this?"

"Payback," Robert said and ducked.

The lieutenant's eyes widened an instant before the bottle exploded.

"Run!" Robert shouted to Lily in English.

The concussion of the blast struck her like a fiery fist. Lily was so stunned that for a moment she couldn't move. She watched in amazement as the lieutenant reeled backward, cursing in Rebelian, howling in pain.

"Go!" Whipping a revolver from the waistband of his jeans, Robert took aim and fired. One of the soldiers fell. The others scattered like ants, shouting, raising their weapons. The rat-tat-tat of an automatic weapon pierced the air.

Wrapping her arms around Jack, Lily ran headlong toward the line of trees a few yards away. When she was halfway there, a second explosion rocked the night. Lily looked over her shoulder in time to see a plume of smoke rise from the nearest jeep. Flames shot from one of the tires. Several of the soldiers were doubled over and coughing violently.

Robert was a few yards behind her, running like a sprinter. Behind him, the lieutenant had fallen to the ground, his uniform charred and smoking. Lilly watched in horror as he rolled and came up with a pistol aimed directly at Robert's back.

"Look out!" she screamed.

Robert's gaze met hers, but he didn't stop running. She saw fear in his eyes, felt the same fear grip her. A shot snapped through the air. Robert jolted, but he didn't slow. Knowing she didn't have a choice but to defend herself, her child and the man who'd probably just saved both their lives, she slowed her pace, lifted her skirt and tugged the tiny chrome .22 caliber handgun from its holster at her thigh. Twisting in midstride she fired four times in quick succession.

Out of the corner of her eye she saw the pistol fly out of the lieutenant's hand. She reached the line of trees a moment later and burst through the low-growing brush. She ran blindly, branches clawing at her face, roots grabbing at her feet like frantic fingers. She ran until her lungs threatened to burst, until her legs quivered with exertion. Then Jack began to cry and a terrible new fear crept over her.

Terrified that he'd been hurt by a stray bullet, she stopped and looked at him. Her hands shook uncontrollably as she ran them over his little body. "Hush, sweetheart. Everything's okay. I'm sorry you had to go through that." Leaning forward, she kissed his cheek. "Shh. Mommy's here. Everything's okay, sweet baby."

But Jack wasn't having it and squealed even louder.

Lily couldn't blame him; she felt like crying, too. She could still feel the hot sweep of horror. Still see the terror on Robert's face. She had no idea how he had managed those explosions, but he'd gotten them out of what surely would have been a deadly situation. For that, she would be forever thankful.

"Robert?" she whispered into the surrounding darkness. "Are you there?"

The only answer came in the form of her labored breathing and the cries of her son. Around her the forest pulsed with nocturnal life. She wasn't sure how far she'd run, but she could no longer hear shots or see the fire through the thick trees.

"Robert? Wh—"

She yelped when a dark silhouette stepped out from behind a nearby tree.

"I'm right here," he said.

Pressing a hand to her stomach, she uttered a silent prayer. "Thank God you're okay."

"Are you hurt?" he asked. "Jack?"

"We're fine." She looked at Jack. "Shaken up and scared, but we're—"

He didn't wait for her to finish, but walked over to her and reached for Jack. Lily's first instinct was to hold her son tight and not let him go, but something in Robert's eyes stopped her. His hands trembled as he unbuckled the carrier straps. An instant later, he released the boy and gathered him into his arms. Lily watched, awestruck and moved, as Robert closed his eyes and pressed his cheek against Jack's. He didn't say a word, but she saw the emotion overwhelming him, and only then did she realize that in the last days something profound had occurred between father and son.

"That was close," he said a moment later.

"Too close."

Robert was shaking violently. His face was pale. A sheen of sweat coated his forehead.

"Are you okay?" she asked.

"I'm fine." As if realizing how he must look, he loosened his grip on Jack. "Give me the carrier. We've got to keep moving. Put some distance between us and De-Bruzkya's goons."

Something in his voice warned her not to argue. She eased the straps from her shoulders and passed the carrier to him. He passed Jack to her, then quickly adjusted the straps to fit his larger frame and slipped the carrier over his shoulders.

"Where the hell did you learn to shoot like that?" he asked as he reached for Jack.

"I didn't."

"I saw you shoot the pistol out of the lieutenant's hands."

Lily shrugged. "I was aiming for the tires on the jeep."

"Terrific." He strapped Jack into the carrier. "Okay, big guy. Let's make some time."

Standing on her tiptoes, Lily draped a blanket over Jack's head and over Robert's shoulder. "Maybe he'll sleep once we start walking."

Robert looked over his shoulder, his eyes scanning the darkened forest. "DeBruzkya's soldiers aren't going to give up. We need to cover some ground very quickly." He glanced at the compass in his hand, then started forward. "Let's go."

Uneasiness prickled up her spine as Lily fell in beside him.

"Why didn't you tell me you had a bounty on your head?" he asked.

"I didn't know."

"That could complicate things at the hospital."

"All I care about is Jack. I don't have to be there for him to get treat—"

"I'm not letting you out of my sight," he growled. "Next thing you'll have the entire Rebelian army after you."

Because she wasn't so certain that wasn't already true, she didn't say anything. "Those explosives you used. I've never seen anything like them."

"They're relatively new. Used for personal protection. Last resort kind of thing. I figured that situation qualified." He frowned at her. "Keep walking."

The realization of how things could have turned out shook her. "If you hadn't been there—"

"I was." Robert regarded her with steely eyes. "It's over."

Before realizing what she was about to do, she crossed the distance between them and pressed a kiss to his mouth. He stiffened for an instant, then his mouth relaxed against hers. Before the moment turned sexual, she pulled away. "Thank you."

He raised his hand to wave off her thanks, but she

stopped him. "I mean it, Robert. You saved my life. You probably saved Jack's life, too. I can't tell you what that means to me."

He stepped back, looking a little stunned, watching her like a big male cat that had just been cuffed by a much smaller female. "I think I know," he said.

Thunder rumbled in the distance and the moment was broken. Hefting Jack's carrier higher on his abdomen, Robert looked around. "We've got to keep moving. The soldiers aren't far away, and I would imagine they're pretty pissed off."

"We're not going to make it to Rajalla by morning, are we?" she asked.

"We can't risk traveling on the road. Unless there's an alternative route that's relatively smooth going—or maybe a taxi service—we're out of luck."

"There are trails through the woods, but they're not well traveled."

"That's going to slow us down." He looked up. "And if I'm not mistaken the sky is going to open up in about two minutes."

Lily looked up in time to see lightning flicker. The thought of traveling at night in cold rain with a band of angry soldiers hot on their trail was bad enough, but the thought of Jack getting wet was unbearable. "How are we going to keep Jack from getting wet?"

"Good old-fashioned American ingenuity." Working the carrier off his shoulders, Robert removed his jacket and draped it over the baby. "Water resistant nylon."

Trying not to let it show how much the gesture meant to her, Lily held Jack while Robert slipped the carrier onto his shoulders, then put the baby into the carrier.

"How well do you know the area?" Robert asked.

"I've taken this route to Rajalla several times."

"Is there someplace where we can take shelter?"

Lily thought about it for a moment, pulled a dusty fragment from her memory. "There's a mine not far from here.

It's old and the entrance is boarded up, but I think I can find it.''

"As long as the roof doesn't leak."

She didn't relish the idea of spending the night in a dark and dusty mine, but it beat the alternative of sleeping in the rain. "This way," she said and started down the trail.

Robert knew things could always get worse. That seemed to be the only rule he'd been able to count on since arriving in Rebelia. Of course it was little consolation when 2:00 a.m. rolled around, the skies opened up and the rain began to fall in sheets. To top things off his leg was aching like a son of a bitch. It had started troubling him several miles back, and the pain showed no sign of abating any time soon. The orthopedic surgeon had told him the pain stemmed from nerve damage he'd sustained from the shrapnel injury. He'd recommended ice, anti-inflammatory drugs and elevation to alleviate swelling and pressure on the nerves. Robert didn't think he was going to get any of those things any time soon, so he'd just have to grin and bear it.

He hadn't even bothered to tell Lily about the bullet wound in his shoulder. Mostly because he knew it was superficial and he didn't want her fussing over him and risk slowing them down. But it was starting to hurt, too.

Looking up at the sky, he let the cool rain wash over his face. Jack had been sleeping uneasily for the last two hours, but Robert could tell the baby was getting uncomfortable with the constant motion and cold, damp air. They needed to camp for the night. More pressingly, they needed to get out of the rain. It was barely fifty degrees. Once they were wet, it wouldn't take long for hypothermia to set in.

"How much farther?" he shouted over the din of rain.

Lily turned to him, looking miserable and wet and uncertain as hell. "I'm not sure."

"Let's keep moving."

She narrowed her eyes. "What's wrong? Are you in pain?"

"I'm fine. Keep walking."

"Robert, you've been limping for the last couple of miles. Do you want me to take Jack?"

"No, damn it." He hadn't even realized he'd been limping. He was so accustomed to the pain, he compensated almost automatically by keeping as much weight off his leg as possible.

"If you need to stop—"

"What I need is a dry place to spend the night, okay?"

"No need to get so testy about it." Lifting Robert's jacket, she peeked beneath it at Jack. "Poor little guy."

"He's dry for now, but we need to find shelter," Robert said. "It could rain like this all night."

Cupping her hand over her brow to shield her eyes from the downpour, she scanned the surrounding forest, looking a little bit lost and a whole lot hopeless. "I don't understand. It seems like we should have come to the mine entrance by now."

Robert looked at her and wondered how long her teeth had been chattering. Guilt tugged at him that he hadn't been able to come up with a better plan than the one he'd offered. "Maybe we need to backtrack a little," he said.

Even with her hair soaked and plastered against her head, she looked beautiful. He felt another tug, stronger this time, deeper. He wanted to put his arms around her. He wanted to comfort her and tell her he was sorry for getting her into this. He wanted to reassure her and tell her everything was going to be all right. He wanted to kiss her again. Lose himself in the lush softness of her mouth. He wanted to touch her the way he had the night before, make her lose control...

"There's a village a few miles from here. Maybe if we keep walking..." Brushing wet hair off her forehead, she sighed. "Damn it. I don't see how we missed it."

"How long has it been since you've been here?"

"Since before Jack was born."

"The entrance could be overgrown with foliage." He followed her gaze with his eyes. "What about landmarks?"

"I remember the mine entrance being near the little wooden bridge we crossed a while back."

"How far off the trail?"

Turning, she pointed toward a jut of earth and rock tangled with vineage and saplings and dry leaves. "In that general direction."

Aware of Jack's little body soft and warm against his abdomen, Robert walked over to the jut of earth. Cold rain trickled down his neck and back as he stooped to pick up a broken branch. The rain burned the bullet wound in his shoulder as he began breaking off the smaller twigs.

"What are you doing?" Lily asked.

"This jut of earth looks man-made." Using the stick, Robert poked at the tangled foliage. He walked several yards and poked again. Nothing but rock and earth and winter-dead foliage. Damn it.

Rain poured down his face and into his eyes. Jack felt so warm and delicate, he couldn't stand the thought of the baby getting wet. He couldn't let that happen. He poked again with the stick. This time, a hollow thump sounded.

Tossing the stick aside, he fought through the brush, tearing the vines and branches away, eventually locating an ancient wooden door. "Bingo."

But Lily was already beside him. He glanced at her out of the corner of his eye. Rain poured down her face, but she didn't seem to notice as she tore aside the tangled branches and vines. "This is it!" she shouted excitedly as the wood planks of the door came into view.

"Stand back." Quickly, Robert unbuckled the carrier and carefully passed Jack to her.

"What are you going to do?" she asked, taking Jack.

"I'm going to kick in the door."

"Wouldn't the knob be easier?"

Robert blinked the rain from his eyes and looked at the rusty knob someone had nailed to one of the planks. Trying not to feel like an idiot, he twisted it and shoved. The door creaked like ancient bones and swung open to reveal an ink-black tunnel.

"What do you see?" Lily asked, craning her head to see over his shoulder.

"Not a damn thing."

"Do you have a flashlight?"

"Hey, I'm a Boy Scout, remember?" He dug the halogen flashlight from his backpack and shone it into the depths of the tunnel. The beam revealed a narrow chasm carved into rock and earth that went on for as far as the powerful beam penetrated. The passageway was seven-feet high and ten-feet wide. Ancient wooden support beams a foot in diameter had been set into the walls and ceiling at four-foot intervals. Cobwebs hung down like Spanish moss. Broken rails and rotted ties littered the floor where mining cars had once hauled ore from the bowels of the earth.

"Home sweet home," Robert said, stepping inside.

"I wonder if they deliver pizza."

"In-room movies would be nice."

"Gone With The Wind."

"I was thinking more along the lines of *The Matrix*."

She smiled at him.

Robert knew it was a stupid moment, but he couldn't help but smile back. She was standing so close he could see the water beading on her eyelashes. He could smell the subtle scent of her shampoo coming off her wet hair. Her eyes were luminescent in the light of the beam. He was aware of Jack sleeping soundly between them, that Lily was close enough to touch, and an odd sense of rightness settled over him.

The moment shouldn't have meant anything—they were cold and tired and hungry with a band of hostile soldiers hot on their trail—but the moment did mean something. It meant a lot. More than he could put into words. A hell of a lot more than he wanted it to.

As he stood there looking into her beautiful eyes, the

realization of just how lucky he was to have found them, regardless of the circumstances, hit him like the business end of a cane. Lily stared back, her eyes wide, her lips trembling with cold. A single drop of water hung from her earlobe. Robert wondered what it would be like to lean down and catch that tiny droplet with his mouth. If she would allow it. If it would taste like her.

Before he realized that he was going to touch her, he reached out and caught the drop with his thumb. She flinched, then opened her mouth as if to speak, but no sound came out. Lord, he wanted to kiss her. Wanted to devour that mouth. Pull her to him. Finish what they had begun the night before. Damn it, he wanted to know if there was a future for them.

"Now might be a good time to pull that door closed," he said gruffly.

"That'll make it awfully dark in here."

"You're not afraid of the dark, are you?"

"No, I just…don't like it."

He thought about what it would be like to be in a dark room with her, decided it was something he'd be better off not thinking about at the moment. "Leave it open a few inches. I'm going to build a fire. We'll use it as the chimney."

Lily turned quickly away and pulled at the door.

Robert let out a long breath and wiped the rain from his forehead, wondering how the hell he was going to get through the rest of the night without doing something he was going to regret.

Chapter 10

Lily sat on the small tarp Robert had laid on the floor trying not to shiver, trying even harder not to think about how she was going to get through the night when she was cold to her bones and her life had just taken a hard left turn straight into disaster. She couldn't believe DeBruzkya had put a price on her head. One hundred thousand dollars was an outrageous sum of money in Rebelia. A lot of people would do a lot of things to earn it.

The possibilities made her shudder.

She looked at Jack snuggled in Robert's jacket next to her, and another layer of fear lanced through her. Robert was right; she'd put her child at risk. The thought struck her like a punch. He was the most precious thing to her in the world. A sweet, innocent baby—and she'd put him in danger. Not only Jack, she realized, but Robert, too, and guilt wrapped gnarly fingers around her and squeezed.

For several long minutes she sat next to Jack and watched him sleep. He'd wakened for a few minutes when she'd changed him; he'd even taken a little bit of the goat's milk, then quickly fallen back to sleep. Lily wished sleep would come to her as easily. Wished she wasn't wet and cold and still shaking from their brush with DeBruzkya's soldiers.

A few feet from the mine entrance, Robert fed ancient wood planks to the small fire he'd built. Lily watched him, a new trepidation creeping over her. She'd never been particularly claustrophobic, but for the first time since they'd set foot inside the mine some twenty minutes ago, she felt hemmed in. Trapped. Not only by the dangers lurking outside, but by her feelings for Robert.

No matter how badly she wanted to deny it, there was something powerful and undeniably profound between them. A tangible connection that pain and grief and distance hadn't erased.

''The fire should warm it up in here a little.''

She started at the sound of Robert's voice and looked up to find him silhouetted against the fire, facing her. His wet hair looked black in the flickering light. He'd slicked it back, revealing sharp cheekbones and angular planes that lent him a menacing countenance. His face was in shadow, but she knew he was watching her. She could feel his eyes sweeping over her as surely as she could feel the welcome heat from the flames.

''It's going to be a long night,'' he said. ''This might be a good time to see what we can do about drying our clothes.''

''I'm fine.'' She knew the instant she said the words how silly they sounded.

''Wet clothes are fine if you're a fish. But you're not, and I don't have to tell you about the dangers of hypothermia,'' he said. ''Do I?''

When she didn't respond, he frowned and walked over to the fire. She knew what he was going to do next—take off his sweater. And while she knew that was the practical thing to do, the side of her that wasn't feeling quite so practical jumped into panic mode.

"What are you doing?" she snapped.

He scowled at her. "Getting dry."

Feeling awkward and silly and terribly uncomfortable, she looked away. She didn't want to see Robert Davidson without his shirt. Seeing him shirtless and brooding would make her remember, and the last thing she wanted to do was remember how things had once been between them.

But for all the warnings blaring inside her head, she couldn't keep her eyes off him for long. She turned her head and watched him drag the sweater up and over his head. Her mouth went dry as his flat abdomen came into view. She saw black hair and taut flesh, and sudden heat flashed through her. He winced a little as he worked the sweater off his shoulders and draped it over a makeshift clothesline he'd fashioned from a coil of old wire.

Aware that her heart was hammering, she stared at the red slash just above his bicep for several long seconds before realizing it was a wound. "What on earth happened to your shoulder?"

Frowning as if the bullet wound were nothing more than an annoying bee sting, he looked at it. "It's nothing."

"*Nothing?*" Rising abruptly, she crossed the short distance between them. Shock rippled through her when she realized the damage had been done by a bullet. "My God, you've been *shot.*"

"It's a graze, Lily. Hurts like the dickens, but it's not serious."

"How can a piece of lead tearing through flesh at a high rate of speed not be serious?"

"The medical term for it is flesh wound."

"Why on earth didn't you say something?"

"I didn't want to distract you."

"Distract me?"

He shrugged. "I didn't think you could run and fuss over a flesh wound at the same time."

A noise of exasperation escaped her. "I thought doctors were supposed to be smart about injuries."

"We don't panic."

"For God's sake, Robert, you could have been killed."

"Any of us could have been killed," he returned evenly.

The words chilled her because she knew they were true, and the guilt twisted brutally inside her. Because she didn't want to think too hard about all the terrible things that could have happened, she turned her attention to the wound. The sight of it made her wince. The bullet had opened a two-inch-long gash. It wasn't deep, but the surrounding flesh was swollen and badly bruised. She could tell by the stain on his sweater that it had bled quite a bit. "At least the bleeding has stopped," she said.

He shot her a canny look. "Think you can butterfly me?"

Lily jerked her head. "Of course I can."

Scowling, he limped over to Jack, knelt and set his hand against the baby's plump cheek. Lily watched as Robert's features softened, and in an instant he went from annoyed man to gentle father. "He's sleeping well," he said softly.

"Up until recently he was always a good sleeper," she said, coming up behind him. "The vitamins really helped."

Robert picked up one of Jack's tiny hands and inspected his fingers. "Nail bed coloration is good."

Kneeling beside him, Lily brushed her hand over Jack's forehead. "Is he going to be all right?" she whispered.

For several moments, the only sound came from the crackling fire and the incessant rain outside. "He's going to be fine," Robert said.

"Promise me," she said.

"I promise."

She knew it was a promise he couldn't ensure, but she desperately needed to hear it, needed even more desperately to believe it. "Thank you."

The fire had eased the dampness from the cave. Slowly, Lily felt the tension at the back of her neck begin to unravel. It seemed like the most natural thing in the world when Robert reached out and brushed the wet hair from her cheek.

"Are you holding up okay?" he asked.

Lily nodded, resisting the urge to press her cheek against his hand. The backs of his fingers were warm and dry, and his touch reassured her as nothing else could have. Her heart beat a little unsteadily against her ribs when he brushed his thumb over the scar at her brow.

"I wouldn't have left you that night," he whispered. "If I'd been able to stay. I would have found you."

Lily saw something she couldn't quite identify in his eyes. Tenderness, perhaps. Affection tempered with caution. She wanted that to be enough, but it wasn't. "I know."

Taking her hand, he rose, and she rose with him. Need and the sweet ache of memories past tangled within her. She knew it was a dangerous thought, but she wanted to step into his embrace. She wanted to be held. She wanted to be kissed. For a short while she wanted to forget about all the troubles in the world. The dangers she had brought down on them.

"You're shivering," he said quietly.

"It's cold." But Lily knew damn good and well she wasn't shivering because of the cold.

His gaze dropped to her mouth, but he made no move to get any closer. "We need to get your clothes dried."

"I think that might be a little awkward."

"Hey, I'm a doctor, remember?" He grinned. "You can wrap Jack's blanket around you until your sweater is dry. He's got my jacket to keep him warm."

She had absolutely no desire to walk around with nothing more than a threadbare blanket to cover her. But Lily knew it would be silly to spend the night in wet clothes and risk hypothermia when she could dry them over the fire.

"I brought some dried fruit and nuts," Robert said. "Let's get your clothes hung and then we'll eat."

"We'll eat after that wound on your shoulder is cleaned and bandaged," she said firmly.

Robert smiled. "Yes, ma'am."

At that moment he looked very much like the man she'd fallen in love with two years earlier. So much that it frightened her.

Moving away from him, Lily stooped and eased the blanket from Jack, replacing it with Robert's jacket. "Sleep tight, sweetheart."

Blanket in hand, she left the warmth of the fire and walked to a dim corner where the air was cold and damp. In her peripheral vision she saw Robert rummaging in his backpack with his back to her.

"Stay right there and don't turn around," she said.

Robert straightened, but kept his back to her. "No problem."

Never taking her eyes from him, she swiftly lifted the sweater over her head, then unhooked her bra. Her skirt was wet, too, so she stepped out of it. Shivering against the cold, she withdrew the mini Magnum and unbuckled the holster from around her thigh. Wearing nothing except her panties, she wrapped the blanket around her and started toward the fire.

Aware that her heart was beating too fast, she risked a look at Robert—just to make sure he still had his back to her. But the sight of his muscular back and broad shoulders stopped her cold. The fire cast a warm glow that turned his skin golden. His jeans were wet. He hadn't yet removed them, and the wet material hugged every toned muscle of his backside. She tried hard to deny the sharp zing of awareness that crept over her, but she didn't have much luck.

Lily reached the fire and looked at the soggy clothes in her hands. "Where's a clothes dryer when you need one?" she said, trying not to feel awkward.

Robert turned. She couldn't bring herself to look at him,

but she felt his gaze sweep over her as surely as if he'd touched her.

"I'll hang them for you," he said.

She did look at him then, and the contact was as shocking as the snap of a bullet through the air. She saw the quick flex of his jaw. The jump of heat in his eyes. She was aware of that same heat jumping through her blood, warming her from the inside out. Aware that her knees had begun to shake, that neither of them had made a move to close the short, dangerous distance between them, she looked away. "I can do it."

She concentrated intently on draping her sweater and skirt over the wire, but she was starkly aware that he was standing just a few feet away. That he was watching her every move. That he hadn't said a word. And that if they didn't do something about the tension, the air around them was going to shatter.

As she smoothed out the wrinkles in her skirt she heard Robert move away. Her nerves settled a bit when she looked over her shoulder and saw him spreading a second tarp on the ground.

Leaving her clothes hanging, she crossed to him. "How's your shoulder?"

"Flesh wounds always hurt the most."

"It's going to be stiff tomorrow."

"I don't think I'll be playing basketball for a while." He rolled the shoulder in question as if testing it and ended up grimacing. "It could use a bandage if you're up to it."

Bandaging the wound wasn't the problem. Standing scant inches from a bare-chested man to whom she was incredibly attracted while she was wearing nothing more than a threadbare blanket was the problem. "I'm up to it."

He sank onto the tarp and dug into his medical bag. Lily watched as he removed a roll of gauze, first aid tape, antibiotic cream and a small container of peroxide.

"Unless you've got really long arms, you might try coming over here," he said. "I don't bite."

Feeling herself flush, she stepped over to him and knelt. "I think we both know your biting isn't the problem."

He frowned at the wound. "Clean it up with a little peroxide, add a thin glaze of the antibiotic ointment, cover it with a bandage. Think you can do that?"

"Of course I can." Lily hoped he didn't notice that her hands were shaking when she tore open an alcohol pad and sterilized her hands. Robert didn't so much as wince when she drizzled peroxide over the wound. She twisted the cap off a tube of ointment, then applied it directly to the wound. The graze wasn't deep, but the bullet had definitely done some damage. He would have a permanent scar. If the bullet had been a couple of inches deeper, it would have shattered his shoulder.

"You're incredibly lucky this wasn't any worse," she said.

"I'd say all three of us were pretty damn lucky."

He made a sound that was more annoyance than pain when she laid the gauze over the wound and pressed the tape over it.

"Sorry," she said. "I know it hurts. I'm just about finished."

"Take your time," he said between clenched teeth, then glanced at her handiwork. "You ever consider taking up medicine?"

Smoothing the last strip of tape, she sat back on her heels. "I'm much too good at journalism."

Working his shoulder, Robert rose and walked to his backpack.

"I'm hoping you have a couple of filets mignons and a bottle of Merlot in there," she said.

"Close." He grinned. "Almonds and dried apricots."

"That'll do in a pinch." She watched as he withdrew a tiny computer and headset.

"I need to check in with Dr. Orloff at the hospital," he said.

"That's pretty high-tech gear for a doctor on a human-itarian mission," she said.

Instead of acknowledging the statement he carried the tiny computer several feet away, slipped on the headset and tapped several keys.

Because she needed an outlet for the nerves snapping through her, she rose and walked to where he'd set out a bag of almonds, a smaller bag of dried apricots and a bottle of water. As she opened the bags and twisted off the bottle cap he spoke in very low tones to whomever was on the other end of the line. Not for the first time she wondered about the air of secrecy that had surrounded him since he'd arrived in Rebelia. If he were here on a humanitarian mis-sion, why all the secrecy? Where on earth had the high-tech communication gear come from? What about those eraser-size explosives he'd used to escape the soldiers? Or was there more going on with Dr. Robert Davidson than he was letting on?

Several minutes passed before he snapped the computer closed and returned to where she sat near the fire. He didn't look at her as he stowed the computer in its case.

"Is everything all right with Dr. Orloff?" she asked, passing him the water and a handful of almonds and dried fruit on a napkin.

She knew something was wrong the instant he looked at her. As hard as he might try to hide his emotions, there were some things a man couldn't hide. Some things a woman sensed instinctively. Lily wasn't sure what was go-ing on, but she knew it wasn't good.

"What's wrong?" she asked. "Is there a problem at the hospital?"

Sitting on the tarp with his elbows on his knees, Robert looked down, then his eyes met hers. "Do you want the truth? Or do you want me to pretty it up for you?"

"You know me well enough to know I want the truth." A terrible thought struck her. "It's not about Jack, is it? Robert, please, if it's—"

"DeBruzkya raised the bounty to five hundred thousand dollars," he said.

The words struck her with the force of a speeding tank, shocking her with fear and a cold, hard reality she hadn't ever wanted to face. "That's outrageous! And how did he know—"

"The soldiers told him we were together," he cut in. "They told him we have a child." He shot her a canny look. "The bounty is for the three of us."

"Oh, God." Rising, Lily turned away from him and pressed her hand to her stomach. She felt physically ill. "He knows about Jack."

"He doesn't know where we are, but I'm sure he's got a vague idea."

"I've put you in danger."

"No. DeBruzkya put us in danger," he growled.

"My God, I've put Jack in danger." The realization tore through her like sharp claws. She'd done this. It was her fault. She'd put not only a man she cared deeply for in danger, but her precious son, as well.

She jumped when strong hands closed over her shoulders. Lily hadn't heard him rise, hadn't noticed his approach. "Don't do this to yourself, Lily."

"This is all my fault," she said.

"This is DeBruzkya's fault."

"I've been blind." She looked at him. "I've been lying to myself. I've been in this country not to free her people, not to give the orphans food and medicine and hope, but because I'm afraid to leave."

"Any sane person would be afraid of DeBruzkya."

"That makes me a coward."

"Stop it, damn it. You're one of the bravest people I know."

For the first time, the reality that she'd failed stared her in the face. She'd failed the Rebelian people. She'd failed herself. But worst of all, she'd failed Jack. Sweet, precious Jack. The taste of that failure was bitter.

Determined not to cry, she blinked back tears. "I wanted to make a difference."

"You did."

"I wanted to bring him down. That monster DeBruzkya. I wanted that so badly it blinded me to the harm I was doing to my own child."

"Honey, you didn't harm Jack. He's fine. You've been a good mother. But you can't do it all by yourself."

She raised her clenched fist. "I was so close. But I'm not going to get him, am I?"

"No, you're not." Robert's jaw flexed. "It's time for you to go home, Lily. It's time for you and Jack to go back to the United States."

"DeBruzkya will never let me leave," she whispered. "I know him, Robert. He's crazy and cruel and obsessive."

Using a firm touch, Robert turned her to him. When she refused to look at him he put his fingers under her chin and forced her gaze to his. "I can get you out."

"He has an entire army looking for us." She squeezed her eyes close to lock in the tears, but they squeezed through her lashes. "He'll kill you. I know it. He'll kill you just to get at me."

"DeBruzkya isn't going to do anything."

A sob escaped her when she thought of who else was vulnerable. "He'll hurt Jack."

"He's not going to get near my son," he said, his voice taking on a dangerous edge.

"DeBruzkya doesn't care about you or Jack, Robert. The only reason he wants either of you is to get to me. I'm the one he wants."

"Damn it, Lily, don't go there."

But Lily already had. She didn't have a choice. She'd been fooling herself to believe she could outmaneuver a master. To actually believe she could bring down someone as diabolical and cunning as DeBruzkya. All she'd managed to do was put Robert and her son in danger.

"I've got to turn myself in," she said after a moment.

"No."

She tried to twist away from him, but his hands tightened on her biceps. "There's no other way."

"Listen to me." Grasping her arms, he gave her a little shake. "You don't have to sacrifice yourself to do this."

"I'm not willing to risk Jack." She looked into his eyes. "I'm not going to risk your getting hurt, either."

"DeBruzkya will kill you!" he shouted.

"No, he won't," she said.

"How can you possibly know that?"

"Because he's in love with me."

His lips drew back in a snarl. "That doesn't matter."

"How can you say that? I'm the only person who can get close to him. I'm his weakness. How can you deny that using me isn't the best way to get to him?"

"Because I love you!" he shouted. "And I'll be damned if I'm going to let you get yourself killed because you don't have the good sense to know when you're out of your league."

Chapter 11

Robert stared at her, breathing as if he'd just run a mile, his heart pounding pure adrenaline. Lily stared back, her eyes wide with shock, her face as pale as death. All the while the words he'd just uttered ricocheted between them like a hollow-point slug.

I love you.

Shocked by what he'd said—deeply disturbed because he'd meant it—he gathered the tattered threads of his dignity and grappled to focus on the issue at hand. "What did he do to you that made you hate him so much?" he asked roughly.

His emotions shifted dangerously when she winced, and Robert realized he'd hit a nerve. A live nerve that jumped when prodded. She tried to twist away, but he held her gently, sensing she needed to talk but knowing the words wouldn't come easily for her.

"Lily, it's me. Come on. Talk to me," he pressed.

Lily looked at him, her eyes stricken. "He...murdered

someone I cared about very much. Her name was Alina,"
she whispered.

"A child?"

"She was seven years old. An orphan in a village not
far from Rajalla. Her mother had been killed by a land
mine. Her father went to fight in the war, but he never came
home. Alina was sent to the orphanage when she was five.
I met her a year later when I was tutoring some of the
kids." She smiled, but he saw the pain in her eyes. "She
had strawberry-blond hair, like mine." She choked out a
laugh. "As silly as it sounds, I think that's what drew her
to me. I started calling her Strawberry. My little Strawberry."

Robert could feel the tremors moving through her. He
loosened his grip, but she didn't pull away. It was as if she
needed his support just to stand as she remembered. "Tell
me about her," he said gently.

"She liked dolls. Plastic or porcelain or wooden, it didn't
matter. I bought her a Raggedy Ann at a tourist shop in a
border town over in Holzberg. It was just a cheap, poorly
sewn doll. But Strawberry didn't care. In her eyes, that doll
was made of gold. She loved her. Took Raggedy Ann everywhere."

A breath shuddered out of her. "I tutored her two days
a week. She wanted to learn English. So she could be a
schoolteacher. She was so sweet. So innocent and smart
and so undeserving of all the terrible things that had happened to her."

The tears flowed freely down Lily's cheeks, and she let
them fall. The sight of her pain moved him. He hurt for
her. He could feel the pain curling inside him. And even
though he didn't yet know what had happened to Strawberry, he hurt for that little girl, too, because he knew the
outcome hadn't been good.

"Then one day I went to the orphanage to pick her up.
We were going to go to the park. Strawberry and Raggedy
Ann and I. But when I got there, the building...it was gone.

Leveled by a bomb. I stood there in the rubble and fell to my knees and I cried like a baby. I looked for her but never found a trace.'' She raised ravaged eyes. ''But I found Raggedy Ann. That's when I knew.''

''Lily…''

''That's when I knew she was dead.'' A sob escaped her.

''Shh. It's okay.''

''No, it's not.''

He could feel the pain coming off her, like heat rising from the desert floor in shimmering waves. He didn't even realize it when his arms went around her. ''I'm sorry, honey.''

''Something died inside me that day, Robert.''

''Nothing died inside you,'' he said.

''I couldn't believe anyone could harm innocent children. I can't reconcile myself to that.''

He pulled back slightly. ''DeBruzkya?'' he asked.

She nodded, tears glistening on her cheeks. ''He murdered that beautiful child. He murdered all of them. I can't forget about her, about them.''

''No one expects you to.'' Feeling helpless and ineffectual, he caressed the back of her head, wishing he could take away her pain, knowing he couldn't. ''You never told anyone this?''

''I never spoke of it after that day. It's like I locked it away and pretended it never happened. But inside I was seething.''

''It's not good to hold something like that inside for so long.''

''I know, but…I couldn't accept it. And I couldn't walk away.''

He knew she was referring to the day he'd asked her to leave with him. He'd known her for a couple of months at the time. Odd that he'd never had a clue she'd been hurting so desperately. And for the first time her refusal to leave with him made sense. ''Why didn't you tell me?''

''I don't know. The time just never seemed right. What

we had…it was really good. The emotions inside me were ugly. Hate. The need for revenge. I just couldn't bring those into what we had.''

''You lost someone you loved. It's okay to grieve.''

''I hate him,'' she said. ''That's not grief.''

''Sometimes it's hard to tell one emotion from another when you're hurting.'' When she wouldn't look at him, he put his fingers under her chin and forced her gaze to his. ''You were very brave.''

''I hurt you. I'm sorry.''

''It's okay.''

''No, it's not. It's not okay.'' Pulling away slightly, she shook her head. ''Now I've put you at risk. I've put my own son at risk. All because I've been blinded by hatred—''

''Not hatred,'' he said firmly.

''It's in my heart, like a black hole in my soul, bottomless and terrible and—''

''Love was part of it, too, Lily. You loved Strawberry.''

''Yes, I did, but—''

''You stayed because you didn't want another child to suffer the same fate. If that's not love, I don't know what is.'' Unable to bear to see her hurting like this, he took her face in his hands and stared into her eyes. ''Come on, Lily. You did what you could.''

''I failed.''

''No.''

''I've put my own son at risk. I've put you at risk. And it's all been for nothing because DeBruzkya is going to win.''

''No, he's not.''

''How can you know that?''

''Because I'm not going to let him.''

Robert hadn't intended to go there, but he didn't regret the words, because he meant them. Still, the conversation had strayed into territory he couldn't ever discuss with her. Lily didn't know about ARIES. She had no idea he was an agent. To tell her now—especially now—would put her in grave danger.

"Trust me," he said gently. "And leave it at that."

"I do."

"I wish I could have been there for you."

"You were," she whispered. "You were always there. What we had…sustained me when I felt as if I couldn't go on."

Robert closed his eyes against a hot burst of emotion he didn't want to feel, against words he wasn't sure he was ready to hear.

"When you said you loved me—"

"Don't." Leaning forward, he set his forehead against hers and tried desperately not to feel what he knew to be true in his heart.

"I have to," she whispered. "I have to say this."

He pulled back slightly to meet her gaze and waited.

"After the missile hit the pub," she began, "when I was lying in the rubble, waiting to die, waiting for the soldiers to take me…" Her voice broke, but she struggled through the words. "I dreamed you came back. You picked me up out of the rubble and carried me away from the horrors of that place. When I came to and I was alone, I realized I'd made a terrible mistake. I thought I was going to die. I waited for you, but you never came. I thought you'd deserted me."

"Oh, honey, no. If I'd been able, I would have come back for you, even if I had to crawl. I thought you were dead."

"DeBruzkya did that to us," she whispered. "I can't let him get away with that. I'm sorry if that's not what you want to hear, but I'm not going to let him walk away."

"I'm not going to let you sacrifice yourself." But even as he said the words, Robert could see she'd made up her mind. She had every intention of using her connection to DeBruzkya to take him down. He could feel his control over the situation slipping through his fingers, like sand through the inept fingers of a child. He was a doctor and scientist, a highly trained ARIES agent; he'd accomplished some amazing things. And yet something as simple—and as complex—as keeping this woman safe eluded him.

They were standing face-to-face with scant inches separating them. But Robert knew those inches were fraught with a chasm of pain. A chasm he had every intention of traversing no matter what the cost.

Need twisted brutally inside him, as painful as any wound, as dangerous as any bullet. He didn't intend to kiss her. But one moment he was holding her lovely face in his hands, wanting—needing—to ease her suffering. And in the next instant his mouth was on hers. He tasted tears and grief, but both those things were laced with the heady spice of desire. And in an instant the moment transformed, from one human being comforting another to a man kissing a woman he cared deeply for.

The earth moved beneath his feet when she made a sound at the back of her throat and opened to him. He hadn't expected her to kiss him back, and for an instant he was stunned. The rush of pleasure made him dizzy. He'd known kissing her would be good, but he hadn't expected it to burn. He hadn't expected it to shake his world. Turn him inside out. Make him forget all the reasons he couldn't get involved with her.

He marveled at the silky feel of her tongue against his, the taste of almond and apricot mingling with the sweet taste of her mouth. Gentle was forgotten as desperation and the need to protect what was precious, the need to possess what was his, took over. She matched him strength for strength, returning everything he gave her and adding something more that was uniquely hers. The combination took his breath.

Robert wasn't a fast lover. He preferred to take his time with a woman. But when she moved against him, when she sighed in his ear and made a mewling sound in her throat, his control broke. He ravaged her mouth. His teeth clicked against hers. He knew better than to rush this moment. But the urgency pushing through him was more powerful than any need for restraint. When she threw her head back, he kissed the delicate line of her jaw, her throat, the point of her chin. He ran his tongue along the ridge of her collarbone until she went liquid in his arms.

Aware that he was breathing hard, that his pulse was raging out of control, he took her hands in his and backed her toward the support beam a few feet away. All the while he kissed her deeply, never giving her respite or time to change her mind.

The support column stopped her backward progression, and he pressed against her. Her body was as soft and warm as a breath. His senses drank in the essence of her like a man dying of thirst. A few feet away, the fire seemed to swell and spark, filling the room with heat. Aware of the pump of blood through his veins, the hot burn of lust in his groin, he loosened the blanket she'd anchored just above her breasts. A violent shiver ran the length of her when it slipped down and dropped at her feet.

Her beauty impacted him solidly, humbling him, and for an instant he felt like an inexperienced teenager. "I'd forgotten how beautiful you are," he said.

"You always make me feel like the most beautiful woman in the world."

"You are."

"Meaningless flattery." She smiled, but he could see the zing of nerves in her eyes.

"Meaningful," he corrected. "Very meaningful."

Her body was familiar and yet it wasn't. Her pregnancy had produced subtle changes that intrigued him so that he wanted to explore every exquisite inch of her. He touched the tiny mole just above her left breast and remembered touching it a hundred times before. He ran his fingers over the thin white scar on her right hip. The scar hadn't been there before, and he wondered if the injury had been one of the horrors she'd suffered the night of the explosion.

Wanting to take away all the old pain—the new pain, too—he touched it gently, lovingly, and tried to erase the injury it had left upon her heart.

Her breasts were fuller, her nipples larger and fully erect. He thought of her breast-feeding their baby and he marveled at the miracle of it, and found himself wishing he'd been there to share that moment with her.

She gasped when he gently cupped her breasts. A cry escaped her when he molded her with his hands. So soft and warm and perfect. She moved restlessly when he brushed his thumbs across the sensitized tips. Dipping his head, he kissed the darkened peak, laving it with his tongue. She cried out when he took her into his mouth and began to suckle. Something primal broke free inside him when she arched. He ran his tongue along the valley between her breasts and flicked the tip of her other breast. His vision dimmed when she reached for him. A hot rush of blood burned him when her fingers closed around his shaft through his jeans.

"I want you," he heard himself say. "I've never stopped wanting you."

"I'll hurt you again."

Pulling away slightly, he took her by the shoulders and eased her back. Her eyes were dark and luminous in the firelight. Her pupils were dilated. Her mouth kiss-bruised and wet. Her breath shallow and fast.

"Why?" he asked.

"I can't leave with you."

"I'm not going to let you stay."

"DeBruzkya will kill you if he knows we're…together."

A quick rise of anger had him pulling away. But Lily stopped him. "Please, don't stop," she whispered. "We have this moment. I don't want to lose it. Robert, I need you."

She kissed him, and Robert knew he was going to do exactly what he shouldn't. She slipped her tongue into his mouth, and he felt the contact all the way to his soul. The

soft pressure of her mouth against his. The brush of her
breath against his cheek. Arousal burning low and hot in
his groin. Twenty-one months of grief and frustration and
anger cut loose inside him. Love and fear and the terrible
realization that the situation had spiraled out of his control
gripped him.

He closed his eyes against the starburst of emotion. He
could feel it tearing him up inside, a wild animal with sharp
claws that refused to be caged. All the while she made love
to his mouth, driving him mad with the need to have her,
to keep her safe, to love her. He kissed her back, gently at
first and then with all the desperation inside him. He felt
her fingers fumbling with his belt and zipper. Every searing
touch set him on fire, tested his control.

When her hand wrapped around his shaft his restraint
broke with an audible snap, and Robert knew he'd lost the
battle. He knew it was going to cost him something precious. Something he wouldn't be able to get back.

He wanted forever.

All she could give him was a moment in time.

And Robert knew that would have to be enough.

Lily had never felt so swept away. For the first time in
her life she needed this. Needed Robert. His touch. The
feel of him against her. She needed all those things as much
as she needed her next breath. As much as her heart needed
to beat.

Even as sensation ebbed and flowed through her body,
she wondered how a touch that felt so right could be so
wrong. She didn't want to hurt him. Not any more than she
already had. But she knew where this would lead. And she
hated herself for not being strong enough to stop it.

Never taking his mouth from hers, Robert worked his
jeans down his hips. She touched him there, marveling at
the thick length of him, the sheer beauty of his body. She'd
forgotten so much about what it was like to make love to
him. The lean flex of rock-hard muscles. The way he trem-

bled with restraint when she teased him. She'd forgotten how powerful a moment like this could be, what raw desire could do to a woman's judgment.

But his kisses intoxicated her as thoroughly as any liquor. She drank them in, and they fed something ravenous and insatiable inside her. His hands were warm and calloused against her flesh, and every touch took her breath away.

A shiver went through her when he slid his hand down her pelvis to cup her. Her heart stopped for an instant and then began to rage. Her mind cried out against the vulnerability of opening herself up to him in this way. But her body reacted instinctively. She heard her name on his lips, and then he separated her and touched her most intimate place.

His touch was electric. She felt her body go rigid. He stroked her once. Twice. And she melted and contracted around him. She heard herself say his name, wanted to say it again and again as his finger moved within her, but she couldn't get enough oxygen into her lungs.

He never stopped kissing her. Never stopped touching her. It was as if there were too many sensations for her mind to process at once. Her brain overloaded. Shorted out. Until there was nothing except the man holding her, stroking her and the sensations streaking through her like white fire.

She heard an echo, realized belatedly that she was crying out. He stroked her deeply, knowing instinctively where to touch, when to tease, when to satisfy. The waves built, a relentless tide calling to the moon. She fought the current, not wanting to let herself be totally swept away. But he smoothed out her fear with his voice, soothing her, stroking her endlessly.

"Let go," he whispered.

"I'm...falling."

"I'll catch you."

Her trust in him solidified. She closed her eyes against

the knowledge. The pain it would bring them. Against the tide of sensation surging through her body, her heart. She rode the tide, and it took control of her, a riptide taking her out to sea. She no longer had the strength to fight it, like a fatigued swimmer caught in a dangerous undertow. She felt herself coming apart in his arms.

Lily let go of her control and shattered. Completion bore down on her, a rogue wave crashing against a rocky shore. White light flashed behind her lids. She felt the fierce power of it tumble her end over end, but she was weightless. She cried his name, heard the whisper of her own in her ear.

It was too much, and yet she knew it was not enough.

"Wrap yourself around me," he said, lifting her.

Her reflexes were so sluggish, and she'd barely gotten her arms around his neck when she felt his hands on her hips, pulling her against him. The suddenness of the act stunned her. She felt the rough column against her back. Cool air against wet heat as she wrapped her legs around him. The zing of anticipation when he opened her.

"I never stopped loving you," he said.

"Robert—" Lily cried out when he entered her. There was an instant of discomfort as she adjusted to his size. Then a hot rush of ecstasy. He captured her cry with his mouth. The shock of pleasure stole her breath as he began to move within her. Rapture turned every muscle in her body to water as he filled her and began to move within her. Never in a thousand years would she believe it could be like this. That she would trust him so fully. That the pleasure would be so great she would lose control. That she would feel so much in her heart that the moment would bring tears to her eyes. Or in her soul she could love him so much, and yet never allow herself to give her heart fully.

A second orgasm rocked her system, shook her from the inside out. Thoughts fluttered in and out of her mind. She grappled for control, but he refused to give her a respite. He moved within her, setting her ablaze all over again. Every nerve ending in her body screamed with pleasure.

And while her heart raged against his, the emotions inside her reached their breaking point.

She held on to him tightly, trying to hold it all inside, knowing there was too much. A sob broke from her lips, a cry wrenched from somewhere deep inside her.

"Lily?" Robert froze, his muscles going rigid. "Honey, what's wrong? Did I hurt you?"

"Don't stop." He was still deep inside her, a steel shaft throbbing with heat.

He didn't move. "Why are you crying?"

Embarrassed because she didn't have the slightest clue how to answer, she tried to look away. He cupped her cheek and forced her gaze to his. "If you want to stop—"

"I don't."

He looked at her as if she'd just asked him a question in Swahili. Blinking back tears she wasn't sure how to explain, she kissed him softly on the mouth, keenly aware that she was aroused, that she'd never been more moved by an experience in her entire life.

She moved tentatively against him, taking him more deeply inside her. His jaw went taut. His pupils dilated. He never took his eyes from her.

"Oh, Lily…"

"Robert, you make me feel so much. I mean, not just physically, but emotionally. It's like I can't hold it all inside me." She choked out a laugh. "That doesn't make any sense."

"It does." One side of his mouth curved. "Sort of."

She looked at him through her tears, taking in the concern and confusion in his eyes. "You moved me."

Cupping her face with his hands, he thumbed a tear off her cheek. One side of his mouth curved. "I think I'm flattered."

She smiled back. "There's something between us."

"I've always known that."

"Make love to me," she whispered.

"Not like this."

She gasped in surprise when he swept her into his arms. "What are you doing?"

"I'm going to finish what we started."

Lily felt as if she'd just snapped out of a dream. A very erotic dream that had left her shaken and weak and burning with need. A dream that had taken her to a place beyond her wildest imagination. She glanced around to get her bearings and realized he'd carried her to his tarp near the fire. Gently, he laid her down. "Don't go away," he said. "I'll be right back."

She drew her knees up to her chest, wrapped her arms around them and watched him walk naked to where they'd dropped her blanket. He scooped it up along with another tarp, then turned toward her with both in hand. He was still fully aroused, and heat coiled deep in her womb at the sight of him.

He sat beside her, draped the blanket over them and then lay down. "Come here," he whispered.

It was the most natural thing in the world for her to go into his arms. Lily closed her eyes against the rightness of it. The solid length of his body against hers. The brush of his chest hair against her sensitized nipples. The nudge of the velvet tip of his penis against her abdomen. She put every nuance to memory because she knew the moment was fleeting. Nothing this perfect lasted forever. If Lily had learned anything in her life, it was that the good things didn't last.

"What are you thinking of?" he asked.

She looked into the vivid blue of his eyes, felt another pang of longing deep within her. "You," she said, scooting closer to him. "Us." Touching her nose to his, she smiled at him, but it felt a little sad on her face.

He kissed her then. A soft, lingering kiss that was so sweet it brought tears to her eyes. A kiss that held the promise of heat and a thousand other things she would have sold her soul to accept.

He whispered her name as he entered her, saying it over

and over again as he moved within her. Lily accepted him into the deepest reaches of her body, giving him everything except the one thing she knew he wanted most.

Her heart.

Chapter 12

Robert stood at the mouth of the mine entrance and watched the rain sweep over the forest in sheets. He didn't relish the idea of going back into the storm. It was too damn cold for him, let alone for a one-year-old baby, but he knew there was no way they could avoid it. Dawn would arrive in a couple of hours. It was only a matter of time before DeBruzkya's soldiers found them. With topographical maps of the area, they could already be on the way.

Troubled and restless and more uneasy than he wanted to admit, Robert closed the door and turned. The fire burned low, casting yellow light on the jagged rock walls and ancient wood beams. He looked at Lily sleeping several feet away. She was lying on her side with Jack curled against her. He stared at them, keenly aware of the swift rise of emotion at the sight of mother and child. And he wondered how in God's name he was going to keep them safe.

He stood there for several long minutes, shaken by the power of his emotions. He couldn't stop thinking about what had happened between him and Lily just a few short hours ago. The way she'd come apart in his arms. It was as if all the months of pain and grief had erupted and spilled over into passion. When the emotions had become too much for her to contain, she'd cried. He'd held her tightly, but it hadn't been enough, and he couldn't ever remember feeling so helpless.

He wanted to believe the experience had moved him so profoundly because it had been such a long time since he'd taken a lover. But Robert had never been able to lie to himself, especially when it came to Lily. He knew why their lovemaking had shaken him so profoundly. Knew it had nothing to do with the physical—and everything to do with his heart.

He'd fallen in love with her all over again. Something he swore he'd never do after what she'd put him through. He hadn't the slightest idea how to handle the situation. Lily wasn't an easy woman to love. She was stubborn and headstrong and independent to a fault. But she was also generous and kind and more fragile than she would ever admit. Her childhood had shaped her, damaged her, made her the beautiful person she was, and he loved the good right along with the flawed—no questions asked.

Once she had her mind set, there was no stopping her. He knew she wasn't going to leave Rebelia. The truth of that twisted him into knots. Made him feel powerless and inept and so frustrated he wanted to shake her.

He thought of his mission and tried not to envision how this was going to end. Robert wasn't very good at losing people. He'd lost his father to hemoedema when he'd been ten years old. He'd lost his brother two years later to the same disease. He'd be damned if he'd let this woman rip out his heart.

Feeling the weight of the world settle onto his shoulders, Robert walked over to Lily and Jack and knelt. For several long seconds he watched them sleep. They looked peaceful in the flickering light from the fire, and his heart stumbled hard at the thought of losing them. He loved her. He loved the child they had created. He wished it was enough.

But it wasn't.

Robert would find a way to be in Jack's life. He would find a way to know him. To guide him and love him and be the best father he could. That wasn't what Robert wanted—he wanted a hell of a lot more—but it would have to be enough.

"Hey."

Robert glanced at Lily to see her smiling at him. The firelight turned her hair to silk and shone like tiny lights in her luminous eyes. Her beauty, the depth of his need for her shook him. For a moment he was so taken aback by his feelings for her that he couldn't speak. All he could do was look at her and want her while knowing that if he went to her now, it would be a mistake from which he would never recover.

Casting him a concerned look, she propped up on an elbow, careful to keep the blanket over her. "Are you all right? You look...troubled."

"We have to go," he heard himself say.

She looked uneasily toward the mine entrance and sat up straighter. "What is it? What's wrong?"

"It's only a matter of time before DeBruzkya's soldiers find us here. We can't risk staying. And we can't travel during the daylight hours."

She glanced over at Jack, brushed her hand across his cheek. "What time is it?"

"Almost five." He rose and walked to where their clothes hung on the wire above the fire. Her skirt and sweater were dry for the most part, so he took them down and handed them to her.

"Thank you," she said, not meeting his gaze.

Robert turned and walked away, careful to keep his back to her. He heard the rustle of clothes and wondered if he would ever make love to her again.

"Robert?"

Something in her voice spun him around. She was holding Jack, staring at him, her face ashen.

"What is it?" Robert asked, but he was already moving toward her.

"He's cold." Laying the baby down, she put trembling hands on his face, ran them gently over his body. "Sweetheart, what's wrong?"

Panic resonated in her voice. Robert could see it in her eyes. He knelt beside her. "Let's get him out of his carrier so I can see him."

"Oh, my God. Oh, no. Oh, Jack."

"Stay calm, Lily." Robert saw immediately that the child was lethargic and having a difficult time waking up. He picked up one of Jack's chubby hands, pressed down on the tip of his fingernail. "Blood return is delayed."

Lily's eyes were huge and frightened when she turned to him. "What does that mean?"

"That means we need to get him to the hospital."

"What's happening?"

Robert worked quickly to free Jack from his carrier. Once he was out he laid him on his back on the tarp and checked his pulse. "Grab my bag," he snapped.

She jumped to her feet, scooped up Robert's bag and brought it to him. "Tell me," she demanded. "What's wrong with him?"

"He may be going into anemic shock."

"Shock?" Falling to her knees next to her child, she looked at his still little body and put her hand over her mouth to smother a cry. "Oh, no. Oh, God, no."

Robert reached into his medical bag for a syringe. He tore the wrapper off, then removed the small bottle of vitamin B-12 from its box and inserted the needle into the protective rubber stopper.

"What are you doing?"

"I'm going to give him some B-12 to see if I can get his red cell count up. That should help." He hoped it would.

Tears streamed down her face as she watched Robert turn the child onto his stomach and inject the vitamin. Jack let out a healthy-sounding wail, and Lily choked back a sob that was half pain, half relief.

"Sorry about that, big guy," Robert said as he withdrew the needle and dropped it into an orange biohazard cup. "I know it smarts."

"I didn't think I'd ever be so happy to hear him cry," Lily said.

Robert looked at her, saw the fear etched into her every feature, and his heart broke for her. "He's going to be all right," he said. "But we need to get him to the hospital as soon as possible."

She wiped the tears on her cheeks with her sleeve, then leaned forward and gathered a crying Jack into her arms. "It's going to be all right, sweetheart. Shh, don't cry. It's okay. Daddy's going to fix you right up."

Daddy.

The word jolted him. It was the first time either of them had used it, and it hit him in a place that was vulnerable and raw. He sat back on his heels and watched her dress Jack, wondering if she realized what she'd said. If she had any idea how much that single word had affected him. How much it hurt.

"I've only got one more bottle," she said, taking a small plastic bottle of milk from her backpack. "I'll need to pick up some baby food and goat's milk at the market once we get into town."

Robert glanced at her, realized belatedly that she'd been speaking to him. "I checked the map while you were sleeping. Rajalla is only a couple of miles away. If we maintain a good pace we should be there in half an hour or so."

"All right." Lily rose, scooped up Jack and secured the straps of his carrier.

For an instant, Robert considered carrying Jack. Then he realized that no matter how much he held his child now, it wasn't going to help when he had returned home, an ocean away, and his heart was once again empty.

The city of Rajalla rose out of the valley like a flotilla of crisp white sailboats tossed about on an ocean of green and winter-gray. Lily's spirits lifted as she stood on the bluff overlooking the city and took in the sight of the cobblestone streets packed with horse-drawn carriages, small, sputtering cars of indistinguishable origin and vendors pushing carts filled with wildly blooming flowers, hand-painted pottery and fresh meats from local farms.

She'd always loved Rajalla. The people were friendly. The city was chock-full of ancient buildings, beautiful architecture and quaint shops. The smattering of cultures formed an interesting melting pot of languages from all over Europe—German, French, English and several dialects of Rebelian. Lily had loved the bustling confusion, the old-world charm, the beauty of the countryside upon which the city was nestled.

All of that had changed since DeBruzkya's soldiers had moved in. Most of the restaurants and cafés had closed. Many of the buildings were damaged. There were a lot more funerals.

But while the war might have damaged the city, she thought, it had done nothing to dull the spirit of the people. Some of the buildings might lay in ruin, but the city had already begun to rebuild. The church in the southern sector sported a new bell tower. The rococo fountain in the town square had been repaired. No, she thought, DeBruzkya and his war machine might be able to damage wood and brick and concrete, but they could never take away the spirit of the Rebelian people.

Lily knew that beneath the old-world charm and friendly smiles, the freedom movement thrived. The thought gave her a smidgen of satisfaction because in her heart she knew that one day DeBruzkya would fall. She only hoped it didn't come too late.

Trying not to think too hard about the role she would play, she looked down at her child, felt the familiar swell of love in her chest. He'd improved throughout the early morning hours. He'd taken half a bottle of milk and an entire jar of *pavio* and *pois*—turkey and pea baby food manufactured and packaged right in Rajalla. His color had returned to normal, and he'd been chattering for the last hour. Realizing how lucky they were, she pressed a kiss to the top of his head and thanked God for taking care of them.

"This way."

She jolted at the sound of Robert's voice. Turning from the vista, she risked a look at him, felt the now familiar tug of an emotion she refused to identify. He looked haggard, a little dangerous and more handsome than any man had a right to after what they'd been through during the long night. She wondered if he'd gotten any sleep. Wondered if he was as troubled—as scared—as she was.

"What are you looking at?" he asked nastily.

"I was just admiring your scowl."

"That obvious, huh?"

"Yeah." She knew he wasn't happy with her, but there was no way she could turn her back on the Rebelian people now. She wished she could make him understand. Wished she could convince him that once this beautiful country was liberated, when her people were free and her children safe, then she could fly to the United States and they would live happily ever after.

Taking her time, she walked over to him. Snuggled against her abdomen, Jack kicked his legs and chattered. She stopped a foot away from Robert, aware that he was watching her closely, that he looked cautious and edgy and tired as hell.

He glanced at Jack, and his expression softened. "I can carry him for you."

"It's all right."

"I want to."

Realizing belatedly that Robert wanted to carry his son, she unfastened the carrier straps and passed Jack to him. Her stomach fluttered when he grinned at him, then brushed his mouth across Jack's forehead. She knew it was stupid to read more into the moment than was there. Lily could lie to herself until she was blue in the face. But deep inside she knew it wasn't simple affection she saw in the vivid blue depths of Robert's eyes, but love.

The realization of what she'd allowed to happen struck her like a well-aimed kick. Aware that her chest was tight, that her mouth had gone dry, she watched him heft the carrier onto his back and adjust the straps to fit his larger frame.

"We're going to have to be careful," he said. "Rajalla is crawling with soldiers."

"I know, it's just that—" She broke off, embarrassed because her emotions were spiraling out of control. She wasn't sure why, but she suddenly felt uncertain and overwhelmed and more afraid than she'd been in a long time.

She walked a short distance away and looked out over Rajalla. "I love this place," she said, struggling not to cry. "It's hard to believe someone would want to destroy it."

She heard Robert come up behind her but she didn't turn around. "This isn't your war to fight, Lily."

"It wasn't Strawberry's war, either."

"You have a son to think about now."

That stopped her. It always did. It was the one point that was inarguable. The subject that caused her the most pain when she thought of what she had to do. There was never a time when she didn't think about Jack's safety. When she didn't consider his future. Once the rebels were in power and a democracy was restored, she could go on with her life and concentrate solely on being a mother to her precious son. But until then…

"It's hard to do the right thing sometimes." She looked at Robert, found his eyes already on her. She didn't think she'd ever seen him so tense. His jaw was tight, his brows drawn together, his mouth pulled into a severe line.

"If anything happens to me," she began, the words coming in a flood, "I want you to promise me you'll take care of J—"

He moved so quickly she didn't see it coming. One moment she was standing alone, and in the next instant her body was flush against his. He stared at her with a fierce expression, his nostrils flaring.

"Don't ever say that," he said between clenched teeth.

"It has to be said."

"Damn it, Lily—"

"I need to know Jack will be—"

Her words were cut off abruptly when he crushed his mouth to hers. Anger that he would kiss her when she was trying to say something so important sparked at the back of her brain. But that spark was quickly doused by the feel of his mouth against hers. The taste of desperation on his lips. The emotion pounding through her with every beat of her heart.

He released her an instant later. Lily stumbled back, stunned by the truth of the moment, shocked even more by how badly it had shaken her. Robert stood a few feet away from her, breathing hard, looking every bit as shaken as she felt.

"It doesn't have to be like this," he said.

"Once the transfusion is complete, I'm going to meet with the rebels."

"No, damn it."

"Robert, I need to do this. I have to." But even as she said the words, Lily sensed danger. She felt the black presence of impending doom pressing down on her like a thunderhead.

And even with the sun shining and the man she loved close enough to touch, she knew that all would not end well, just as it had not ended well for a little girl named Strawberry.

Chapter 13

The Hospité de Rajalla was in dismal condition, Robert thought as they entered the building through a rear exit. Two years ago it had been a bustling city within a city, with a state-of-the-art surgical center and two hundred beds. But, like the rest of Rebelia, the civil war had made its mark. The south wing, once the maternity ward, had been so badly damaged it was closed and cordoned off with wooden horses and great sheets of polyurethane. Several of the windows had been broken and hastily repaired with cardboard and tape.

He squashed the uneasy desire to look over his shoulder as they walked down the wide hall toward the bright overhead lights of the nursing center. He felt relatively certain none of DeBruzkya's soldiers had spotted them, but there was no way he could be absolutely sure. He would do everything in his power to expedite Jack's transfusion, then he planned to take Lily and Jack to the ARIES base camp he'd set up when he'd arrived.

If a man and a woman traveling with backpacks and an

infant were out of place, no one gave any indication. Nurses in white uniforms rushed down the wide hallways with purposeful strides, their shoes muted on the tile floor. A female voice blared in rapid Rebelian over the intercom system.

Upon entering the city limits, they'd stuck to the back streets and alleyways. But they'd passed very close to a group of soldiers several blocks from the hospital. Four of them, wearing camouflage and the identifying black berets. They'd been smoking cigarettes and drinking black tea, but Robert hadn't missed their watchful eyes or the automatic weapons strapped to their shoulders.

"Do you think those soldiers noticed us?" Lily asked.

Robert looked over at her, felt the familiar pull and tried hard not to think about all the things that could go wrong while they were here. "I think they were too busy showing off those nifty new uniforms to the women at the café across the street."

She shot him a quick smile. "Especially the one in the short skirt."

"She had nice legs."

She arched a brow.

He rolled his shoulder. "Hey, I'm a doctor. I appreciate fine anatomy."

She huffed. "Well, she didn't look very impressed."

If he hadn't been so tense he might have laughed. Even in a time of war life went on, he thought. Young men tried to impress young women. People laughed and cried and overcame.

Men and women fell in love.

He looked at her, felt an odd quiver in his gut. Several strands of hair had broken free of the ponytail and curled around her face. A face that was pale and smooth and so beautiful he couldn't take his eyes off her.

For a crazy moment he wanted to stop her, draw her to him and kiss her until she forgot all about the rebellion. Until she forgot about everything except him and Jack and a future that was growing dimmer with every step they took. But he knew even if he kissed her now, she would still do what she deemed necessary. No matter how many times he asked her not to. No matter how dangerous.

He looked down at Jack, and a different kind of emotion gripped him. The baby stared at him with guileless blue eyes and reached out to grasp his chin with pudgy fingers. Turning his head slightly, Robert kissed his son's tiny hand and tried not to think about how badly it was going to hurt to lose him.

They reached the nurse's station, and a pretty young woman with dark eyes and a friendly smile greeted them in Rebelian.

"We're looking for Dr. Orloff," Robert answered in perfect Rebelian.

"I just saw him a few minutes ago," she said. "Let me page him for you."

Several minutes later Dr. Roman Orloff came through a set of double swinging doors. He was about six feet tall and wore the traditional white lab coat over dark slacks and a colorful sweater. He spotted Robert immediately and headed in their direction at a determined clip.

"Dr. Mercier! Good to see you. I trust you didn't have any problems getting here?" He was grinning a bit too brightly. His eyes swept to Lily and Jack then back to Robert.

"Thanks for seeing us, Roman," Robert said quietly.

Dr. Orloff extended his hand. "Don't say anything," he said in a low voice, never losing his overzealous smile. "Follow me. Smile a lot. Don't look directly at anyone."

A surge of adrenaline skittered through Robert. "What is it?"

"You two are wanted. There are signs everywhere."

"Have soldiers been here?"

"Not yet, but I'm sure they'll come eventually."

Robert felt Lily's eyes on him, but he didn't look at her. The weight of the decision he was about to make weighed down on him, staggering him. "Do you have a safe room?" he asked.

Orloff nodded. "It's in the basement."

"Can we do the transfusion down there?"

"Yes."

"Good. The baby took a turn for the worse earlier," Robert said and followed him into the elevator.

The basement made Lily feel claustrophobic. The ceilings were low. There were no windows. Dim overhead lighting revealed water stains on drooping acoustic tiles. As she and Robert and Dr. Orloff walked down the narrow hall, she cuddled Jack and reminded herself that they were safe here. Still, those internal reassurances did little to alleviate the knot of fear in her stomach.

It had taken them nearly ten minutes to reach the safe room. The main elevator had taken them to the third floor, where part of the wall had been damaged by some kind of explosion. From there they'd taken a narrow stairway down to a freight elevator. The car had rattled and shook as it lowered them to the basement.

"The procedure room is very well maintained." Dr. Orloff removed a set of keys from his trousers and inserted a key into a locked door. He shoved it open and hit a light switch set into the wall.

Lily blinked against the sudden bright light. The room closely resembled an operating room. Two beds dominated the center of the room. Gleaming stainless steel counters surrounded them on three sides. A double stainless steel sink was set into the opposite wall. Floor-to-ceiling glass-front cabinets comprised the wall to her right.

"I'm impressed," Robert said.

Orloff grinned. "It's not George Washington University, but it'll do in a pinch."

"And then some."

"We've treated our share of rebels in this hospital." Dr.

Orloff looked at Lily. "Doesn't do much for our funding to advertise that sort of thing."

"What are your capabilities?" Robert asked.

"We've got it all. Oxygen. X-ray machine. MRI room two doors down. Refrigeration for blood storage, though our supplies are critically low." He motioned toward the cabinets. "Our medications are low, but we've got the essentials."

"I can donate blood," Lily blurted.

Both men looked over at her.

"I mean, for your blood bank," she said.

Robert looked at her. "Both of us can donate."

"I'm not going to turn you down. We need blood desperately." Dr. Orloff shrugged. "Of course, we're fresh out of juice and cookies."

Lily choked out a pent-up laugh. She looked at Jack, realized she'd been so preoccupied with getting him to the hospital safely, she hadn't yet asked about the transfusion. "How is the transfusion done?"

"Very simple," Dr. Orloff said. "We're going to sedate Jack and transfer a very small amount of blood-bank blood to him."

Robert walked to Lily and eased Jack from her arms. "Because of the hemoedema, Jack's circulation is affected, and his organs aren't getting the amount of blood they need to function properly. He needs a bone marrow transplant, but a transfusion will increase his red blood cell count and his blood volume. It should last several weeks."

Lily's arms felt empty without Jack. She'd told herself she wasn't going to let this upset her, but as she watched Robert lay her baby on the bed, a stab of melancholy went right through her center. All she'd ever wanted was for him to be healthy and happy and have all the things she hadn't.

Like a mother and father.

The thought seemed to come out of nowhere and hit her with surprising force. Vaguely, she was aware of Dr. Orloff scrubbing with iodine soap up to his elbows, humming a

tune that was much too cheery for this dreary basement
room. Unbearably anxious, she stood next to Robert and
watched him administer the sedation. Jack cried briefly,
then settled, his eyes drooping. "He looks so tiny lying
there all alone," she said.

"He's not alone," Robert said. "We're with him. He's
going to be fine."

She looked at him and in the blue depths of his eyes she
saw the truth of those words, felt it in her heart. And as
impossible as it seemed, she knew that somehow things
were going to work out.

"Here we go."

Lily stepped back when Dr. Orloff walked over to them
with the tray upon which was the intravenous needle.

"Let me," Robert said.

Dr. Orloff passed the needle to Robert. Lily watched,
transfixed, as Robert expertly inserted the IV into Jack's
tiny vein. She winced when Jack whimpered. She leaned
toward him and put her hand on his forehead. "It's all right,
sweetheart," she said quietly. "Mommy's right here."

"He's doing great," Robert said once the needle was in
place.

"I think I'm the wreck," she said.

"You're doing fine."

"I'm glad it's you who's doing this."

Her heart beat a little fast when he smiled at her, but the
moment was broken when Dr. Orloff rolled the wheeled IV
tree and collapsible bag of donor blood. "Thirty milliliters.
Type A."

Robert double-checked the label, then attached the length
of tube to the IV needle in Jack's arm. "Right."

"How long will this take," Lily asked.

"About an hour." Without looking at her, Robert
crossed to the second bed, kicked the brake up and rolled
it closer to the bed where Jack lay. "You're exhausted.
Why don't you lie down and try to get some sleep?"

She shook her head automatically. "There's no way I can sleep with Jack—"

"Dr. Orloff will be here to monitor him."

"Where are you going?"

Robert grimaced. "I've got to check in with one of my colleagues."

Lily wasn't sure why, but she didn't believe him. Ever since he'd come to her door she'd sensed that he was keeping secrets from her. She couldn't imagine why. But if she'd learned anything since coming to Rebelia, it was that ignorance was never bliss.

"You're lying to me," she said quietly. "And I don't understand why."

Dr. Orloff looked at them sharply from his place at the counter across the room, then returned his attention to the chart as if realizing he was eavesdropping on a personal conversation. Glancing over his shoulder, Robert took her arm and guided her to the door, then into the hall and closed the door behind them. "Don't ask any more questions, Lily. I'm not going to answer them."

"You're not telling me something."

"I'm not telling you a lot of things."

"That makes me feel a hell of a lot better."

"You're going to have to trust me on this."

"I do. I just…don't like being kept in the dark."

He stared at her for a long time before speaking, then removed a tiny disk the size of a watch battery from his breast pocket. "I want you to keep this on you at all times," he said.

Lily opened her hand and he dropped the disk into her palm. "What is it?"

"Don't ask me that, Lily," he said. "Please. Just…trust me. Keep it for me, okay? Keep it with you at all times no matter what."

"All right," she said, baffled and growing increasingly anxious.

"When I come back, I want you to come with me to give a statement to some people I've been working with."

"*Statement?* What are you talking about?"

"I'm talking about Bruno DeBruzkya." He raked a hand through his hair. "I think you know him."

"What's going on, Robert?"

"I can't tell you."

"Damn it—"

Jaw tight, he yanked open the door and crossed to where his backpack leaned against the wall and hefted it over his shoulder. "Dr. Orloff, if you need me for any reason you've got the number to my satellite phone."

Orloff looked up from the counter where he was hunched over a board, scribbling. "Yes, of course."

Robert turned to Lily. "Stay with Jack. Try to get some rest."

A swirl of panic coiled inside her. "Where are you going?"

Instead of answering, Robert leaned close to her, cupped the back of her head and kissed her hard on the mouth. The question fizzled, and for a staggering moment all Lily could think about was the way his mouth felt against hers. The gentle pressure of his lips. The taste that was uniquely his. The firm press of his body against hers. The reassuring strength that seemed to emanate from him. And the myriad emotions uncoiling inside her every time she was close to him.

An instant later he released her. "We'll finish this when I get back."

"Don't leave," she said.

"I'll be back." He raised his hand, brushed his fingers gently across her cheek, then looked at Orloff. "Keep an eye on them."

The urge to rush to him and keep him from leaving was strong, but Lily held her ground. Feeling desperate and helpless and unreasonably frightened, she watched him walk out the door.

* * *

Robert skirted the main street, sticking to the alleys, bombed-out buildings and interior courtyards whenever possible. There seemed to be an inordinate number of soldiers in the city—a hell of a lot more than he'd expected. He tried to reassure himself that the soldiers had nothing to do with two wanted Americans, but he didn't believe it.

Even though the morning was cool, he was sweating profusely as he made his way up the narrow wooden staircase and used his key to open the door. The apartment smelled of old wood and dust motes, but Robert barely noticed as he crossed to the satellite radio he'd set up on the floor.

Yanking off the cover, he dropped to his knees in front of it and hit the power button. Only then did he realize that his hands were shaking. That his heart was pounding. At first he didn't understand it; he knew he wasn't in imminent danger. But he sensed it coming. Like a dark storm on the horizon full of violent wind and killer lightning and heading in his direction. Or maybe toward Lily and Jack.

He loved her and that little boy more than anything in the world. More than he'd ever believed possible. He knew Lily loved him. There was no way in hell she could look at him the way she did, make love to him the way she had if she didn't feel something powerful and real and soul deep. How in God's name was he going to make her see that? How was he going to make her see past what she deemed as her duty to a little red-haired girl named Strawberry? How was he going to keep her and Jack safe when her sense of responsibility kept putting her in harm's way?

"Damn, it, Lily," he muttered, his voice sounding strange in the dead silence of the room.

Shoving the thoughts from his mind as best he could, he set up the digital camera and hailed ARIES headquarters. "This is PHOENIX, do you read?"

"Got you, PHOENIX." It was Hatch's voice.

Robert tapped on the monitor, and the older man came into view.

"What do you have for me?" Hatch asked.

"DeBruzkya's headquarters is in the old Veisweimar Castle."

"Satellites have seen some activity there," Hatch said. "The place has been derelict for years. Now that activity makes sense."

"He's probably using underground tunnels to store tanks and missiles, to keep them out of sight of the spy satellites."

"Not to mention the weapons inspectors from the United Nations. Good work."

"He is, indeed, amassing gems, but this is where things get funky."

"Funky?"

Robert told him about the old Rebelian Gem of Power legend. When he was finished, Hatch scratched his head and said, "DeBruzkya doesn't strike me as the superstitious type."

"You think there's more to it?"

"Don't you?"

"You mean aside from his being a lunatic?"

Hatch smiled. "What about Dr. Alex Morrow?"

"My contact couldn't place the name but said it sounded familiar."

Hatch regarded Robert with sharp eyes for a moment. "You look strung out as hell."

Robert didn't have anything to say about that so he remained silent.

Sighing, Hatch flipped a switch on his end. "Okay, Davidson, off the record. What the hell's going on?

"I don't know what you're talking about."

"You know exactly what I'm talking about. Damn it, when my agents are in the field, I like to know what's going on inside their heads. I have no idea what's going on inside yours right now."

Robert rolled his shoulder. "I've been busy. Haven't had much sleep—"

"You look like hell. You've checked in all of three times since you've been there."

"I'm a little...distracted. That's all."

"A little distracted can get a man killed, Robert. What gives?"

For an instant, Robert was tempted to sign off. To turn off the radio and end the questions. The last thing he wanted to do was make a fool of himself in front of his boss. How stupid was it for an agent to get involved with his contact while on a dangerous mission? Plenty stupid. Imbecilic if he wanted to be truthful about it.

"You going to talk to me or are we going to burn up the satellite waiting each other out?" Hatch snapped.

"My contact," Robert began. "She's a woman."

Hatch's eyes sharpened. "I'm listening."

In all the years they'd worked together, Robert had never discussed his personal life. He was a private man and he'd always sensed Hatch was the same.

"Lillian Scott," Hatch said after a moment. "An American journalist. I know all that."

"She has a son." Sighing, Robert looked out the window, realized it had begun to rain. "He's mine."

Now it was Hatch's turn to curse, and he did so quite thoroughly. "I knew you knew her. That's one of the reasons I chose you for this mission. But I had no idea you two were involved."

Robert looked at the monitor to see Hatch thumb an antacid from his pocket and pop it into his mouth. "I guess there are some things even ARIES intelligence can't know in advance."

"I guess so," Hatch agreed.

The rumble of thunder broke the silence, and Robert found himself thinking about Lily and Jack in the basement of the hospital all alone.

"I'm bringing you in," Hatch said.

Robert's hackles rose. "No, you're not."

"It's done. Cross the border into Holzberg. There will be a jet at the airport waiting to take you to Paris."

"I haven't found out about Dr. Morrow yet."

"You've set up base camp. You've obtained information about the gems. You've discovered the location of De-Bruzkya's headquarters. That's enough for me to deem this mission successful." He glanced at his watch. "It's oh ten hundred there in Rebelia. I want you at the airport in an hour."

Robert stared at him, aware of the steady thrum of his heart, keenly aware that he was about to disobey a direct order and more than likely screw up his career. "I can't do that."

"Why the hell not?" Hatch snapped.

"I'm not leaving without her." Robert reached for the keypad to sign off.

"What do you need, PHOENIX?" Hatch asked quickly.

Robert moved his hand away from the keypad. "I need a chopper with night vision and a winch."

"You got it. Just tell me where and when and I'll have someone there."

"I'll let you know." Robert hit the keypad and the screen faded to black.

Chapter 14

Lily lay on her side in the narrow bed and snuggled Jack against her. Exhaustion dragged at her, both physically and emotionally, but her thoughts refused to let her rest. She couldn't get Robert out of her mind. Couldn't stop thinking about all the things that had happened between them since he'd walked into her cottage just two short days ago. Every time she closed her eyes, she saw his face. The way he'd looked at her when he'd walked away. The way his eyes darkened when he touched her. The emotion in his eyes when he'd told her he loved her. He was a good man, and he loved her. But it hadn't mattered to her. She'd hurt him anyway.

Shifting restlessly beneath the blanket, she eased Jack's little body more closely against her and closed her eyes tightly. Dr. Orloff had left one of the overhead lights on. Just enough for her to make out the clock on the wall, and she'd spent the last forty minutes watching the second hand sweep endlessly around the dial.

The transfusion had taken forty-five minutes. Once the

bag of donor blood had emptied, Dr. Orloff had removed the needle from Jack's arm and applied a small pressure bandage. Lily had spoken softly to her son while the doctor checked his blood pressure and took his temperature. She'd been inordinately relieved when he'd told her Jack appeared to be tolerating the transfusion well and that he didn't expect any complications. The mild sedative he'd given Jack would wear off in a few hours, and Jack would be back to normal shortly thereafter.

But as Dr. Orloff had scrubbed down, he also reminded her that at some point Jack would need a bone marrow transplant. While her son might be the picture of health now, he could relapse in a few weeks. Leaving her with that unsettling thought, he'd told her to get some rest and then left.

That had been nearly an hour ago, and she still couldn't quiet her thoughts. Robert had always told her she had an unreasonable conscience. She felt too much for others. Not enough for herself. A flaw that had cost her plenty over the years. But Lily had always been an old soul. She'd been born knowing things—feeling things—that normally came with experience or age or both. Closing her eyes, she thought of Robert.

I love you.

His words echoed inside her head. She told herself she didn't want him to love her, but she knew that was a lie. She wondered when she'd gotten so damn good at lying to herself. She wanted him to love her. Wanted that desperately. She loved him, too. Had loved him since the day she'd met him over two years ago in that smoky little pub. She wanted a future with him. A father for Jack.

But what about your work here, Lily? Are you going to walk away from it? Are you going to walk away from the children? From Strawberry?

Closing her eyes against the barrage of thoughts, the stab of pain in her chest, she listened to the drip of water in the sink. The tick of the clock on the wall. The occasional thump of a water pipe in the corridor beyond. Fatigue dragged at her, a turbulent river sucking her into its murky depths. She fought the current but felt herself slipping into darkness. Too much to think about. Too much to do. *I love you....*

Lily jolted awake, aware that she was breathing hard, that her body was slicked with sweat despite the basement chill. She wasn't sure what wakened her. Maybe the dream she'd been having about the gun. The soldier wearing the black beret...

Turning her head slightly, she glanced over at the clock, realizing only fifteen minutes had gone by. She sagged into the bed, set her hand against a soundly sleeping Jack. A series of loud pops from the corridor shattered the silence. Lily bolted upright. She'd been in Rebelia long enough to be intimately acquainted with the sound of gunfire. But she'd never grown used to it, and the sound brought goose-flesh to her arms. Next to her Jack stirred and began to whimper. Scooping him into her arms, she hugged him to her and set her hand gently over his mouth.

Her heart slammed against her ribs when she heard another series of pops, then the shuffle of boots on tile outside the door. Angry voices followed and Lily knew the soldiers had come to the hospital looking for her. Terror knifed through her at the thought. Not because she feared for her safety, but because of the child she held in her arms.

Vaulting from the bed, holding Jack against her with one arm, she kicked the pedestal brake and shoved the bed toward the small storage room. If she could get it out of sight and hide beneath it, there was a chance they wouldn't find her.

The door swung open before she'd made it halfway across the room. She looked up, saw the silhouettes of a dozen men, heard the sound of steel against steel as automatic weapons were cocked. Her only thought was that they would shoot her—shoot Jack—before even knowing who she was. Razor sharp terror cut through her. The rush of adrenaline came so hard it made her dizzy. "Don't shoot!" she screamed in Rebelian. "I've got a baby!"

Her heart beat a hard tattoo against her ribs as several men shuffled into the room. She could tell by the black berets they wore that they were part of DeBruzkya's army. They had a distinctly cruel, ragged look about them. The look of men who'd lost a little bit of their humanity.

A tall, thin man with a goatee stepped forward, his eyes skimming the length of her and landing on Jack. Without speaking he reached into the pocket of his torn jacket, withdrew a badly wrinkled sheet of paper and showed it to the man behind him.

"En hur." It's her.

The man behind him was overweight and pale. A cigarette dangled from the side of his mouth. He looked at Lily and smiled. "General DeBruzkya is going to be very pleased."

Lily glanced over her shoulder, but she knew there was no escape. She thought about the doctors and nurses aboveground and wondered how many of them these men had killed. Aware that she was shaking uncontrollably, that Jack had started to cry, she watched, horrified and transfixed, as the crowd of men parted. Her knees went weak when she saw the reverence in their eyes. Only one man she knew of could command that kind of respect—even if it wasn't earned.

Shock rattled her entire body when General Bruno DeBruzkya entered the room. For a moment, she couldn't catch her breath. Her vision tunneled on his face. A wave of disbelief swept through her. His gaze sought hers. An emotion she didn't understand touched his eyes briefly but was gone so quickly she couldn't be sure she'd seen it at all.

"Lillian Scott."

DeBruzkya was a short, rotund man, but he had the voice of a giant. She jolted at the sound of it, then silently berated herself because she saw clearly the moment of twisted pleasure her fear gave him. His boots clicked smartly on the tile floor as he walked to her.

"How did you find me?" she asked in a voice that sounded amazingly calm considering she was coming apart inside.

"Ah, such a lack of manners." He tsked. "You Americans. All business. No time for small talk."

"My son is sick," she said, praying that would touch him in a place that was still human. That even if he killed her here and now, he would spare her son. *Please, God, don't let them hurt Jack.*

Robert, where are you?

A shiver went through her when DeBruzkya reached her. He wore a snug brown-and-black uniform. Ribbons and medals adorned the left shoulder just above his heart. She thought of the pistol strapped to her thigh and wondered if she could get to it and shoot him down before the other soldiers opened fire.

He stopped a foot away from her and studied her the way a potential buyer might study an expensive piece of real estate. "You're beautiful, as always," he said.

"What are you going to do with me?"

The hairs prickled at the nape of her neck when he walked behind her. Vaguely she was aware that the room had gone silent. That her heart was beating out of control. That her precious son was warm and soft against her breast.

"A little pale. A little thin." He came in front of her and cocked his head. "You've lost weight since I last saw you. Are you feeling well?"

A quiver ran the length of her when he raised his hand and caressed her cheek. His hand was inordinately soft, and she wondered how such a cruel man could have such a gentle touch. Because she knew he would draw pleasure from any show of emotion, she endured his caress, steeling herself against the revulsion it brought her.

"You left me with the impression that you were going to write my autobiography," he said. "I'd been looking

forward to working with you. And then suddenly you simply dropped out of sight.'' Dropping his hand, he looked
at Jack. ''Nice-looking boy. I didn't realize you'd had a
son.'' He eyes snapped to Lily's. ''I didn't realize you
were…married.''

Without warning he grabbed her left hand, baring the
ring finger, squeezing painfully. ''Why no wedding band?''

''Let go of me.''

He squeezed with so much force that his jowls shook.
Pain radiated through her finger and wrist, but she endured
it without crying out. She refused to give him that much
satisfaction. ''I—I'm not married.''

Once again calm, he released her then leaned forward
and lightly pinched Jack's cheek. A doting uncle visiting
his favorite nephew. ''What's his name?''

''Please don't hurt him,'' she said.

''What's his name?'' he repeated.

''Jack.''

''Rebelia is a dangerous place for a child.'' He stepped
back and folded his arms, studying them both. ''I've seen
terrible things happen to children.'' He shrugged as if that
were out of his control. ''If the parents aren't careful.''

Her heart pounded furiously. ''Don't you dare threaten
me.''

DeBruzkya raised his eyebrows as if the thought had
never occurred to him. ''Such fire.''

''Don't hurt him,'' she repeated.

''The rebels, Lillian. They're the ones causing all
this…violence. They're out of control.''

Lily thought of Strawberry and felt her hands curl into
fists. She could hear her breath coming swiftly. She tried
to calm herself, but the combination of fury and terror
pumped pure adrenaline through her veins. ''What do you
want?''

He smiled, like a rodent that had made off with the
cheese an instant before the trap snapped closed. Leaning

close, well out of earshot of his men, he whispered, "You will know in due time, Lillian. It is our destiny."

She flinched when he raised his hand abruptly and snapped his fingers. "Search her for weapons, and then they will be coming with us!" he barked in Rebelian.

"No," she said. "Please, no."

Glaring at her, DeBruzkya grasped her bicep and jerked her toward him, so close their faces were nearly touching. "Do you think you can make of fool of me?"

"Please, just let us go."

"I'm never going to let you go. That's the one thing you can count on." Cruelty glinted within the depths of his eyes. He pulled away. "Be careful with her," he said to his men. "I don't want either of them injured."

Trembling and incredulous and more terrified than she'd ever been in her life, Lily watched as two soldiers started toward her. She had no idea if DeBruzkya knew that she was part of the rebellion; he'd given her no indication. If he did, she felt sure that she was as good as dead—or worse. The thought sent a bitter rise of bile to the back of her throat. She'd heard the stories of what happened to rebels who were captured. Most kept a final bullet in the chamber of their pistols, preferring death over capture.

If there had been an avenue of escape at that moment she would have taken it. She would have risked a bullet in her back simply to escape whatever they had in mind for her. But with her child in her arms and a dozen soldiers surrounding her, she knew it was useless. There was no escape, and she wasn't yet to the point of suicide.

She stood motionless, her heart banging against her ribs like a mad drum. The two soldiers approached her, their faces completely devoid of emotion. Lily looked at the youngest of the two men. He couldn't have been much over twenty, and she found herself wondering if he had any idea what kind of man DeBruzkya was.

"Don't do this," she said.

Grimacing, the younger man took her arm while the

other quickly and impersonally ran his hands over her body. Lily closed her eyes when he discovered the pistol strapped to her thigh. "General!"

But DeBruzkya was already at her side, his eyes amused and unnervingly cruel. "Ah, Lillian, you have many surprises in store for me, no?"

Because her heart was in her throat, Lily didn't answer. Just stared at him, horrified by the realization that if he took her pistol, she would have no way to protect herself or Jack.

Never taking his eyes from hers, DeBruzkya yanked up her skirt. She tried to shift away when he ran his hand over her thigh, but the soldier holding her squeezed her arm painfully, and she stilled. The general's fingers lingered inches from her panties, then quickly unholstered the tiny pistol. Smiling, he examined it and shoved it into the waistband of his slacks. "I'll keep this for you," he said, then to his men, "let's go!"

The soldier holding her arm forced her toward the door. Lily clutched Jack tightly and tried hard not to think about what DeBruzkya had in store for them. More frightened than she'd ever been in her life, she pressed her face against the top of her son's head and began to pray.

Robert had learned to trust his instincts over the years. As he made his way to the hospital, he couldn't shake the feeling that something was wrong. He felt it as clearly as he felt the light rain on his face.

One block from the hospital, he ducked into the alley across the street and looked at the three-story structure, his eyes moving to the top floor, the third window over from the south side. His blood stalled in his veins when he saw the white length of curtain flapping in the breeze. It was a signal he'd discussed with Dr. Orloff. If there was a problem—any kind of problem—while Robert was at base camp, Dr. Orloff was to open that window and put out a white flag to warn him.

Blood zinging through his veins like a spray of bullets, Robert broke into a dead run, a hundred scenarios flashing through his mind. He tried to comfort himself with the knowledge that Lily and Jack were in the safe room in the basement, but he knew DeBruzkya was a master at getting information, at making people talk.

Ice pick jabs of pain flared in his thigh as he ran, but the fear clenching his chest dwarfed it. He sprinted down the street with the speed of an Olympian athlete, then took the crumbling steps of the hospital three at a time to the top. He didn't think before bursting through the doors. He knew better than to enter a building without knowing who was inside. But it was emotion driving him now, not logic.

Pulling the revolver from the waistband of his jeans, he entered the lobby, found it eerily quiet. He heard someone crying, then spotted a young nurse sitting on the floor behind the desk. Next to her a man in a white lab coat lay on his back in a pool of blood.

Robert sprinted over to her, speaking in Rebelian. "What happened?"

She looked up at him with tear-filled eyes. "The soldiers came. Several people were shot. Please, help me. He's been shot."

"I'm a doctor." Robert knelt, but knew immediately there was nothing he could do for this man. Setting his hand against the man's throat, he felt for a pulse. When none came, he sat back on his heels and shook his head. "I'm very sorry, but he's gone."

Putting her face in her hands, the woman sobbed.

Robert put his hand on her shoulder and squeezed, outrage and anger burning through him. "Are the soldiers gone?"

"They left about ten minutes ago."

"How many soldiers?"

"I don't know. Fifteen or so. Maybe more."

"Where's Dr. Orloff?"

"I don't know."

"Did the soldiers take anyone with them?"

Her gaze snapped to his. "There was a woman and a child."

Robert didn't hear the rest of the sentence. He jumped up, felt the world rock beneath his feet as his worst nightmare became a reality. For several long seconds he stood there, breathing hard, trying to decide what to do next.

DeBruzkya had Lily and Jack. The woman he loved and his innocent son were in the hands of a madman.

And suddenly Robert knew what he had to do. He knew it would be the most dangerous mission of his life. Only he was no longer acting as an ARIES agent, but a man who would do anything to save his family.

Chapter 15

Lily should have realized where DeBruzkya would take them. That like the spider he was, he would take them to his lair where he would have complete control and the freedom to do with them as he pleased. But her mind was so cluttered with emotion she wasn't thinking clearly. She could handle becoming a prisoner. But the thought of DeBruzkya hurting Jack was too much to bear. As the soldiers had marched them through the forest toward the Veisweimar Castle, she decided she would do anything—including giving up her own life—to keep him safe.

The castle was like something out of a medieval movie replete with a moat, gargoyles and a drawbridge. The place was huge and surrounded by high stone walls. It had been built during medieval times, then fell to ruin and was swallowed by the forest. During World War II, the Nazis had transformed it into a prison. After the war, it had once again fallen to ruin. Lily had never imagined DeBruzkya transforming the place into a modern-day fortress.

The soldier behind her snapped something in Rebelian

and prodded her between the shoulder blades with the muzzle of his gun. Lily stepped onto the drawbridge, shuddering at the sight of the black water below. Her arms ached from carrying Jack for so long. She was glad her son had been given a sedative; she didn't know how these hardened men would react to a crying baby. In the back of her mind, she wondered how much longer the drug would last.

The soldiers marched her into a large courtyard. Even though it was afternoon, it had grown dark. Black clouds roiled in the sky to the north, and she knew the storms would arrive soon. Before her, the tall doors of the castle yawned, like a monster with great jaws about to devour them.

"Walk!" the man behind her shouted.

Lily snapped a very American expletive at him. Several of the soldiers laughed, but the word earned her a hard shove.

She hadn't seen DeBruzkya since the scene in the hospital. Belatedly she realized a man of his stature would never march with his soldiers. He would travel by jeep. Chances were, he was already here.

She thought of Robert and closed her eyes against the jab of pain. She knew he would come for her. Knew he would search for her and Jack—or die trying. She'd told him about the Veisweimar Castle, so he would know where to look. If the soldiers found him, she knew DeBruzkya would have no mercy.

The thought tore her up inside. She loved him. He was kind and gentle and would be the perfect father for Jack. Yet Lily had let him go. She'd chosen the solitary life of an underground rebel leader. And for what? she asked herself.

But Lily knew the answer. She'd spent her entire life alone and unloved. Shuffled from one foster home to another. It had hurt knowing there wasn't a soul on this earth who'd loved her. But Lily had loved. She'd loved with the purity of heart of the child she'd been. She'd fallen in love with her prospective parents and siblings. Their backyards with swing sets and trees and little black pups. Still, they'd let her go. She was too old. Too strong-willed. And so they'd deserted her, they'd walked away, filling her young heart with the agony of the unwanted.

That night in the pub, when she'd been badly injured and lying amid the debris, she'd felt that same pain. The pain of knowing someone she'd loved had deserted her.

Only he hadn't.

Lily closed her eyes against the pain that knowledge brought her. Regret squeezed her heart. She'd made so many mistakes, she couldn't begin to correct them. She wouldn't even know where to begin. God, she'd been such a fool.

"Stay here," one of the men ordered her.

Except for the two soldiers who had been assigned to guard her, the men dispersed in the courtyard. The two men accompanied her into the grand foyer. Lily couldn't believe the opulence of the old castle. Flickering gas lamps mounted on the walls lighted the room. High ceilings lent the place a cavernous feel. The air was cool and slightly damp, but she could smell the crisp scent of eucalyptus in the air.

A young woman with crystal-blue eyes, clad in traditional Rebelian garb, approached them. She couldn't have been much over twenty years old. Lily stared at her, wondering what role she played and how she fit into DeBruzkya's game plan.

"General DeBruzkya would like her taken to the guest suite adjacent his," she said in Rebelian, then glanced at Lily. "The child comes with me."

"No." Breaking free of the guard, Lily stepped back, clutching Jack to her chest. "No!"

"Please," the young woman said softly. "It is General DeBruzkya's wish. I am only going to bathe him and allow you time to prepare for dinner."

The words barely registered in Lily's mind. "He stays with me."

The young woman looked over at the soldier. "I can assure you, Madame Scott, you and your son have nothing to fear from me." She glanced quickly over her shoulder, then whispered in English. "You have much to fear from the general. Please, do as I say."

Lily heard the words. She saw the sincerity in the young woman's eyes. But she couldn't bring herself to part with Jack. She would rather they cut off a piece of her flesh than take her child away. "Don't take him," she heard herself say.

The young woman nodded to the soldier.

Lily knew what would happen next, and she dreaded it with every fiber of her heart. The man approached her and reached for Jack. Panic sprang through her like a wild animal released from its cage. Lily lurched, but the soldier snagged her arm. He jerked her around to face him. Simultaneously the second soldier moved forward and wrapped a strong arm around Jack.

Lily could have fought them, but she was terrified a struggle would hurt Jack. That it would frighten him. She cried out as her son was taken from her arms. "Don't take him!" she screamed in grief and fury. *"Give him back to me!"*

Blinking back tears, the young woman rushed forward and gently took Jack from the soldier's arms. "I will take good care of him."

Lily's control left her, replaced by a mother's instinct to protect her young. Twisting, she tried to lunge toward the woman, but the soldier holding her was faster and stronger. Screaming, she fought him, lashing out at the second soldier with her boots. A fleeting sense of satisfaction flashed through her when her boot connected with something solid. The soldier yowled and danced back.

"Give me my baby!" she screamed.

But the young woman hurried away from them and down

a long stone corridor. ''Bring him back,'' Lily whispered as her son and the young woman disappeared.

''Calm down!'' the soldier snapped, giving her a hard shake.

Lily barely felt her head snap back. Despair pressed down on her like a giant, smothering hand. Her arms felt cold and empty without Jack. Feeling the tears build in her eyes, she looked at the soldier. ''I want my baby back,'' she said.

His eyes skittered away. And even though his inability to meet her gaze told her this young man was still human, that he could still feel the need for basic human kindness and dignity, she also knew it wasn't enough to save her.

''Take her to the guest suite adjacent General De-Bruzkya's,'' said the second man.

Taking her arm firmly in his, the young man guided her in the opposite direction from where the woman had taken Jack. Lily looked over her shoulder, hoping to get one last look at her son. But he was gone. She felt Jack's departure like a saber slashing through her heart. The pain was so intense and so deep she could barely draw a breath. She felt physically ill as the soldier guided her up massive stone steps. Her despair darkened. She knew it was fruitless for her to cry, knew it wouldn't make any difference to her captors, but she couldn't hold back the tears. A sob wrenched from her by the time they'd reached the first landing. Lily cried openly, stumbling on occasion, feeling as if her heart were being torn from her body. Of all the things that could have been done to her, having Jack taken away was the worst.

She thought of Robert, and fresh pain slashed her. She felt it well like blood on a wound, spill over and burn a path down her heart. She lost her sense of direction as they walked down a wide, dark hall and turned onto yet another winding staircase.

''He won't hurt you,'' the young soldier whispered as he

guided her toward the top landing. "He won't hurt your son."

Lily looked at him through her tears. "Let us go," she said. "Please. I'll die without my son."

The soldier looked away. "I can't do that."

"Where are you taking me?"

"Your suite."

"You mean my cell?"

"Call it what you like."

At the top of the landing, Lily looked around to get her bearings and shivered. The hall was made of stone, dank and dark and cold. A gaslight flickered high on the wall but cast very little light. The soldier guided her to a door. Keys jangled as he removed a round ring from his uniform pocket and opened the door.

"Step inside," he said.

When Lily didn't move, he put his hands between her shoulder blades and shoved her. She stumbled into the room, but a quick spurt of anger spun her toward the door—just in time to see it close. She reached for the knob only to hear the lock click into place.

Feeling more helpless than she'd ever felt in her life, she turned and scanned the room. Surprise rippled through her when she realized she had, indeed, been locked in a suite. The room was befitting an expensive Paris hotel. Glossy mahogany furniture glimmered in the dim light. There was a sleigh bed with a high mattress. A chest of drawers. A bureau with a beveled mirror. A writing desk with a gas lamp beneath the single window—which was at least fifteen feet up.

To her right a door opened to a luxuriously furnished bathroom. She entered to find the small room endowed with brass fixtures and marble and stone. A sunken tub dominated the floor beneath a second window. The glassed-in shower was immense. Feeling trapped, furious that she'd been separated from Jack, Lily left the bathroom and strode into the bedroom. For a moment, she considered destroying the room. Then she spied the note on the bed—right next to a dozen bloodred roses.

Feeling a little sick, she crossed to the bed and snatched up the single sheet of paper. *My darling Lillian, I fear you will be quite upset upon reading this letter. Please rest assured that your infant son is in good hands. My staff has been instructed to treat both of you with the utmost kindness and respect. I hope you find the suite to your liking. My goal is to make your stay here at Veisweimar as comfortable and pleasant as possible.*

I would like to discuss some business with you this evening over dinner. Feel free to use the shower. There are several gowns and shoes stowed in the closet, which I had flown in from Milan. I hope the styles and sizes are to your liking. Dinner is served promptly at seven o'clock. If you're on time, I'll make sure you get the opportunity to spend some time with your son later.

Until then, Bruno.

Vaguely, Lily was aware of the paper shaking in her hands. Of her pulse raging like a white-water river down the side of a mountain. For the first time she realized just how delusional DeBruzkya was, how dangerous. He was living out some kind of sick fantasy.

And she was right in the center of that fantasy.

Robert looked at the global positioning system in his palm and tried not to notice that his hand was shaking. He'd given the miniature GPS radio to Lily so he could track her if they were separated. He hoped she still had it. Hoped the soldiers hadn't found it and taken it away from her. He thanked his lucky stars Hatch liked to arm his ARIES team with high-tech toys.

Robert had been running on adrenaline since leaving the hospital an hour earlier. He considered himself in pretty good physical condition, but after nearly two miles of running, his leg was beginning to cramp. And he knew if he wanted to make it to the Veisweimar Castle before dark he would have to get his hands on some type of vehicle.

Around him rain fell in sheets, but Robert barely felt the chill or the wet cling of his clothes. He stepped onto the dirt road and looked both ways. He'd been on that particular road for nearly an hour, and all of two cars had gone by during that time. Not a good number considering he needed a car five minutes ago.

The passage of time taunted him as he pulled out his compass and headed north. Lily and Jack had been missing for nearly two hours. Every time he thought of them he had to fight a surge of panic. He could only imagine what she was going through. She might be a strong woman— tough even, and fast on her feet, to boot—but she was no match for a brutal man like DeBruzkya. Robert had seen what the dictator was capable of, and even a courageous woman like Lily didn't stand a chance against a sociopath. What the hell did DeBruzkya want with her? Had the dictator somehow found out Robert was an ARIES agent and intend to use her as leverage? Or were his intentions of a more personal, more twisted nature?

The possibilities made his heart pound with a helplessness he'd never known before. He thought about Jack and felt his gut twist into a knot. Urgency was like a fire raging through him, spreading and gaining momentum, threatening to burn him alive. He needed to move. To do something. To bring them home. He loved Lily more than life. He loved his child. His *son*. He refused to consider the possibility that DeBruzkya would hurt them. The thought was simply too much to bear.

Robert was so embroiled in his thoughts, he almost didn't hear the rumble of an engine, the sound of tires sloshing through mud. He blinked rain from his eyes and looked over his shoulder to see dual headlights cutting through the rain and fog. Running on fear and desperation, he put his hands over his head and stepped into the beam of the headlights. The brakes squealed. Tires slid in thick muck. But the vehicle—an old car of indistinguishable origin—slid to a stop.

A man in a raincoat rolled down the window. "Are you drunk, man?" he shouted. "What's seems to be the problem?"

"There's been an accident," Robert said.

He saw the other man's eyes sweep the area, obviously looking for a vehicle that didn't exist. "My wife is badly injured," Robert added.

The car door opened. Robert's heart pounded as he reached for the pistol. Turning his collar up against the downpour, the man approached him. "Where is she? Does she need to go to the hospital?"

"I need your vehicle," Robert said.

The man's eyes widened. He turned to run to the car, but Robert was faster, grabbing his arm and spinning him around. "I just need your car. A young woman's life is at stake."

The man's eyes flashed to the pistol. "The car is yours."

Robert slapped the last of his cash into the man's hand. "Thank you," he said in Rebelian and got into the car. Looking at the lightning flickering in the sky, he hoped the rain would hold until he reached the castle. Rain made good cover.

"Hold on, Lily," he whispered and jammed the car into gear.

The winding stone staircase seemed to go on forever. Lily's dress was so long, she had to lift it to avoid stumbling over the hem. The only sound came from her shoes, the shoes of the young woman who'd come for her and the boots of the soldier accompanying them.

The knock on her door had come precisely at 6:55 p.m. By then, Lily had showered and dressed. She'd chosen the black gown. It had seemed only fitting since she was probably going to meet her death in the coming days. The gown was a tad too large, but the silk draped nicely—not that she gave a damn. She'd chosen shoes with low heels—just in case she needed to run for her life.

Once on the ground level, the young woman and soldier escorted her through ancient arched doorways and past darkened stairwells toward a brightly lit chamber at the end of the hall. Just outside the door, they stopped. "General DeBruzkya waits for you in the formal dining hall," the young woman said.

It was the same woman who'd taken Jack from her an hour earlier. Lily looked into her eyes, searching for a seed of compassion, something she could reach. "Where's my son?"

"He's in the nursery, sleeping," the woman replied.

"I want to see him."

"The general will see you first."

"Please, take me to see my son—"

The soldier gave her a warning look. The young woman shook her head. "Please, madame, go to the general. Talk to him about seeing your son. It is out of our hands."

Frustrated and angry and more frightened than she wanted to admit, Lily turned toward the door and forced herself to walk into the cavernous room. A fire blazed in the giant stone hearth. Lily could feel its warmth even from twenty feet away. Upon its mantel a dozen candles cast soft shadows on the stone walls, lending the room a feeling of warmth and opulence. A glossy mahogany table with a white linen runner down the center stretched like a sleek cat to the left of the hearth. A bouquet of white and red roses adorned the center of the table.

General DeBruzkya sat at one of the high-back chairs with a stemmed wineglass in his hand, watching her with predatory eyes. Lily felt his gaze follow her as she crossed to him, felt the gooseflesh raise on her arms, the chill sweep down her back. The intensity of his gaze unnerved her, so she concentrated on the table. There were two formal place settings. Matching stemmed Waterford wineglasses. Wedgwood china. White linen napkins. Gleaming silverware with ornately designed handles. Expensive French wine. She hated all of it. The opulence. The beauty. The man who watched her as if she were nothing more than a pretty piece of crystal that had caught his fancy, or a rare wine that was to be sampled and then consumed.

DeBruzkya stood. "Ah, Lillian, you look ravishing."

Her skin crawled when his gaze swept over her. He licked his lips and used his napkin to blot sweat from him forehead. "The black suits you."

"I want to see my son," Lily said.

Amusement entered his eyes. "Please, sit down. Share a meal with me. Some of this French wine. I had my chefs prepare the food specially for tonight."

She looked at the silver servers spread out on the table like gaudy ornaments. Even though she hadn't eaten the entire day, her mouth soured at the sight of the food.

"Beef Wellington with asparagus and hollandaise," he said. "Field greens with raspberry vinaigrette. Sorbet if you like. Truffles."

When she remained standing, he frowned. "Please. I'd like to discuss something important with you." He leaned closer to her and whispered in a conspiratorial voice. "The sooner you talk with me, the sooner you'll see your son."

The words brought a dangerous rush of anger. Lily stared at him, hating that he would try to control her by using her son for leverage. In the back of her mind, she wondered how he would react if she snatched up the silver pitcher of water and splashed it in his face.

"Please." DeBruzkya rounded the table and pulled out her chair. "Sit."

Knowing anything but cooperation would be fruitless at this point, Lily lowered herself to the chair.

"Thank you," he said. "That wasn't so bad, was it?"

She watched him round the table, inordinately relieved that he was sitting across from her as opposed to right next to her. She truly didn't think she could bear to be touched by him. Even a casual touch would send her into a rage she wasn't sure she would be able to control.

She watched as he spread the white linen napkin in his lap. He reached for the bottle of wine and filled her glass. Topping off his own, he leaned back and studied her.

Lily stared back at him, aware that her heart was pounding. She couldn't fathom what he could possibly want from her. Couldn't imagine what was going on in that twisted mind of his. The possibilities made her shudder.

"I'm sure you're wondering why you're here."

"The thought did cross my mind."

He smiled, but cruelty glinted in his eyes. "I enjoy a woman of your…fortitude. It's refreshing. Most women are afraid of me. Most men are afraid of me. Are you, Lillian?"

"No," she lied.

"I'm going to enjoy our dinner very much, indeed." Smiling, he picked up his fork and knife and began to cut the tender pastry. "Eat," he said. "Enjoy this decadent food. My chef is from Paris. One of the best in the world."

"While your people starve."

"The Rebelian people must learn to bow to their government. I mean only to help them. To lead them. To take them into the twenty-first century as a powerful nation."

She didn't know why her mind chose that minute to think of Strawberry, but she did and had to blink back the uneasy burn of tears. Hating it that her hands were shaking, Lily picked up her silverware and began to cut, back and forth, barely aware of what she was doing. Because she didn't quite trust her stomach she started with water, then a small piece of the asparagus.

"The last time we sat down to a meal, you agreed to write my autobiography," DeBruzkya said matter-of-factly as he salted his food.

When Lily didn't answer, he raised his head and glared at her. "Then you dropped out of sight."

"I—I had a baby," she said. "My…focus changed after Jack was born."

"Ah. It is difficult being a new mother, no? Being alone with a child?"

"No, I just…put my writing on the back burner."

His black eyes flashed to her. "Ah, Lillian, don't lie to me."

"I—I'm not."

"I know about the *Rebellion*. I've been reading it for weeks now. It's quite…entertaining."

She tried to swallow the fear rising inside her, but it swamped her, a dangerous river flooding its banks, threatening to drown her. She looked at her food, felt a swirl of nausea and set her fork down.

"I didn't mean to ruin your meal."

He knew about the *Rebellion*. That could only mean he knew she was involved with the freedom fighters. She knew what happened to the rebel leaders. They were shot or hanged—if they were lucky. The unlucky ones were imprisoned and tortured until they gave up the names of other rebel leaders.

She jumped when he abruptly stabbed his knife into the wooden tabletop. Fear and dread flashed inside her when he rose and rounded the table to stand behind her. Her pulse roared in her ears. She tried to calm herself with deep breaths, but she couldn't seem to get enough oxygen into her lungs. She thought of Jack, alone or growing up in orphanages the way she had, and her heart simply broke.

She closed her eyes when he leaned forward, trapping her by bracing an arm on either side of her. He was so close she could smell the wine on his breath, discern the crisp tang of Italian aftershave.

"You're shaking," he whispered, running his finger from her shoulder to her elbow then back up. "Are you afraid of me?"

"I know what you do to rebels."

"Are you a rebel, Lillian?"

"No."

"Don't lie to me."

"I'm a…a journalist." She flinched with she felt the brush of his lips against her ear.

"You played me for a fool."

"No—"

She yelped when he grasped her arm and pulled her out of the chair and to her feet so that she was facing him. A dozen emotions skittered through her brain, but simple terror took center stage and rendered her helpless. "Let go of me," she said after several long moments.

His eyes glinted. "I'm never going to let go of you, Lillian. I'm going to keep you here, as my wife. You're going to write the autobiography you promised all those months ago. I'm going to raise your son as my own. We're going to have other sons together. Lots of them."

The words curled around her like a snake, choking her. She tried to shove away from him, but he easily held her against him. Panic zinged through her, and she began to struggle in earnest, but she was no match for him.

"I'm a powerful man, Lillian. I have plans for the future. Not only for Rebelia, but all of Europe. Once I get my hands on the Gem of Power—"

"The Gem of Power doesn't exist."

He laughed. "Ah, but it does. If you let yourself believe. I believe, Lillian. I'll make you believe, too."

"You're delusional," she whispered.

"I have something the Americans want very badly. With the Gem of Power and the help of Dr. Alex Morrow, the sky is the limit."

The mention of Dr. Morrow gave her pause. She remembered Robert mentioning the American doctor who'd disappeared in nearby Holzberg. "I don't know who Dr. Morrow is," she said.

"You don't need to know. But Morrow's here. In my headquarters." He sighed. Lily felt the warm brush of his breath against her ear and shuddered. "Ah, Lillian, I'm going to do great things," he said. "I need a wife with strength and courage and vision. You have all of those things." His gaze swept down the front of her. "And so much more."

Lily knew then that if she was going to get out of this alive, if she was going to save her son, she was going to have to use her head and not her emotions. She had to stop being afraid.

"You may not love me," he whispered. "But I can give you everything you've ever wanted. You'll learn to compromise."

Lily thought about Robert and closed her eyes. "Love is…important to me," she said, not wanting to sound too eager lest he realize she was playing him in a desperate attempt to buy time.

"Lillian." He leaned toward her, brushed his lips across her temple. "I've dreamed of touching you like this for so long." His hands trembled as they slid from her shoulders to brush the outsides of her breasts. "War can be a very lonely time for a man."

She fought the rise of revulsion and endured the contact, trying desperately to think of a way out of this. "This is happening…too fast. I—I'll have to think about it." She looked at him and tried desperately to smile. "You understand that a woman likes to think about these things."

For a moment she wasn't sure if he was buying into it. She'd never been a good liar, even worse at hiding her emotions. She stared into his black eyes, terrified he would see the lie for what it was. That he would see right through her to the terror in her mind, the hatred in her heart.

Instead, he leaned forward and set his mouth against hers.

Chapter 16

Robert took out the first sentry with the miniaturized stun gun that doubled as a watch. One instant the young man was raising an ugly-looking Chinese-made SKS-47, the next he melted to the ground like a blob of gelatin.

"Thank you, Hatch," Robert quietly muttered.

Glancing over his shoulder, he worked off his sweater and jeans, then quickly gathered the young soldier's uniform and put it on. The trousers were too large, but he didn't plan on running into anyone who might question the fit.

He found a set of nylon cuffs stowed in a pouch in the soldier's belt and secured the man's wrists to a steel bar on the window. He used his T-shirt for a gag, then picked up the gun and headed into the castle.

Robert had never been inside Veisweimar Castle, but he'd taken several minutes with his computer to pull up a set of blueprints that were stored on the ARIES database and put them to memory. He'd hoped to enter the behemoth structure on the south side, but sentries had been concentrated there, so he swam the moat and went in from the north. With the help of an aluminum grappling hook, he scaled the twelve-foot wall, then climbed a pine tree and entered through a second-level balcony.

His leg ached with breathtaking ferocity as he jogged down the dimly lit corridor, but Robert had long since grown used to the pain. Pain was tangible. He could deal with it. What he couldn't deal with was the fear of not knowing where Lily was. Not knowing where Jack was. Not knowing what DeBruzkya had in mind for either of them.

Robert had seen the torture and the executions. If De-Bruzkya somehow found out Lily was involved with the freedom fighters… He couldn't finish the thought. Terror slashed through him with such force that his stride faltered. Panic warred with the need for a level head. Panting as much from the run as the adrenaline streaking through him, he reached the end of a corridor then looked down at the GPS tracking device in his hand. The device showed that he was right on top of the transmitter. He was close, but the device wasn't sensitive enough to pinpoint her exact location. Left would take him to the main section of the castle where the kitchen and ballrooms were located. Right would take him into the basement that held the prison cells and interrogation rooms which, in Robert's mind, translated as torture chambers. More important, the generator room was also located in the basement.

He took a right. The corridor was narrow and dim and very damp. He could see an arched entry at the end of the hall. He was halfway there when he heard the voices. Glancing around, he realized there were no alcoves or doorways for him to duck into. Two soldiers were coming up the stairs. He saw the tops of their heads, then they spotted him. Robert didn't hesitate. Raising his hand, he greeted them in Rebelian, using the slang term for *slow night*.

They met at the top of the stairwell. Robert noticed one

of the soldiers watching him intently and grinned. "Anyone got a smoke?"

The younger of the two immediately dug into his pocket and withdrew a small tin of brown cigarettes. Robert accepted one and put it to his lips. He'd never been a fan of tobacco, but leaned forward eagerly when the younger man struck a match.

"What's your name?" the older man asked.

"Bane," he said.

"You new?"

"First night on the job."

"What are you doing down here?"

He smiled. "I was on my way to the nursery."

The soldier's eyes narrowed. "The nursery is on the third level."

Robert let his smile turn sheepish. "The sentry told me it was down here."

The two men looked at each other and laughed. Robert laughed along with them, wondering if they could see the sweat that had popped out on his forehead. Because he couldn't think of a damn thing to say—because his Rebelian left something to be desired—he puffed hard on the cigarette, then doubled over in a fit of coughing.

Laughing, the younger man slapped him on the back. "Maybe you need women's cigarettes."

"Or mother's milk," the other man chimed in.

While they laughed Robert worked his hand into the breast pocket of the shirt he wore, then straightened. The younger man was still cutting up, but the older one was staring at the watch Robert held in his hand.

"What is that you have there?" he asked, his smile fading.

Grinning like an idiot, Robert leaned close to him. "You ever see a James Bond movie?"

"Sean Connery," the younger soldier said, grinning.

"Pierce Brosnan," Robert corrected.

The two men leaned close to the watch, looking curiously at it. He touched a tiny button at the crown of the watch's face. The charge whistled. Out of the corner of his eye, he saw the older man's hand tighten around his rifle. An instant later, he pressed the face of the watch against the older man's neck. One hundred thousand volts of electricity snapped, dropping him like dead weight.

The younger man lurched back, fumbling for his rifle. "What the *hell?*"

Robert lunged, tagged him with the watch. "Sorry, man," he growled as electricity cracked through the air.

The young soldier hit the stone floor like a bag of potatoes. Looking left and then right, Robert stuffed the watch into his pocket. Knowing that in a matter of minutes the castle would be crawling with heavily armed soldiers, he sprinted to the stairwell and took the steps two at a time into the basement. According to the blueprints, the generator room was halfway down the corridor and to his right. Robert sprinted to the door, but it was locked. He backed up slightly, kicked the door and it flew open, banging hard against the stone wall. Heart pounding, Robert quickly located the generator at the rear and fished out two of the miniature explosive charges. He planted one on the underside of the generator. Because the castle also used natural gas, he searched for the feed pipe and planted the second device there, then set the timers for thirty seconds.

Knowing the blast was going to be huge because of the gas, he sprinted from the room, slamming the door behind him. He was halfway down the hall when the stone beneath his feet shuddered. An instant later the concussion struck him in the back like a giant fist and sent him flying. He saw debris, felt the heat of fire and hoped to God he could stay conscious long enough to find Lily.

Revulsion swamped her as DeBruzkya pressed his mouth against hers in a sick imitation of a kiss. Lily endured the contact but fought a greasy rise of nausea. Panic threatened, and she tried desperately to separate her mind from what was happening to her, from the very real fear that this could escalate into something horrible. Just when she thought she couldn't bear it any longer, the floor shuddered beneath her feet, followed by an ominous rumble. At first she thought it was thunder from the coming storm, then the lights flickered and went out, plunging them into darkness.

"What the..." DeBruzkya pulled away, but he didn't release her.

Insistent pounding sounded at the door. Lily could hear shouting beyond. DeBruzkya turned to her, his rodent's eyes seeking hers. In the thin light cast by candlelight, Lily could see the hunger, the disappointment and thinly concealed cruelty etched into his features. Slowly, he released his grip on her arms, then ran his hands to her shoulders and squeezed hard enough to make her wince. "Stay here," he said and started toward the door.

Lily sagged against the mantel, stunned, trying to decide what to do next. She watched DeBruzkya cross to the door and yank it open. She heard voices as he conversed with his men. She couldn't make out the words, but in a sudden burst of insight she knew Robert had come for her and Jack. The realization filled her with hope and the strength to do what she needed to do next.

Pushing away from the mantel, she darted to the table and quickly extinguished all but one candle. Behind her she could hear DeBruzkya barking out orders. She snatched the last lit candle, then started toward a door at the rear of the dining hall. If DeBruzkya or one of the men were to shine their flashlights in her direction, she would be in plain sight. She twisted the knob. *Please don't be locked.* Relief swamped her when the door swung open.

Lily smelled olive oil and garlic and yeast from the day's cooking as she stepped into what appeared to be the kitchen. The light from the candle in her hand flickered off the stainless steel work areas. Two industrial-size stovetops and ovens lined the wall to her left. Straight ahead, another door beckoned. Spotting a metal folding chair, she quietly closed the door behind her, dragged the chair over and wedged it tightly beneath the knob. It wouldn't hold them for long, but it might buy her a few minutes.

Her heart raged against her ribs as she snatched the candle and jogged through the room toward the door on the other side. She yanked the knob, but the door was locked. "Damn!" she whispered.

She looked wildly around for something with which to pry it open. She could hear a cacophony of shouts coming from the dining room. Fear and urgency sent her across the room where she began yanking open drawers. She pulled out towels and gadgets, finally coming upon knives. Her gaze landed on the butcher's ax, and she snatched it up. Setting the candle down on the counter, she faced the door and swung the ax as hard as she could. Wood splintered with a loud *crack*. The sound seemed deafening in the stark silence, but she didn't stop. She swung again and again, animal sounds erupting from her throat as she pounded at the lock and surrounding wood. Panic and fear and a mother's desperate need to save her child drove her.

After endless minutes the door swung open. One moment she was swinging the ax, the next she was standing there, breathing hard, and looking down a long dark stairwell that seemed to go into the very bowels of the castle. She snatched up the candle, entered the stairway and took the steps at a dangerous speed even though she couldn't see more than five or six feet in front of her. The stairs seemed to go on forever. The shoes she wore were loud against the stone steps and hindered her progress, but she didn't dare risk kicking them off.

The stairs opened to a narrow corridor where the air was musty and cold. Lily could hear water dripping and echoing off the stone walls. Venturing into the corridor, she passed several ancient wooden doors on her right before noticing that the tiny windows set high on the doors were barred. Only then did she realize she'd entered what appeared to be the dungeon. The thought of all the things that had happened within these walls made her shudder.

Holding the candle in front of her like a weapon, she walked into the inky blackness. The thought of being trapped in a catacomb without light or fresh air unnerved her. Surely there was a back exit, wasn't there? Panic pressed down on her. Lily broke into a run. She could hear herself breathing hard. The click of her heels against the stone floor. She felt as if the low ceiling and walls were pressing down on her, smothering her. She ran faster, the doors blurring past. The candle flickered wildly, casting bizarre shadows on the ceiling.

The hands came out of nowhere, strong and overpowering. One instant she was sprinting down the narrow passageway, the next strong arms wrapped around her waist and pulled her into a darkened alcove. The candle clattered to the floor, plunging her into darkness. Lily screamed, but the sound was cut short when a hand clamped over her mouth.

DeBruzkya, she thought, and panic overwhelmed her. She twisted, but he yanked her against him. A scream echoed inside her head, but his hand over her mouth prevented her from screaming. She lashed out with her feet, missed his shin and ended up losing one of her shoes.

"Lily! Easy. It's Robert."

His whisper lapped over her like a gentle ocean wave over sand, smoothing out her terror. She went still. The relief swamped her with such power that her knees went weak. "Robert? Oh, God."

"I'm here, honey. Easy, it's me. You're okay."

"I can't believe you're here." The words tumbled out brokenly. "DeBruzkya—"

"Shh. Just calm down. Everything's going to be okay."

Turning in his arms, her body flush against his, she looked at him. "We have to find Jack. They took him from me."

"That's exactly what we're going to do."

She didn't expect him to kiss her. Not at a moment like this when they risked discovery at any moment. But he did, and the kiss took down her panic. Eased her fear. Filled her heart with hope. Her soul with love for this man. He kissed her long and deep, stirring her and rousing her. And at that moment Lily knew in her heart that somehow everything was going to work out.

His jaw was taut with tension when he pulled back. "Are you all right? Did they hurt you?"

"I'm okay."

"Jack?"

"I don't know. I don't know where he is. I think he's in the nursery."

"That's where we'll go next. Where's DeBruzkya?"

"We were in the dining room when the lights went out. There was some kind of explosion." Lily wasn't sure why she was telling Robert about the explosion when chances were he knew a hell of a lot more about it than she did.

"Hopefully, that will keep them busy for a few minutes," he said.

"He's crazy, Robert. I mean, we were…he wanted to…" She couldn't finish the sentence. "He has this sick fantasy that there's something between us."

"He didn't…"

"No."

"That son of a—"

"He mentioned the Gem of Power." The words were coming in a flood. She couldn't seem to get them out fast enough. "He mentioned Dr. Alex Morrow."

Robert's gaze snapped to hers. "How so?"

"Just that he's here, in the castle."

"Crazy bastard." He paused, deep in concentration. "We find Jack first. Once the two of you are safe, I'll come back for Morrow."

"DeBruzkya will kill—"

"Shh." He pressed a kiss to her mouth, her jaw, her temple. "Trust me, Lily. I know what I'm doing."

She didn't doubt that Robert knew what he was doing; he'd proven it to her time and time again. But that didn't mean she was going to sit back and let him walk into a dangerous situation alone.

"Did he force you to wear that?" he asked, referring to the gown she wore.

Lily nodded.

Taking a deep breath, he glanced nervously over his shoulder. "We don't have much time. This place is going to be crawling with soldiers as soon as they put out the fire."

She slipped her foot into the shoe that had fallen off in the struggle. "How are we going to find Jack?"

"The nursery is on the third level."

The thought that finding her son could be as simple as that sent a jolt of hope straight to her heart. "Do you know how to get there?"

"Yeah, but we've got to hurry." His eyes skimmed down the slinky gown she was wearing to her shoes. "How fast can you run in those shoes?"

"Fast enough." She looked at the long gown. "The dress is the problem. Hinders my stride."

"Not for long." He pulled a knife out of his pocket, and a four-inch blade snapped into place. She jolted when he leaned forward and slashed the material to midcalf. "Sorry about the dress."

"I prefer denim over silk, anyway."

"But you have great legs." His eyes were dark and knowing when they met hers. Raising his hand, he touched the side of her face with the backs of his knuckles. "Let's go find our son," he said and took her hand.

He guided her down the narrow passageway at a dead run. At the end of the hall, he paused briefly at the doorway, then they went up the narrow, winding stairs. Lily considered herself in relatively good shape, but the climb seemed endless. For several long minutes the only sound came from the pounding of their shoes against stone, their labored breathing and the rush of blood through her veins.

Robert stopped abruptly on a small landing outside an ancient wooden door. "This is the third level." He turned to Lily and set his hands on her shoulders. "You stay here while I get Jack."

"I'm going with you."

"This isn't a good time for you to argue."

"I'm not letting you go alone."

"Damn it, Lily, I'm wearing a uniform. That'll keep me out of trouble."

"DeBruzkya will kill you." The thought shook her so profoundly that for a moment she couldn't speak. "He won't kill me."

He didn't say anything when he turned away from her, but his expression was a dangerous combination of fury and frustration. Giving her a last, lingering look he eased the door open several inches and looked out. Behind him, Lily listened for voices, but couldn't hear anything over the pounding of her heart.

"It's clear." He glanced at her. "Follow me."

Like a big, predatory cat, he slipped through the door and into a hall. He pressed his back against the wall and moved stealthily toward the opposite end. Taking her cue from Robert, Lily did the same. Halfway there, she realized he was limping badly. That he had a sheen of sweat on his forehead even though the castle was chilly, and she wondered how much pain he was in.

They were nearly to the end of the hall when a faint sound echoed off the stone walls. The sound went through Lily like a knife. Jack, she thought, and everything inside her went utterly still, her every sense honing in on that sound.

"That's Jack," she whispered.

"Lily, just stay cool. Don't do anything—"

She knew better than to run into a dangerous situation unarmed and with absolutely no idea what to expect. But the need to reach her son was so overwhelming she couldn't stop herself. She left the relative protection of the wall and sprinted down the hall. Vaguely she was aware of Robert moving behind her, but she didn't slow down.

She tried the first door she came to only to find it locked. The next door stood open several inches. Lily sprinted to it, shoved it open, heard it bang hard against the wall. Standing beneath a stone window, the young female servant spun to face her. Lily stared at the other woman, her eyes going to the child she held in her arms.

"Give me my son," Lily said.

"Wh—what are you doing here?" the young woman cried.

Lily was across the room and reaching for Jack before she realized she was going to move. There must have been something in her eyes, because the servant relinquished the baby without a word.

Taking her son into her arms, Lily looked into his innocent face, felt the part of her heart that had been missing since he'd been taken from her slide back into place. She held him close, kissing his plump cheeks and forehead, barely aware that he'd stopped crying. "It's okay sweetheart," she whispered. "Mommy's got you. Everything's going to be all right."

The sound of steel against steel snapped her head up. Lily watched as DeBruzkya stepped out of the shadows, a shiny chrome pistol trained on her chest. "Ah, Lillian, your love for your child makes you very predictable." Cruelty glinted in his eyes as he started toward her. "If I weren't so very fond of you, I'd put a bullet through the both of you right now."

Terror swept through her with such power that for a moment she couldn't draw a breath. Heart raging, she clutched Jack to her chest and stepped back. Vaguely, she wondered if Robert was still in the corridor, if he had any idea DeBruzkya was in the room with her.

"You have no right to keep my son from me," she said.

"Where's the man you were with?" DeBruzkya asked.

She tried to look confused, but she could tell from the general's expression he wasn't buying it. "I don't know what—"

"Don't lie to me!" He shifted the pistol toward Jack. "Where the hell is he!"

Lily choked back a scream of terror. "Don't hurt my baby!"

"I've got you covered, General DeBruzkya!"

Shock rippled through her at the sound of the familiar voice speaking perfect Rebelian. She glanced at the door. Robert, in a Rebelian Army uniform and black beret, burst in, his automatic weapon trained on her chest. "Are you all right, General DeBruzkya?" he shouted.

"Fine," the general spat. "I've got the situation under control."

"Do you want me to take her to her suite, sir?"

"No! I want her male accomplice found, damn it. Now!"

"We've found him, sir!"

For the first time, the general gave Robert his full attention. "Found him? Where is he? I wish to interrogate him immediately. I want to know who he's working for."

"He's been injured."

"Injured?" DeBruzkya lowered the pistol. "No matter. An injury will make interrogating him much easier—"

Robert charged, ramming his head and shoulders into DeBruzkya's midsection. The general brought the pistol up, but he was knocked off his feet before he could aim, and the shot went wide. Lily dropped to her knees and covered Jack with her body. Another shot rang out and zinged off stone. Out of the corner of her eye she saw the female servant flee the room.

She heard a colorful American curse. Heard the hair-raising snap of electricity from Robert's stun gun, then DeBruzkya's body sprawled onto the floor like a fallen bull.

"Robert!" Clinging to Jack, she stumbled to her feet and crossed to him on shaking legs.

Robert reached for her, pulled her to him and kissed her. "Are you all right?"

"I'm fine."

"Jack?"

Lily's hands shook uncontrollably as she ran her hands over their son. "He's okay. Thank God."

"Still groggy from the sedative."

"Thank goodness." She smiled at Robert. "Even though you were wearing the uniform, I thought for sure De-Bruzkya was going to realize you weren't one of his men."

"It was too dark." He grimaced. "Besides, men like DeBruzkya don't care enough about the people under them to know their names or faces."

She looked around. "How are we going to get out of here?"

"There's a stairwell that leads to the roof."

"The roof?"

"There's a chopper on the way." She shot a questioning look at him, and he smiled. "Don't ask."

He started to turn away, but Lily stopped him. "There's something I've been meaning to tell you," she said.

As if realizing what she was about to say, Robert stopped and turned to face her. "Lily, this isn't the time or place. You don't have to—"

"Yes, I do." She stared at him, felt the words tangle in her throat, dangle precariously on her tongue. "I've been wrong," she blurted. "About everything."

"That covers a lot of territory, Lily. Think you can be a little more specific?"

"I can be a lot more specific." She closed her eyes, felt the words solidify. And she knew. She'd always known. "I love you." It was the first time in her life she'd said the words, and the rightness of them brought tears to her eyes.

For an instant, he looked shocked, and she felt a moment of panic when he didn't respond. "You're right," she said quickly. "This isn't a good time—"

She started to turn away, but he stopped her by taking

her shoulders and turning her to face him. "I love you, too," he said. "I always have. I just…didn't think I'd ever hear you say it."

"I'm sorry I hurt you."

"I understand." He let out a breath that wasn't quite steady. "That's enough."

She smiled, even though tears blurred her vision. "Everything is going to work out."

"It always does when it's meant to be." He glanced over his shoulder. "Maybe we can discuss this in more detail once the chopper picks us up."

"Chopper?"

"Friend of mine."

"He just happened to be in the area?"

"Something like that." Taking her hand, Robert started toward the staircase that led to the roof. "Let's go."

Lily followed, keenly aware of how tightly he was holding her hand, that her precious son was pressed snugly and safely against her abdomen. They moved quickly through utter darkness. Robert took her through a narrow door, then to a spiral staircase that seemed to go on forever. At the top, a heavy wooden door blocked their path.

"The roof?" she asked.

Robert nodded. "Stand back."

She moved away. A single, powerful kick and the door swung wide, banging hard against the brick wall behind it. Lily stepped onto the roof, and the cool breath of the night embraced her. The rain had stopped at some point and a three-quarter moon peeked like a shy child through jagged clouds. In the distance, she could hear the whop-whop-whop of a helicopter's rotors. And she knew in her heart that this man had kept his promise. Everything was, indeed, going to be all right. The knowledge sent a starburst of joy straight to her heart.

A few feet away, Robert braced a large timber against the door, then turned to face her. "Chopper should be here any minute."

"I'm not even going to ask how you arranged it," Lily said.

He looked sheepish for a moment. "I have a confession to make."

"You're not going to shock me, are you, Robert?"

"Probably." Crossing to her, he put his arms around her shoulders and smiled. "I'm not here on a humanitarian mission."

"I got that impression once or twice." Her gaze met his. "Why then?"

"I'm an agent with a secret arm of the CIA called AR-IES."

If it hadn't been for all the amazing things she'd seen this man do in the last hours, she never would have believed it. But she did now and she owed him her life for it. "One of the good guys," she said quietly.

"Think you can live with that?" He glanced down at the child between them. "Think Jack can live with that?"

Lily blinked back tears, but felt them squeeze between her lashes anyway. She knew now was a silly time to get sentimental, but she couldn't seem to help it. "I've got something I need to get off my chest, too," she said.

He arched a brow. "You're not going to shock me, are you?"

She choked out a laugh. "Probably."

"I'm all ears."

"Would you like to get married?" she blurted.

"Any particular reason?"

"You mean aside from the fact that I'm crazy in love with you?" She smiled. "I need a father for my son."

He kissed her on the mouth, then leaned forward and kissed his son's forehead. "Maybe we could discuss this in more detail over dinner tomorrow. I took the liberty of making reservations."

She cocked her head. "But don't we need to go into hiding? DeBruzkya's men—"

"The Rouge in Marseilles. Great seafood. Open air.

Right on the water. Great place for a guy to propose to the woman he loves.''

Because her emotions were choking her, Lily could only stand there and wonder how it was that she'd ever let this man go. ''I've already proposed.''

''I'm a traditionalist. I'd like the chance to get down on one knee and propose good and proper.'' He pulled back just enough to make eye contact. ''Besides, we're in no hurry, are we? We've got the rest of our lives.''

''I love the sound of that.''

He took her hand. ''Honey, we've got forever if that's what you want.''

''That's exactly what I want,'' she whispered. ''Forever. With you.''

''You got it,'' he said and lowered his mouth to hers.

Epilogue

It was the first time in the history of his career with ARIES that Robert had to wait for Samuel Hatch to show up for a debriefing. He spent nearly ten minutes talking shop with Carla Juarez in the main office, filling her in on some of the things that had happened in Rebelia. Of course, Carla was a lot more interested in the mystery woman and one-year-old child he had returned home with. She'd been smiling from ear to ear by the time she'd shown Robert into Hatch's inner sanctum—where he'd now been waiting for nearly ten minutes.

Restless, Robert rose from the sled chair opposite Hatch's desk and strode to the credenza where the listless strawberry plant was struggling to remain upright, even though Hatch had added a plant light since Robert had been here last. A bag of potting soil sat at the edge of the credenza next to a small aluminum watering pail. Remembering Hatch's determination to keep the threadbare plant alive, Robert smiled. If anyone could nurse that wretched-looking plant back to health, it was Hatch.

It had been four days since Robert, Lily and Jack had been airlifted from the Veisweimar Castle in Rebelia. Robert still couldn't quite believe he'd found her after all this time. That she was alive. That she'd given him a son. He loved both of them more than life itself, and had no earthly idea how he'd survived all those months thinking she'd been killed.

Just thinking of her made his heart beat faster. He'd only been away from her for a little over two hours—just long enough to drive from his home near D.C. to ARIES headquarters in Virginia—and already he missed her. Already he missed Jack. A sweet ache pulsed inside him with every beat of his heart, as powerful as the need to take his next breath.

After what they'd gone through in Rebelia, Hatch had given them three days of leave in Paris, compliments of ARIES. Decompression time is what Hatch called it. Something deep cover operatives needed after a particularly intense operation. Robert called them the best three days of his life.

The office door swung open. Robert looked up to see Hatch stride in, a small bag in one hand, a tastefully wrapped gift in the other. "I was wondering when you were going to show up," Robert said good-naturedly.

"Damn traffic." Hatch strode to the desk and set the wrapped gift on top of his "out" box. Reaching inside the brown paper bag, he withdrew a small bottle of liquid plant fertilizer and turned toward the credenza. Robert watched as Hatch mixed a few drops of the fertilizer in the watering pail, then poured the mixture over the strawberry plant.

"It's looking better," Robert said, referring to the plant.

"Damn thing's going to die on me." Taking his chair, Hatch scooted up to his desk, pulled a manila folder from his drawer, then opened it. "The gift is for you and Lily," he said without looking up.

Robert glanced at the tastefully wrapped box, noting the white paper and matching satin bow. Because he hadn't been expecting a gift from Hatch, he shoved his hands into his pockets. "Ah, thanks."

"Pretty quick wedding," Hatch said.

"We flew directly to Vegas once we arrived in the States from Paris." Remembering that neither he nor Lily had been able to wait, Robert smiled. "We're going to have another wedding in January. You know, with all the bells and whistles. You're on the invitation list, by the way."

Resting his hands on the file in front of him, Hatch shot Robert a canny look. "I didn't know you were involved with her when I sent you over there."

"I know."

"I'm sorry, Robert. I wouldn't have put one of my operatives through that. It could have been dangerous and must have been hell for you finding out that she was alive the way you did."

"Everything worked out."

"How's the boy?"

Robert thought of Jack, his precious son, and his chest swelled. "He's doing great. The bone marrow transplant is scheduled for next week."

"Let me know how it goes." Hatch's knowing gaze met Robert's and held. "I'm glad everything worked out for you."

"Me, too." Because he wasn't comfortable discussing his personal life with his superior, Robert cleared his throat and went quickly to the next topic on his mental list. "The only thing I regret is that I wasn't able to bring Alex Morrow. We were so damn close."

Something he couldn't quite read flashed in the older man's expression, and for an instant he looked older than his sixty years. "You confirmed the location of Dr. Morrow," Hatch said. "You found out where DeBruzkya's headquarters is located. Those two things are vital and, in my eyes, you did what you were sent over there to do. Operation PHOENIX was a successful mission."

"Morrow's still missing," Robert pointed out.

"True," Hatch conceded, then leaned back in his chair. "Luckily, I have an ace up my sleeve."

Robert contemplated him for a moment, intrigued. "Anyone I know?"

"You ever heard of Jared Sullivan?"

"Everyone even remotely connected to CIA has heard of Sullivan. Best damn search and rescue expert in the business. I thought he retired and went back to Texas."

Hatch waved off the statement as if the operative's untimely retirement were an insignificant detail. "I'll take Sullivan's retirement."

Robert knew he would. Samuel Hatch was an amazing man. He took care of all his operatives the same way he took care of that scraggly strawberry plant.

Rising, Hatch met Robert's gaze and extended his hand. "You take that gift home to your wife. Open it together. I've arranged for you to have as much time off as you need. I suggest you take it."

"I will, sir." Realizing the debriefing had ended, and a new phase of his life had begun, Robert stood and accepted the other man's hand, grasping it tightly. "Thank you."

As he walked toward the door, Robert thought about Lily and Jack and wondered if Hatch had any idea that Operation PHOENIX, one of the most dangerous missions of his career, had made him the happiest man in the world.

Keeping that thought in mind, he left ARIES headquarters and headed for home where his family waited.

* * * * *

The secret is out!

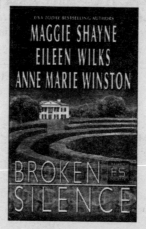

Coming in May 2003 to SILHOUETTE BOOKS

Evidence has finally surfaced that a covert team of scientists successfully completed experiments in genetic manipulation.

The extraordinary individuals created by these experiments could be anyone, living anywhere, even right next door....

Enjoy these three brand-new FAMILY SECRETS stories and watch as dark pasts are exposed and passion burns through the night!

The Invisible Virgin by Maggie Shayne
A Matter of Duty by Eileen Wilks
Inviting Trouble by Anne Marie Winston

Five extraordinary siblings. One dangerous past.

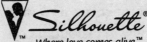

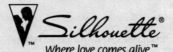

If you enjoyed what you just read,
then we've got an offer you can't resist!

Take 2 bestselling love stories FREE!

Plus get a FREE surprise gift!

Silhouette®

COMING NEXT MONTH

SIMCNM0303

INTIMATE MOMENTS